SAY YOU'LL STAY

CARRIE LOMAX

SAY YOU'LL STAY

Previously Titled Holiday Heat

© 2017 Carrie Lomax.

All rights reserved. No part of this book may be reproduced or used in any manner without the express written permission of the publisher except for the use of brief quotations in a book review.

This book or parts thereof may not be reproduced in any form, stored in any retrieval system, or transmitted in any form by any means—electronic, mechanical, photocopy, recording, or otherwise—without prior written permission of the author, except as provided by United States of America copyright law. For permissions contact: info@carrielomax.com.

This is a work of fiction. Names, characters, businesses, places, events and incidents are either the products of the author's imagination or used in a fictitious manner. Any resemblance to actual persons, living or dead, or actual events is purely coincidental.

Cover by Velvet Madrid.

ISBN: 978-1-7321531-2-7

❀ Created with Vellum

For Anna

1

The buzzer shrieked like a jet roaring down a runway, startling Alyssa as she reached to set her wine on the side table. The glass missed the edge and fell, shattering into a constellation of razor-sharp pieces across the scuffed wood floor.

The noise came again, insistent. Alyssa picked her way carefully over the field of shards to the almond box on the wall. She smashed the button bearing a scratched picture of a key. It had better work because she wasn't going down six flights of stairs to open the door manually. Her mobile phone lay amongst the splinters on the floorboards. She'd knocked it off the couch while trying to save the glass. Gingerly she brushed away the fragments. 12:43 AM.

He'd left her dangling for nearly five hours. Was Zach dead in a ditch?

That afternoon, Alyssa had splurged on a salon blowout. Then she'd come home and painted a dark stripe above each eye, dabbed perfume on her wrists and neck, dressed and waited. Eight o'clock had come and gone. It had been the only available time slot months ago, back when they'd started talking seriously about getting married. He'd insisted the engagement had to happen at *this* restaurant, even if it meant missing Christmas Eve with her family in Florida.

Now Zach, her boyfriend, had stood her up on what was supposed to be their engagement night.

He'd blown her off before but never for something important. Not like this. If there was one time when she needed reassurance about where she ranked on his priority list, then tonight was it.

At a minimum, he could've texted her to let her know he'd be late. Or that dinner was off. A little courtesy shouldn't be too much to ask from someone you were about to pledge your life to.

He was here now, stomping up the stairwell, his steps staggered. Drunk again, though she was hardly in any condition to pass judgment.

His fist landed on the door three times. Resolute, Alyssa flicked open the locks. If she hadn't burned through all her anger hours ago, she might feel a little more prepared for this confrontation. She hoped he hadn't brought some extravagant gift, like he usually did to smooth over major fuckups. Alyssa wasn't letting him buy his way out of this mess.

"Babe, I am so sorry," Zach slurred. "Merry Christmas."

Happy fucking holidays. "Zach. What are you doing? We were supposed to get engaged tonight, remember?"

He nodded. "Cold feet."

She stood there, waiting for the explanation that didn't come. "That's it?"

"I'm not ready to get married." Zach shrugged, his blue eyes unfocused and wary.

"Getting married was *your idea*. It was never something I pushed for. I told you repeatedly I'd rather wait." She backed up a step as he shrugged out of his coat and hung it on one of the hooks behind the door.

Pent-up frustration fueled a new spurt of anger, her voice rising. "I can't believe I was worried about you. You might've been hit by a car or something! I called your parents. I almost called the police. I missed Christmas Eve with my family because you insisted it had to be at this restaurant, and you can't even be bothered to show up?"

Freed of his fine cashmere arm-prison, Zach slumped against the door. "I'm here to make it up to you now."

The fool probably thinks he's getting laid tonight.

Alyssa turned away, staring out the one window her tiny apartment boasted. The sliver-view of Central Park, framed between two buildings, was the pad's only selling point. Well, that and the fact it was cheap enough not to need a roommate. The microscopic hole had served its purpose for the past six years, but she was beyond ready to move out. As soon as she got married.

Now she wasn't getting married.

She'd never been excited about the idea, but Zach pushed and pushed until she gave in, the way she always did with him. For months, she'd ignored the warning signs that things weren't right between them, but this was outrageous even by Zach's standards. No way was she locking herself into a lifetime of this crap.

After a few steadying breaths, Alyssa turned to face her boyfriend like a mature, rational adult. "You said you'd go to your end-of-year work party for two hours and come get me at eight for dinner at eight-thirty. Instead, you show up hours late, and drunk. We're supposed to be at the airport for a 6 AM flight. Do you remember any of this or are you too wasted?"

Zach was silent, scowling like a schoolboy enduring a lecture from a teacher.

Alyssa took another deep breath. "Do you have any idea how frightened I was? Why, after insisting that we get engaged, would you stand me up for the event that *you* planned?"

"Babe," he slurred, pushing off the wall. "I'm sure I texted you. Check your phone."

"I just looked at it. There's nothing."

He shrugged off the lie. "I knew you had reservations about getting engaged so sue me if I wasn't eager to get here tonight. I need to know you're a hundred percent into this. Besides, the more I thought about it, I realized if we got married...the sex might get...boring."

She and Zach hadn't had sex since...before Thanksgiving? Longer. Wrapped up in work and holiday preparations, she'd hardly noticed, which spoke volumes about the state of their relationship. *Of all the pointless excuses.*

She hated how he did this so easily, turning situations where he was completely in the wrong into her fault. This time, she wasn't letting him get away with it.

He stepped closer. Alyssa backed up one step, then another. Zach, several inches taller than her five-foot-seven, loomed over her.

"No," she said forcefully an instant before his mouth landed on hers. Sputtering, Alyssa pushed him away and stepped backward.

"Ow!" she yelled as a shard stabbed her heel.

"I hurt you?" Zach stared, confused, as she bent to check her injury. Zach didn't even offer his arm to lean on. He could be such an insensitive jerk sometimes, and he was on a roll tonight.

"No. Yes. I broke a glass." Grimacing, Alyssa hopped awkwardly toward the bathroom. As if on cue, the neighbor downstairs started banging on his ceiling, her floor.

The white Swiss-dot stockings she'd spent big bucks on because they went so well with her dress had a run halfway to her knee. They were covered in blood, and she'd never even worn them out of her apartment. She pushed the door almost closed and hiked up her skirt.

She stripped off the ruined stockings and tossed them into the trash can. She lifted the ankle of her injured foot and placed it on the opposite knee to examine her heel. "Could you bring me a paper towel?"

Her erstwhile boyfriend barged into the bathroom to proffer a wad. Alyssa reached up to the sink and ran water over it. Teeth clenched, she took the dagger of glass between her fingernails and ripped it from her skin. Blood puddled on the tile.

Zach blanched. "Babe, we gotta talk."

"Please go now." The drops fell one after the other, great globs of bright red. At least something in this apartment was a festive color. She pressed the wet towels to the wound and grimaced.

"Leave the key. Box up the stuff I have at your place and send it to my parents' house. I don't want to see you ever again." She wanted to feel pride in standing strong, but one glance at Zach's expression and unease curdled in her stomach.

She ripped a Band-Aid out of its protective covering and plastered it across her heel. It soaked through in an instant. Alyssa reached for a threadbare but clean towel. Pressing it to her foot, she rummaged in a drawer until she found a tube of expired Neosporin and an Ace bandage with crumbling elastic.

"Babe, you might need a doctor. I don't want to leave you alone."

"I wish you'd considered that five hours ago." Alyssa limped back out wearing a makeshift bandage like an extra from a zombie movie. Her boyfriend was still in her living room. *Ex*-boyfriend. What about *get out* was so hard for him to process?

"Aly, call me when you get to Florida. You'll get your ring. I'm just not ready to get married."

Alyssa closed her eyes, picturing her hands reaching through the collar of his cashmere coat and strangling him with his Burberry scarf. She opened them. "Me neither, Zach. Please go."

He nodded. "I don't want to lose you."

"You just did," Alyssa said tiredly.

He finally left, clomping down the stairs like a Clydesdale with coordination problems. The door slammed shut, which started the downstairs neighbor banging again. Alyssa spent maybe two nights a week in her own apartment, and most of the time all she did was drop into bed. Her usual good nature fractured. She stomped on the floor, hard. Pain radiated up her leg.

"Fuck!" Wincing, she fell onto the couch.

The floor remained strewn with sharp glass. She'd booby-trapped her own apartment.

Alyssa stared out her window for a moment trying to summon the energy to clean up the mess. It was never truly night in New York City. Ambient light washed the landscape in dirty ocher. It wouldn't matter if she never set foot into this apartment after tonight. Her life in New York—she was done with it.

Her body sagged into the ancient IKEA couch, worn out from an evening that had turned emotional for all the wrong reasons. In hindsight, she shouldn't have agreed to skip Christmas Eve with her family. Being so far away, she didn't get to visit as much as she'd have liked, and in recent calls with her sister Janelle, something had seemed off. She'd been weirdly fixated on the engagement.

Alyssa hauled herself up and hobbled around, sweeping up glass.

She should've asked Zach to do it before kicking him out, though she knew he couldn't wield a broom and dustpan.

The Louis Vuitton handbag Zach had given her for her last birthday sat on the desk that doubled as a table. She didn't care for the style, but she'd carried it every day because he'd enjoyed buying her expensive things, and she'd been a little too willing to accept luxury goods as a substitute for genuine affection. She growled and upended it over the battered table.

She couldn't vent at Zach, but anything he'd given her was fair game.

For the next few minutes she sorted the contents into either the garbage can or a stack of things to keep: phone, half a package of gum, dental floss, mascara, several receipts she still needed to submit for reimbursement at work, her zippered Coach wallet still in decent shape despite four years of abuse, and two tubes of lipstick. Oh, and the notebook she never used.

Then she limped to the tiny closet in the alcove she used as a bedroom and took down a cheerful pink Coach bag. The set had been her reward to herself for landing her first job out of college. She carefully placed the pile of items to keep inside.

The Louis Vuitton went into its dust covering and onto the shelf. A fifteen-hundred-dollar bag sitting in a nine-hundred-dollar-a-month studio apartment—how much sense did that make?

It was time to go. Alyssa zipped up her coat and extended the little handle on her wheeled suitcase.

In the foyer, she learned why Zach had taken the stairs. The elevator was out of service. Again. She bumped her luggage down all five flights of stairs, too upset to care about how much noise she was making. No one emerged to yell at her. Most likely, everyone was away visiting family. Except her downstairs neighbor, of course. He *would* have to be the one to stay home.

Outside, the suitcase wobbled drunkenly for a whole two feet before snow packed the wheels and it turned into a sled. Alyssa hoisted it and trudged on. Gray slush piled up along the sides of the road. The city was cloaked in a haunted, almost eerie silence. A familiar form hunched in the corner of the subway stairwell.

Alyssa squinted against the glare of the brightly lit subway station. "Gina? Is that you?"

A woman huddled in the stairwell with two large, battered suitcases forming a barrier around her body. She glanced up. "Yeah, it's me, all right. Aly?"

"Didn't you get an apartment?"

"Had it, but soon as I got the housing voucher set up, I lost the lease. The landlord rented it to someone else. How's that for luck? Got the money to pay but no place to rent." Gina's deeply crinkled face belied her relative youth.

Chronic homelessness had a way of wearing you down. Despite this, Gina usually had a ready laugh and a wide grin. Once, Alyssa had laughed at some joke Gina had cracked, and they'd been talking off and on ever since. Gina's police officer son had died of a gunshot wound, and she'd lost her job a few months later. Though life had spiraled quickly out of control, Gina was tenacious in trying to drag it back on track.

"What're you doin' out this time of night?" Gina asked.

Alyssa leaned against the grimy subway wall. "Taking the train to JFK. Got an early flight home to Florida."

"Long trip."

"Yeah. I have time, though." She'd had a bad evening, but at least she'd never been homeless on Christmas. "Hey, Gina. Are you going anywhere to celebrate today?"

"Nah. Might see some friends at the shelter. I'll get a there bed tomorrow night." She sniffed. "The holidays are rough. I like to be alone."

Alyssa bit the fingertip of her glove to pull it off, tasting wet wool. She fished in the pocket of her handbag, past the laptop in its snug blue neoprene case and her toiletries neatly bagged for security scanning. Her fingers were cold and slow as she unspooled a set of three keys. The woman in two coats and a skirt worn over untold other layers watched her guardedly.

"I have a better idea. No one should be homeless on Christmas, Gina. The big key gets you into the front door of my building. The gold key is for the deadbolt. Silver key is the front door. I'm not back until January first. You can stay until then, if you'll bring in the mail."

Gina eyed the key set like she might snatch it away. "You sure you want some nutty stranger staying in your apartment?"

"You're not crazy. You just have terrible luck. It's sitting empty otherwise. There's laundry in the basement and detergent under the sink. There's a change jar on the closet shelf with quarters for the machines. The man below me doesn't like it when you make noise." She reached for Gina's hand and folded the keys into her palm.

"I'll be quiet as a mouse."

"Great, you'll fit right in with the real mice."

Gina barked a laugh. "Why're you doin' this?"

Good question. Because Gina was her secret friend, someone in her life that Zach didn't know about. As if he'd ever look twice at a homeless woman. It was a small good deed to mark her newfound freedom.

"How long have I seen you here in this subway stop? Four years? Five? I trust you." She shrugged. "The apartment isn't much, but it's a better place to sleep than a subway station, and you'll have all the alone time you need to get through the holidays."

She made Gina repeat the address twice. Together they carried her heavy suitcases up to the street. Alyssa flagged a cab and handed Gina two twenties.

"Merry Christmas." She waved.

"An' Happy New Year!" Gina bellowed out the window as the cab pulled away. Alyssa stood there grinning like an idiot until she realized her feet and fingers were numb. Her happiness at performing a small good deed melted faster than a snowflake on a radiator.

Alyssa's stomach tried to tie itself into a knot. Her parents were going to lose it when she told them the mortifying story of how she'd spent her Christmas Eve. They were in awe of Zach, and Janelle fawned over him like Prince Charming personified.

Forget saying anything about her houseguest. To anyone. Helping someone else put the only bright spot into her holiday, and it was all hers. Zach would never know. She didn't have to worry about him any more, though.

She replayed the evening in her mind all throughout the long trip to JFK airport, but by the time she'd made it through security and to her gate her righteous anger had faded and doubt crept in. Zach wasn't perfect—he'd hardly been an adequate boyfriend—but they'd been together for two years. Maybe she'd been hasty. If he'd had any better excuse than the one he'd offered, she might've forgiven him.

Alyssa settled into her seat, buckled the belt, and yawned. Dawn stained the sky as the aircraft taxied down the runway and lifted off. It circled the city once, finding its flight path. Cold New York stretched out, the buildings like Lego buildings below, getting smaller, turning the big city into a toy. She'd fought so hard for so long to be here. How could she tell her family that, after everything they'd sacrificed, she was ready to walk away?

2

"Aly!" Janelle, her younger sister, wrapped her arms around her neck with a fierceness that made Alyssa choke. It was akin being tackled by a St. Bernard puppy, minus the drool.

"Come on, big sis. Show it!"

"Show what?" Although she was sweating, Alyssa was glad she'd automatically pulled her gloves on while scrambling to get off the plane. She'd finally caught a few hours of sleep during the trip, and now her breath was stale and her throat parched.

"The ring! Speaking of sparklers, where's Zach?"

"He couldn't make it." Alyssa hoped she didn't sound too evasive. She needed caffeine before breaking the news. "Merry Christmas to you too."

"Let's get Alyssa home before we start interrogating her, Janelle." Alyssa's mother reached for a hug.

"Oh, fine." Her sister grabbed for the wheelie suitcase. Alyssa let her take it. She had her shoulder bag and coat to carry.

"How come you didn't fly into Fort Myers?" Janelle asked as they zipped over the tile. They exited the airport without passing a single purveyor of coffee. *Haven't they heard of Starbucks in Florida?*

"Tampa was cheaper. I know it's a drive. Thanks for picking me up."

The boots that had failed to keep her feet warm in New York were roasting them now. In the car, she kicked them off and slipped into cheerful red ballet flats. Her bandage stuck out of the shoe, needing to be changed and ruining the effect.

"Zach would've ponied up for the tickets. What's the point of having a rich boyfriend if he doesn't show you the good life?"

Alyssa sighed. She'd never survive two hours of this treatment.

"We have different ideas about what makes for the good life, Janie." Sometimes Alyssa felt like an alien life form. She could blend in anywhere, but she'd never fit in.

There was no point in continuing to make an ass of herself by wearing the gloves. Her mother zeroed in on the naked ring finger of her left and raised an eyebrow in question.

"Zach's not coming. Work. You know how it is." She shrugged.

"Isn't the stock market closed on Christmas?" Catherine Carlisle eyed her attentively. Like Janelle, she had dark hair and vivid green eyes. Both women sported deep tans, the kind that came from regular activity in bright sunlight all year long. Alyssa shrank down in her seat feeling like a pale ghost who'd showed up to haunt the family holidays.

"Yeah, but you know finance guys, they work all the time." Alyssa watched the rows of palm trees flash by the side of the road. "Hedge funds."

"I've always thought Zach could be self-absorbed," her mother commented. "Is something going on?"

Caffeine or not, she might as well get it over with. "Yeah. We broke up."

Her mother and sister gasped in unison. "When?"

"Last night."

"Totally broke up?" Janelle's shock registered in the review mirror. She'd taken the middle of the back seat so she could peer into the front of the car.

"Done, over, final." Alyssa sat up a little straighter to better project Having It All Figured Out. Confident. In control.

"Oh, no. Honey." Her mother tried to reach across the seat to hug her with one hand and nearly ran into a parked car. "Are you all right?"

"I'm fine. Better than fine. I'm glad I didn't get engaged. You're right, Mom, Zach is self-absorbed and inconsiderate. I can't even believe I dated him. Not getting engaged was a near-miss."

"Who cares? He's rich and only going to get richer." Janelle, who was struggling to make ends meet on a recent graduate's salary, had recently discovered the value of money. "At least if you'd married, him you could've made out like a bandit in the divorce. Although, on the bright side, I don't have to waste money on some hideous bridesmaid's dress."

Alyssa rolled her eyes. "Thanks for caring."

"Janelle, your attitude is appalling. Look, it happened, let's all try to forget about Zach and not let him ruin the holiday. There's still plenty to celebrate, like your promotion."

"Yes, I'm starting a new role at the agency when I go back." Alyssa tried to say it brightly but her words came out flat. It was nothing more than a title bump with more responsibility, longer hours, and no extra pay. "Lead Creative for Direct & Digital on a major client account."

"I don't know what that means."

"It means she designs spam emails and junk mail for a living, Mom." Leave it to Janelle to frame it in the bluntest terms possible. Her sister had a built-in bullshit detector and wasn't fooled by fancy words.

"I sent you to art school to make that stuff?" Her mother was mostly kidding, but the sharpness in her tone said everything about her disappointment with Alyssa's career.

"I'm employed, Mom. Self-supporting. No small feat for an art grad in New York City." Advertising was what happened to good art school graduates who didn't have trust funds or connections in the museum and gallery world. She'd worked hard to get where she was, but it wasn't what she'd thought she would do with her life.

Her mom reached over to squeeze her knee. "In any city, honey. We're so proud of you."

A genuine smile touched her lips. They were the first positive words Alyssa had heard all holiday season. She'd been about to mention the lack of a raise, just to get all the bad news out of the way, but the words died in her mouth.

AT THE SLAM of a car door in the driveway next door, the garden hose in Marc De Luna's hand slowed to a trickle. Janelle's girlish voice carried over the fence. Ever since the Carlisle family had moved next door, his friends had been telling him he ought to make a play for her —or they were threatening to try it themselves.

Yet Marc's attention always skipped over Janelle and landed her sister. He'd know that tangle of hair anywhere. The summer she'd moved in it had been brown, but within a few months the sun had streaked it with gold. After she'd moved to New York she'd dyed it blonde for a few years. Honey blonde, bright blonde, it didn't matter. It all looked good.

When she'd come back last summer it had been brown at the roots again, fading to a dark blonde at the ends. It looked expensive, professionally done. Right now, it was up in a loose ponytail, dangling to the middle of her black shirt.

She never glanced his direction. Alyssa had been his neighbor for less than a year. She'd been home for a summer or two when he'd been busy playing the field and flunking out of college. He'd watched her go from cute high school senior to gorgeous grownup, a little too sophisticated for Florida and a long way from Ohio, where the Carlisles had moved from.

Miss New York. He'd teased her with that nickname once, a few summers ago. Alyssa hadn't spoken to him the rest of the week she'd been home. She never said much, not to him, other than a few occasions when she'd gone on about art and design. It all went over his head, but her enthusiasm made a lump form under his ribcage. The weird sensation returned whenever she did, and when she left, the space remained empty for days after.

She didn't notice him now, either. Nothing had changed.

Marc returned his attention to washing away the bits and pieces of greenery and smudges of dirt leftover from the plants his father had repotted. He wished he could rinse away the tense knot that had manifested in his midsection just as easily.

Alyssa. Engaged. To the douchey finance guy with the too-easy grin she'd brought home last summer. No accounting for taste.

The boyfriend wasn't here though. He hadn't been in the car, and no one had arrived since. Interesting.

"ALYSSA, HONEY." Her mother looked out the window above the kitchen sink as she loaded the dishwasher. They'd finished opening gifts and the living room was a veritable mess. "Would you take out the trash?"

"Right now?"

"Yes, please. We're having a cookout later and your dad invited the neighbors to stop by. You can help clean up, broken heart and all."

"It's not broken, Mom. Seriously, it's not even cracked. Hardly a scratch." Her pride, however, had taken one hell of a beating. It was less that Zach had stood her up—although the episode still stung—than that she'd stayed with him for so long in the first place. It was hard to be devastated about losing someone when there hadn't been anything of substance to lose.

Alyssa hauled herself off the couch, where she'd been on the edge of drifting into a much-needed nap. Her bare feet were slung over one end like a teenager with no responsibilities, but she should be helping out. She pulled herself up without complaint.

She quickly collected all the wrapping paper, bows, and boxes, stuffed them into a garbage bag and took them outside to the recycling bin. It was tempting to sneak in that nap before whichever neighbors her mother had invited over showed up.

From next door, the sharp clatter of bottles bit at her ears. Alyssa glanced up to see her neighbor performing the same ritual.

Being within ten yards of Marc De Luna always made Alyssa feel like she was drowning in lava. Hot didn't begin to describe it. Just seeing him burned away nerve endings. Faded jeans hung low on his narrow hips. The pale blue T-shirt clung to his pectoral muscles and broad shoulders, loose around his body where his waist narrowed. Marc's thick dark hair was just shaggy enough to make her want to run her hands through it.

If he ever looked her way, she'd probably fall into the trash can. She was that suave. And if he spoke to her? She'd swoon and give herself a concussion.

She yanked the lid of her parents' can open, tossed in the bag of paper recycling, and gently closed it. There was no point in trying to attract Marc's attention. For starters, he was the last person she wanted to be around at this exact moment. Ever since her parents had moved to Verona Harbor, Florida, when she was in high school, Alyssa had watched him from afar. He'd been in college then. If he'd gotten as far as declaring a major, it would've been a degree in seducing sorority girls. Despite this, Alyssa still remembered every single syllable he had ever spoken to her.

She glanced up. His intense amber gaze pinned her where she stood.

"Alyssa. I wondered if you were coming home for the holidays." He dropped the lid to the garbage can and shifted his weight onto one foot.

"You did? I mean, of course. I always come back for Christmas." She felt faint. What fresh hell was this speaking words business? If she did fall over she'd blame it on the balmy weather. Marc *never* spoke to her, except to tease.

"You didn't last year."

"I can't believe you noticed," Alyssa blurted. She'd been in Connecticut with Zach's family.

"I've always noticed," he replied with a half-grin that hit her like a tractor-trailer. "I hear we're coming over for dinner later."

"You are? I mean, yes. Right. For dinner." Her voice sounded better, but her words had never sounded so stupid. Her mother hadn't specified which neighbors. Theirs was a social block, and she could've meant anyone ten houses up or down either side of the street. It hadn't occurred to Alyssa to clarify who was coming over.

"See you later," Marc said casually.

Alyssa stumbled into her house, where she caught a glimpse of herself in the hall mirror. Gray smudges lurked beneath her eyes from lack of sleep, her stringy, tangled hair shot from her head in crazy angles, and she still wore the wrinkled, stained black shirt she'd had on since leaving her apartment. Not to mention she hadn't seen a ray of sunlight in about a year.

"Mom! When are the De Lunas coming over for dinner?" *So, what? He talks to you and suddenly you're salivating?*

Also: *Shut up, Inner Critic.*

Catherine stepped out of the kitchen. "Half an hour or so. Why don't you clean up a little before our guests arrive? Janelle, would you help me with the avocado rolls?"

Alyssa squinted at her mother. Could she be…up to something?

Time was a-wasting. Intrigue could wait. Twelve minutes later she wore a white-and-red floral print dress. The sparkly green earrings, bracelet and necklace from her sister complemented the outfit. Thank goodness she'd gotten a manicure in anticipation of her big engagement night. A quick shower and a little makeup went a long way toward erasing evidence of fatigue.

"You look fancy," Janelle told her in the half-complimentary, half-condescending way that only little sisters could manage, no matter how old they were. Janelle was three years younger, and at twenty-four still the baby in the family.

"Thanks!" Alyssa bounded past her to the door. The doorbell had just begun to chime when she yanked it open. "Hi, Ms. De Luna."

"Hello, dear. You remember my sons, Marc and Julian." It wasn't hard to see where Marc got his handsomeness from—he had his mother's eyes. Their father was taller, and thin. Julian favored him, but Alyssa hardly noticed him beyond that fact.

"Where can I put this tray?" asked Mrs. De Luna.

"Over here." She held the door open and gestured for Janelle to take it. Her sister shot her a long-suffering look.

Marc was the last person to enter the house, carrying a large bouquet of flowers. Alyssa couldn't stop a huge grin from overtaking her face. "For me?" she joked nervously.

Whoa, Nellie. Alyssa's stomach churned at her own boldness. It wasn't as if saying hello over the garbage cans had changed anything. *He's always noticed,* a little voice reminded her smugly.

It's Marc. You're fresh meat. Don't get your hopes up. Too late.

"This one is," he replied, separating one huge white lily out of the bunch. He broke the stem with a practiced twist and tucked the bloom behind her ear.

She took a deep breath and imagined braces around her knees. She was not going to collapse from a little neighborly flirtation. Still, if she was the slightest brush of Marc's fingertips against her hair could make her weak-kneed, she'd had no business even thinking about getting engaged to Zach.

"Come this way," she said.

"Any way you want," he replied.

Alyssa stumbled. She must have imagined the smirk in his voice. He could've intended it as a perfectly innocent comment. It didn't stop the blush from creeping over her cheeks. If only she'd gotten a tan before she came here so it wouldn't be so noticeable.

Dirty mind, Aly. Get a grip!

"Marco, want a beer?" Alyssa's dad came over, providing her with a merciful escape.

He handed the bouquet to her mother, who declared them lovely and went in search of a vase. Marc turned and locked eyes with her. The heat went nuclear, spreading from her core into every limb until her spine threatened to melt. The corners of his eyes crinkled, and his sexy mouth pulled up at the corners in a suppressed smile. Alyssa gave her head a tiny shake.

Marc De Luna had intended that comment exactly the way she'd heard it.

3

Away from Marc's flirtations, doubt cat-footed its way through her psyche. Nothing had changed since her last visit, when he'd barely said hello over the fence separating their parents' yards. She was just Alyssa, same person he'd spoken a handful of words to in all the years her parents had lived next door to his. Marc was the kind of guy who made girls' panties wet just by walking into the room—at least the ones like her, who wore undergarments. He might toy with her, but there was no way his interest was serious.

On the other hand, she didn't need serious. She'd had more serious than she could handle until fifteen hours ago. She needed fun. Thinking about it logically, Marc offered the perfect rebound opportunity: he was here, she was in New York. Even if it all went cockeyed, there'd be enough time until her next visit to smooth over the worst of the awkwardness.

She shook her head. She was getting ahead of herself. He'd given her a flower and made a mildly risqué joke. It didn't mean he wanted to jump her bones, no matter how often she'd fantasized about jumping his.

A whisper of warm evening air ran along her neck. She took a seat at the glass patio table. As she sat, the scent of sea and old water whuffed up from the seat cushions. Janelle came back with a bottle and filled her glass with lychee wine. The sweetness made her mouth pucker.

The chair next to hers screeched across the flagstone patio.

"Sorry," Marc said, wincing as he sat beside her. "I was wondering where you'd disappeared to."

"You know me, hiding from the crowd." Alyssa groaned inwardly. She was so bad at flirting. She'd always been the quiet one, the girl whose friends vented about relationship woes.

Quit overthinking it. She sat up straighter. Fine. If Marc wanted a fling, something short-term, she was game. Maybe Marc was just what she needed to forget Zach, engagement rings, and New York.

His gaze touched briefly her cleavage, and she felt it as surely as if it had been his finger trailing over the rise of her breasts. Her mouth quirked up as he glanced away, caught out. Then the air stopped in her lungs as he looked her directly in the eye.

"I don't know you. Not really. I'd like to though."

Alyssa tried to break contact but was instantly pulled back into the tractor beam of his attention. It was no mystery why he was catnip to women. "Let's start with the basics. Seeing anyone?"

"Nope."

Marc's expression was so intense it was like being eye fucked over dinner. In front of her family. Her fingers trembled as she clutched her napkin. Alyssa inhaled and forced herself to let the edge fall. Then she met his gaze full-on. His met hers for a long minute. This time, he turned away.

Better. Definitely an improvement. Maybe she was getting the hang of this flirting business at the ripe old age of twenty-seven. "Me neither."

"I heard you had a boyfriend."

"We broke up." The words shot out of her mouth.

His satisfied smile made her toes curl. "I heard that too."

"Really? How?"

"Our moms talk. They always have."

"News travels fast." Alyssa shot her mother a speculative glance.

Everyone else sat down to dinner, all at once, like a flock of parakeets settling into a tree. Alyssa pushed a strand of hair behind one ear, her stomach too tight to enjoy the meal. Ham and pineapple, huge green avocadoes filled with red salsa, roasted corn, Moros y Cristianos, and shrimp sat wasted on her plate. Marc did not appear to be suffering the same stomach problems. He was a lot more practiced at this, but Alyssa refused to let the thought bother her. It was what she wanted, at least right now.

"A toast." Alyssa's dad held up his glass. "To friends near and family from far, gathered to celebrate. To successes" —he nodded at Alyssa, and her soul shriveled at being publicly honored for nonexistent accomplishments— "and a bright new year to come."

Glasses clinked all around. Marc dropped his arm across the back of her chair. Alyssa leaned back, letting her hair slither across his forearm. In response, he dangled his fingers over her bare shoulder. There was only the briefest contact of skin, but it sent shockwaves through her entire body.

"You gave up on the blonde, I see. What's this style called? Something fancy…"

"Balayage. New York blonde is high-maintenance. This is easier."

He pulled his hand away. "My favorite was when you first moved here and it turned gold from the sun."

What a line that was. She shouldn't encourage it, but her mouth insisted on beaming at him with approval over her internal objections. "I don't believe for one second you've ever noticed my hair color before, Marc De Luna. You're an awful liar."

Marc reached over and plucked a piece of pineapple off her plate. "Scout's honor. Every year, I wonder what color it'll be when you come home to visit. Now that you've conquered the big apple, what's next, Miss New York?"

Alyssa loved it when he called her by the nickname, as if she was some sort of beauty queen. He'd teased her with it once before and she'd been tongue-tied for a week. Even now she missed a beat before responding, dryly.

Conquered New York, my ass. "World domination, of course."

Something flared in his eyes at the word *domination*. "What's it like? I've never been."

"To New York?"

"Nope. Haven't had any reason to go."

He ran his fingers through the ends of her hair and Alyssa shook her head a little, grinning. "Come visit me sometime. I can put you up in my luxurious two-hundred-square-foot apartment."

"So, your boyfriend really isn't going to mind if I come crash on your couch?"

He returned his arm to the back of her chair, and his finger stroked the curve of her bare shoulder. Alyssa wanted to rub against him like a cat.

"No boyfriend, remember? But you wouldn't fit on the couch. I can't stretch out on it, and you're five or six inches taller than me. You'd have to take the bed."

She took a sip of her drink and eyed the other people around table, hoping no one else had heard her highly suggestive words. Janelle and Julian were talking sports with their fathers, and Mrs. De Luna and Catherine were catching up on the latest neighborhood chitchat. No one was paying any attention to her and Marc. She could be bold and no one would notice. To a point.

He chuckled, and the sound made a grin spread over her lips no matter how hard she fought to stay cool. Her heart rate picked up. She was doing this. Flirting with Marc, not standing there gawping while he lobbed overtures.

"Consider it a promise." He pulled his arm away from her shoulders and reached for her hand beneath the table. Long, warm fingers curled around hers. She ran her thumb over calloused ridges on his palm as a kaleidoscope of ideas about where he could put those rough-tipped fingers wheeled through her imagination.

No wonder Marc was popular with the ladies. He knew exactly how to make you feel like the center of his universe, where anything was permissible. She dropped her left hand onto his knee and froze.

Marc inhaled sharply. Maybe she'd gotten ahead of herself. If he'd had any doubts about what she wanted, surely he didn't now. Alyssa swallowed when Janelle speared her with a *what-are-you-doing* scowl from across the table. Their families' proximity was awkward, no doubt.

"Let's take a walk. We could check out the harbor. It's not far," he suggested.

"Sure." Good idea, putting as much distance as possible between them and their families. Alyssa tucked her hair behind her ear. "I'll get a sweater."

On the sidewalk, silence stretched awkwardly between them. For the first block that was all right while they left their family homes behind, but by the second block nerves had choked Alyssa's throat closed. Her foot began to ache the minute they were out of sight of the house. Alyssa shifted her weight to the ball and did her best not to limp.

"Is your apartment really two hundred square feet?" Marc finally asked.

"One hundred and eighty-eight, to be exact," she replied, lunging for the verbal lifeline he'd tossed.

He shook his head. "I've seen larger closets."

"I know. But it's cheap by New York standards, and the location is good. Right by Central Park and close to two subways."

"I have apartments I rent out, but nothing that small."

"Rent out? You own them?" She'd heard something about Marc and real estate, but the De Lunas didn't discuss money. Alyssa's thoughts scattered as she tried to memorize his every movement. She'd never felt like this with Zach. Not once.

Every few steps the backs of their hands brushed together, the space between them magnetized. Or their shoulders touched and her stomach flipped. Alyssa pulled her sweater tight over her chest and crossed her arms, not for warmth, for protection. From what, she wasn't certain.

Rushing into a fling with a guy you've nursed a crush on for the better part of a decade is impulsive, and you don't do impulsive. But was it rushing if she'd known him since high school? Even if he saw her as easy, recently-dumped pickings, any time they had together was on loan from her real life. She shouldn't waste a minute. Yet alone with him, her mind couldn't stop cartwheeling ahead to consequences long enough to enjoy the experience.

"Yeah, that was my drop-out-of-college strategy. Buy cheap real estate, flip it for a profit and reinvest the money in rentals for the long term. I'd rather work with my hands than sit in front of a computer." Marc moved his arm to her waist. Every thought that he might not be into her scattered like a flock of starlings evading a predator. There was a word for it. Murmuration.

Forget the damn birds.

Alyssa leaned into him, partly to hide her limp. She could tell the wound had reopened from the way it throbbed. Sticky liquid sucked at her foot with every step. But mostly because Marc's body was so delicious. A thin layer of cotton was all that separated her fingertips from a six-pack waiting to be discovered. All she wanted to do was unwrap the Christmas gift she hadn't expected to receive.

4

Marc suffered a rare moment of hesitation trying to figure out what he was supposed to do. With any other girl, he'd have been angling to go to her place by now.

But this was Alyssa. She'd always been different. Aly's kindness pulled everyone into her orbit. People just liked her: his mom, his dad, even his older brother, who rarely found much to like about girls. It was amazing New York hadn't beaten that magnetic quality out of her. If anything, it was stronger now.

Or maybe she'd dialed it up for him tonight. She'd been a total vixen at dinner, but since they'd walked out Aly had fallen back into her usual silence. It was frustrating to get a glimpse of her relaxed and then have her clam up again. What had he said wrong?

These situations were why banter had been invented, but Aly never responded to that shallow shit. Until tonight, when she'd humored him for once. Now that she was talking to him, he wanted to push her to keep opening up. He didn't have the first clue how to do that.

"I'd forgotten about the pelicans." The huge birds were gathered at the end of a dock. A few circled in front of the rising moon. Occasionally a dark shape would dive into the water with a silent splash. "I don't think I'll ever get used to warm winters. It doesn't feel like Christmas."

"It's all I know." Their conversation was nosediving. *Fuck.* He'd never had any idea how to talk to this woman.

She was all talent and ambition, and while he'd been too lazy to finish school and had arranged his entire life to revolve around his sailing obsession. He'd been too focused on sex when he should have been studying. He'd outright wasted his parents' investment in his education. It hadn't hurt him. He'd managed just fine playing things his own way. Women came and went, and he'd never much cared how long they stuck around provided they left quietly. Yet he already dreaded Aly's return to New York.

Keep her talking. Better yet, kiss her. He'd waited ages for an opportunity, and he wasn't going to waste it on small talk.

Alyssa stopped, leaning gently against him. His arm fit perfectly into the gentle curve of her hip. He let his palm dangle against her body, imagining what it would feel like to hike up the skirt of her dress and pull her gorgeous leg around his waist and slide…

Way too soon. Alyssa wasn't just any girl. She had talent and ambition, especially compared to him, and was so far out of his league he shouldn't even be playing the game.

Now he had all that determination and creativity tucked under his arm, and damn if it didn't come wrapped in a spectacular package. The lily was still tucked behind her ear, and he hadn't forgotten the look on her face when he'd had the brass to make a crude joke in her parents' foyer. Like she'd wanted to get started right there against the glass and marble console table next to the front door.

He hadn't thought she could hear him. When she'd glanced over her shoulder with questioning hazel eyes, he'd known for sure he had a shot with her.

Finally. If he didn't screw it up.

He frowned. Alyssa was definitely favoring one foot. "Are you okay?"

She limped over to lean against the wall. "I'm fine. Let's pause here."

Alyssa leaned her forearms on the top of the iron wall. Her hair fell in a curtain over her shoulder and halfway down her back. He loved the cascade of thick strands, and one of his favorite fantasies was sinking his fingers into it while kissing her full-on. The things he'd daydreamed about doing to her over the years were too dirty and too numerous to count. Her generous lips curved upward, and all he could think about was them clasped around his dick.

Marc walked over and placed his hands on either side of her. Big mistake. Alyssa's gorgeous butt was now less than two inches from the center of his attention. All she had to do was stand up straight, and her body would be pressed against his from chin to knee.

Which was exactly what she did.

So much for not moving too fast.

Marc inhaled a lungful of cool, salt-tinged night air. With it came a heady dose of Alyssa: the subtle combination of the scent of her hair, some whisper-light perfume, and, most intoxicating of all, the warmth of her skin. He lifted his hand to her shoulder and gently turned her to face him.

She was still as his mouth his touched hers, firm and soft and sensuous. Unhurried, perfect. He forced himself to move slowly as she slid her hands up his chest, over his shoulders, and around the back of his neck.

Too fast. Marc had a fleeting notion of pulling back, but then she sighed and parted her lips, and there was no stopping.

Somewhere behind them the music had started. They were alone on the walkway. Marc had been wanting to take handfuls of Alyssa's skirt and shove them up around her waist ever since she'd bent over the railing. Now he ran his hand down her curves over her hip and gently grabbed a fistful of red floral print silk. Her skirt rose an inch, then another. Her legs were bare beneath her dress.

Alyssa leaned back against the wall. Marc took the opportunity to kiss his way down her elegant neck, tasting the hollow of her throat where her pulse beat like a hummingbird's wings. Lazily he traced a circle against her naked hip with his fingertips. He sank the fingers of his other hand into the silk of her hair, and found the delicate indentation at the base of her skull.

Then he kissed her for real. Full-on, no holds barred, his tongue sliding past hers, lips open and shared breath. The way he'd wanted to for so long.

Alyssa gasped and pressed hard against him. The soft rise of her breasts flattened against his chest. The hard pebbles of her nipples rubbed past his. If she was wearing a bra it didn't provide much in the way of headlight dampening. Forgetting where they were and heedless of how quickly they were barreling forward, Marc slid his hand between Alyssa's inner thighs. She froze.

It was too much, too soon. But the dampness he found there was irresistible, pulling him forward despite common sense screaming at him to back off. He brushed one fingertip across her sex.

Oh, mierda. He'd never felt a woman so aroused. He had no idea what to do. They stood there, foreheads pressed together, as he slowly withdrew his hand and smoothed her skirt over her hip.

"The sex is going to be incredible." He didn't think he'd said it out loud until she nodded, her velvety skin rubbed softly against his in agreement.

A man in skin-tight pink leopard-print shorts on roller blades shot into his peripheral vision. Marc and Alyssa turned away from one another like guilty teenagers.

"Nice night for it!" the body-builder yelled.

"You know, I've seen a nun on roller blades in New York, but nothing quite compares to him," Alyssa said in an almost-normal voice. Marc watched her fingers tremble as she tucked a piece of hair behind her ear. The lily had fallen to the ground. He picked it up and placed it back behind her left ear. She hadn't moved from her perch against the wall, one hip cocked.

Marc glanced down the length of her leg. A dark shadow pooled below her foot. "You're bleeding."

"I am?" Alyssa glanced down. "I cut my foot on a piece of glass this morning before I left. It rubbed open a few blocks ago."

"I'm taking you home."

"Don't." Alyssa placed one palm on his chest, right over his heart. "Please. It's not serious. I'm only here for a week. Let's not waste a minute of it. Take me to your place."

"We should wait until tomorrow, especially if you're hurt." Marc's dick threatened to reach up and strangle him. It was very relieved to hear her next words. All of him was.

"Absolutely not. Where can we get a cab?"

He laughed, startled by her decisiveness. "Around here everyone gets a Lyft."

Alyssa pulled her phone out of the pocket of her sweater. "What's the address?"

"You're serious?"

She peered over the top of her phone, eyes dark. "I am."

"Put that away." Typing in the address was a surreal moment. "Two minutes."

Which he spent kissing her thoroughly. When the car pulled up, he scooped her into his arms. She yelped and wound one arm around his neck. Now he had ahold of her, and there was no way he was letting go. He'd figure out the rest of it later.

The car ride was short. They spent it making out in the back seat of the cab while the driver stoically ignored them. Alyssa let her fingers trail down the zipper seam of his jeans, feeling the swell of his body. The sex *was* going to be incredible. She'd fantasized for years about this, and she wasn't about to back down. But… "Where the hell are we?"

"You told me to take you to my place," Marc said, scooping her into his arms again.

Alyssa settled her arm around his broad shoulders. "Um, this is a marina."

He laughed, a throaty sound that did wicked things to her pelvic region. "I might be the only person in the world who'd tell you 188 square feet sounds luxurious, because I live on a sailboat."

"You live on a what?"

"A boat."

"By choice?"

Marc grinned. "That's a complicated question. The short answer is yeah. I own four properties and I still choose to live on a boat. It's cheap and better living with my parents."

"Show me." Alyssa winced as her feet hit the dock. Marc jumped smoothly onto a white boat that looked like every other one bobbing silently around them. This, she had not anticipated.

"Welcome to the *Escape*." Marc reached out one hand. Alyssa took it and hopped over the six-inch gap between the dock and the deck. This comprised the extent of her nautical knowledge. Well, the word *mainsail* had once won her a 50-point bonus in Scrabble.

"It's beautiful," Alyssa declared, her attention on Marc. It was nighttime, and she'd need considerable explanation before she could tell what differentiated it from the one floating a few feet away. No matter the venue, Alyssa had one thing on her mind: Marc naked. The sooner the better.

"Careful you don't hit your head."

Alyssa maneuvered down a steep flight of stairs into a small room. The boat hadn't seemed large enough to have a living space. Her eyes widened as they adjusted to the darkness. To her left was a gleaming compact kitchen and to the right a narrow door. In the middle of the cabin was a table surrounded by benches. At the front of the cabin was a triangular bed with drawers beneath it. Around the edges of the cabin were small oval windows open to let in the night breeze, which let in the harsh glare of sodium lights. Beneath them were shelves bearing neat rows of books.

She knew firsthand how organized you had to be to live in a small space for any length of time. Marc had clearly mastered it. There wasn't a single item out of place.

"This is wonderful." Alyssa shrugged out of her sweater and tossed it over the dining banquette.

"I like it." Marc had kicked off his shoes and gestured for her to sit down. "There's a first aid kit here. Let me take care of your foot."

"It's nothing. Feet bleed a lot, that's all." Nonetheless, she perched on the opposite seat and let him slide his hand under her ankle. He pulled a small yellow bag from a cabinet and tore open a gauze pad. While he was setting out supplies, she bent her knee for a better view. It did look gory. Maybe she should've gone to a doctor.

"Better?" Marc asked when he had applied the last bandage. She nodded.

"Good. Where were we?" He leaned across the divide and kissed her.

"We left off at this." Alyssa took a fistful of his shirt and dragged it upward. Marc took the hint and pulled it over his head. Then they were kissing again, openmouthed and hungry. A cursory exploration of the ridged contours of his abdomen made the blood pulse in her veins, and the hard, long ridge of his erection made her mind blank.

Alyssa sat up and unzipped her dress. Marc's expression was unreadable as he sat back and pushed the straps down her shoulders. She pulled it over her head and tossed it on the floor by his shirt. Embarrassment radiated through her body as she sat there in her best bra and underwear, waiting for him to react. He'd been with a lot of women. There was no way she measured up.

Marc ran his hands over her bare calves, hooked his hands behind her knees and pulled her slowly down until her back was flat against the seat with her head propped on the arm rest cushion. Alyssa held her breath as he hooked one finger on each side of her underwear and pulled it over her bent knees.

They were really doing this.

He stripped them down over her ankles and tossed them onto the pile of clothing that now dominated the floor.

"Open your legs," he demanded, running a knuckle down the inside of her thigh.

"Why?"

Marc's expression was obscured by shadow, but he chuckled. "You need to ask? I want to go down on you."

Alyssa swallowed. Zach had done it occasionally. Not often, not recently, and not happily either. "I thought guys hated giving oral."

"I don't." He ran his finger over her sex and up the inside of her other leg. Alyssa parted them fractionally.

"Why?" she asked suspiciously. Couldn't they get on with the main event?

Marc propped his chin on his hand. The posture tilted his face into a patch of orange light filtering in through one of the small windows.

"Do you ever give oral sex?"

"Sometimes. Yes." Was he asking for a blowjob? Disappointment stole over her.

"Do you enjoy doing it?"

Trick question. "Occasionally. If it's with the right person, and I'm in the right mood."

"When you enjoy it, why do you like it?"

Alyssa swallowed, grateful for the darkness. Her face was hot in a way that nothing to do with her desire to get it on with Marc. "Because I get to feel powerful. I can make someone I care about feel good."

"Mmmhm."

Oh.

"You don't have to do anything you don't want to."

"I want to."

This time, when he ran his knuckle down her thigh, her knee fell all the way open. She'd never been so exposed. Her breath caught as Marc bent his head, parted her, and ran his tongue straight down the seam of her body. Alyssa moaned.

He'd had some practice with this, and that bothered her a lot more than it had any right to.

"Do you like this?"

"Yes," she whispered, her ability to speak gone.

"Do you want more?"

"Yes, *please.*"

Moments later she buried her fingers in his hair as he pushed his fingers inside her and stroked in rhythm with his tongue. Alyssa clutched his shoulder and experienced his pure mastery. He grazed her labia with his teeth, which sent a shudder through her body. He followed that with focused attention to her clit, and the shudder became a ripple and a breathless moan.

"Good?"

Alyssa made a sound that could've meant *great, yeah,* or something in between. She was accustomed to perfunctory tolerance of oral sex from her partners, not skill and enthusiasm. That alone made tonight worth the risk she was taking.

While she was still recovering, Marc shucked his jeans, pulled her up and leaned her against the waist-height captain's bed. With one hand, he rummaged through a tiny cabinet until he found a package of condoms.

Relief loosened any remaining tension in her body. It would've been maddening to have to walk away if he'd tried to pull the *I hate condoms* whine. Instead, he was being a perfect gentleman about it. She didn't have one because she hadn't exactly planned this, not that she was complaining about the direction her evening had taken.

"Are you sure you want to keep going?" he asked, rolling one over his engorged cock.

"Best Christmas present I've ever received," Alyssa replied, pressing kisses along his collarbone. She liked how he'd asked again.

His chuckle rumbled through her. He was *really* good at this. Then her hands were busy memorizing every contour of his chest and the glorious flat stomach she'd often glimpsed and dreamed of touching. She'd never whispered a word of her secret obsession to anyone. It was too obvious. Crush on Marc? You and every other female for twenty miles in any direction.

With one quick motion, he slipped his hand beneath her knee and pulled her leg up. The hard wood edge of the hip-high bed dug into her naked ass, holding her up as Marc thrust hard. Alyssa gasped. Nothing had ever felt as good as the sensation of him sliding into her, full and hard, stretching her body.

She made a sound that would've been embarrassing if her brain cells still functioned. Who was this version of her, lost in pleasure, not thinking three steps ahead? All that mattered was the exquisite sensation of Marc's body within hers, his weight and warmth centered on pleasing her. She ran her hands over the taut roundness of his buttocks, followed the planes of his back, and buried her fingers in his thick dark hair as he molded her breast with one hand.

He wasn't done either. He turned her against the bed and curved against her body. Alyssa shuddered as Marc entered her from behind, grabbing fistfuls of the bedsheets when his teeth grazed the nape of her neck. One broad hand splayed over the small of her back as he pumped and reached around her with his other hand to rub her clitoris. Alyssa's back hollowed, giving him better access. Oh, it was so damn good.

Fizzy little sparks popped behind her eyes as the orgasm rolled over her. Her head tilted so her hair fell back. Their mouths were an inch apart over her shoulder as he leaned in and coaxed her body toward a second climax.

When she could breathe again, Alyssa realized he was a few beats behind. He moved urgently inside her. Purely by accident, their eyes met as the orgasm caught him. A smile crept over her as she pushed back to meet his frantic pumps and watched the emotions swirl in his amber eyes. It touched her in a tender spot she'd forgotten to guard.

For a long minute, they were still. Breathless, he hauled her into the tiny captain's bed and pulled her close against his body. They lay boneless and recovering in the stuffy cabin.

Her heartbeat slowed as she traced the lines of his small nipples and the breadth of his chest. Foolish organ, getting all worked up over a hookup. This was *Marc*. She had tonight, if she were lucky, maybe a few more nights. Failing to remember who and what he was would lead to a whole lot more pain than Zach ever had.

Her ordinary self was not invited to this evening. She'd think through how to deal with the fallout in the morning. Considering she'd disappeared with the playboy next door on Christmas Day, her family was bound to rain holy hell on this parade.

5

Marc stepped away to dispose of the condom. When he came back Alyssa's gorgeous body sprawled lazily over his bed. His balls tightened, already interested in more.

Most of her face was hidden in shadow. Judging from the way her lips curved upward as he approached, Marc guessed she wouldn't mind another round either. He reached for another condom package and climbed into the cozy space next to her. There wasn't enough room to do anything except cover her body with his. Neither of them could sit up without risking a concussion.

The closeness was fine with him. He couldn't get enough of the velvety texture of her skin, the silk of her hair, or the sweet scent of her body. If it weren't for the irritating seagulls outside he'd think he was dreaming. Marc ran his palm up her ribs, his fingers tracing each indentation, savoring the experience of touching her. Damn, he'd waited so long for this.

Alyssa shifted, drawing her leg up over his thigh and propping her head up on one hand. She reached between them with her free hand and grasped him gently. Too gently. He pressed against her fingers and her grip firmed. Better. Marc ran his hand down her leg and pulled it up. She settled it around his waist. He slid his hand over her hip and down her ass to her center, inching her body closer to his while he explored her wetness.

"Don't suppose you have another condom handy?" Her voice was breathy and raw.

He reached for it and handed it to her wordlessly. All reserve remaining in her body eased. She relaxed, opened it, and rolled it on. Her fingers sent flares of arousal down his shaft and into his body like comets.

Marc leaned forward and pinned Alyssa against the mattress with a grin. She opened her knees and tilted her pelvis as he inched inside her. The space didn't allow for creative positioning. Vanilla as it was, this was even more intense than the gymnastics they'd done before. The sensation as her body gave way, tight and hot, crashed over him like waves over a rock.

He pulled out and pressed forward again. Aly bit her lower lip in concentration, her eyes lively and wondering as she locked her legs around his waist, pulling him deeper. Marc dug his toes into the fabric, the sight of her even teeth on her lip doing strange things to him. His breath caught in the airless space. Her chin tilted back, her eyes drifting closed.

"Keep them open," he demanded roughly.

Her lashes fluttered up, revealing hazel eyes flecked with gold streaks, radiating like sunlight out from her pupils. Mascara smudged a little around the corners of her eyes. He'd messed up her makeup. He'd tangled her hair and put the soft haze in her expression. For once, she wasn't distant or sophisticated or polished, and it was hot as fuck.

Instinctively, Marc's hips flexed harder. Alyssa gasped and met him, an inarticulate throaty growl as her eyes drifted closed again.

"Look at me," he demanded. "I want to watch." The way she'd watched him. He'd never been this connected with a woman before. It made him hungry. Wolfish. He needed to see it again.

Alyssa frowned. He placed his hand along the side of her head, his thumb on her chin, so intent on the storm he saw breaking over her he hardly noticed how close to the edge he was.

She closed her eyes and buried her face in his shoulder, panting hot against his skin. The pleasure and frustration were almost unbearable as the orgasm ripped through him at hurricane force.

He'd wanted to be there with her, and she'd hidden herself at the last possible moment. He couldn't say why he wanted it so badly. Marc didn't want Alyssa to hide anything from him, especially not herself when he was balls-deep inside her.

THAT WAS NOT ONE-NIGHT-STAND SEX. Her luck that the best sex of her life was with the one man immune to relationships. It was too good to be temporary, but temporary was the whole reason she was lying beneath him, clutching his shoulders as colors popped behind her eyelids while her entire body strained against his. The way he filled her made her brain short out under the onslaught of sensation.

Sure, he'd turned the art of orgasms into a science. It meant nothing. He made every woman feel like this. Didn't he?

It was rebound sex. A little gift to herself. Yet it had also been soul-searching and raw and perfect. The kind of sex one should be having with a real partner. Not with the guy you were screwing on a vacation rebound. His scent hit her nostrils as breath returned to her lungs, penetrating her body in the most ephemeral way.

At least she hadn't compromised in going after what she wanted, for once. How messed up was she that a one-night stand felt like an achievement?

ALYSSA LAY in bed for a long time after Marc had awoken, kissed her, and climbed out. She'd almost fallen asleep again, until the memory of what she'd done jerked her upright so fast she cracked her head against the ceiling.

She'd disappeared *with her neighbor* on Christmas night. Her family was going to kill her dead for acting so out of character.

Alyssa scrambled out of the bed, naked. Oh, so naked. Remembering the way Marc had awoken her this morning, his rough stubble as he kissed along her neck, made her feel all warm and gooey south of her navel. Marc knew exactly what buttons to push on a woman's body, and she was going to enjoy it for as long as she could. When it ended, he was going to be the gold standard for any future boyfriend.

Not that they'd exactly discussed expectations, but Alyssa understood Marc's implicit rules. Keep it light and temporary. She could always ghost it back to New York, and any messy loose ends disappeared. By her next visit he'd be onto the next girl, no hard feelings. Right?

Maybe if she played her cards right, maybe they could hook up again on future visits. This was absolutely worth a repeat. Lots of repeats. As many as possible before he tired of her company. Considering they communicated better with their bodies than with words, that moment might come sooner than she'd like.

Alyssa pinched the straps of her dress and pulled it up over her shoulders with distaste. In bare feet, she climbed the steep stairway, unsure what to expect. The sun blinded her as she stepped over the high ledge. Shading her vision, she found only glittering sea stretching into the distance.

"Watch your head!" Marc shouted. Alyssa ducked. A large beam whizzed by, missing her by inches. When she popped up again he was two feet away wearing a relieved expression.

"A little warning, next time?" she suggested.

"I gave you one." He grinned. He moved past her and pulled a rope down, winding it around some sort of two-pronged protuberance.

The boat tipped sideways. Alyssa reached for the nearest solid object and found herself clinging to smooth varnished wood behind the leather seat. Marc moved back to the steering wheel. A moment later the ship leapt forward over the waves. The sail snapped in the morning light.

Alyssa threw out her arms, like she was flying. Her belly dropped as the boat crested a wave and landed again.

"This is amazing!" she shouted over the wind.

"Ever been sailing before?"

"No!"

"Here, I have something sexy for you to wear."

When she'd raked her hair out of her eyes enough to see what he was holding, Alyssa laughed. It was an orange life vest. "If you insist."

"I do. I never take chances on the water, and I'm not going to start with you." He pulled the straps tight around her waist, then kissed her hard. "Now that you're not going to drown if you fall in, try going to the front of the boat."

"Where's yours?" she asked petulantly as he buckled it around her. He pointed to the unobtrusive harness around his chest.

"It inflates when immersed in water. I don't have an extra, though." He kissed her cheek. "Try going out there. You'll like the view."

A very narrow rail wrapped around the front tip of the ship. Carefully Alyssa edged her way out onto it.

"Hold on," Marc called behind her.

The ship leapt forward like a racehorse. Alyssa gasped. Though it was a warm day, the air was cool and sea spray hit her arms. Within moments, she was shivering. Yet she stayed, entranced by the endless horizon and the waves playing beneath the bright sunlight.

When her skin had been thoroughly scoured by seawater and sun, Alyssa crawled back to the steering area. She couldn't remember ever feeling so dirty. Her dress was stained and wrinkled, her wind-whipped hair a hopeless tangle of salt and sex.

Yet her shoulders moved freely without any of the tension from a long day hunched over a computer. It was invigorating. She wished she could stay on the *Escape* forever, with nothing but the sea and the sky to interrupt them from doing whatever they wanted to.

They bobbed on the ocean, apparently at a standstill. Marc's sunglasses hid his eyes as he scanned the horizon. "The wind's shifting. We'll hang out here for a while and then head back to shore."

"Okay. Here. Take a picture?" She unbuckled the orange life vest and dropped it to the deck. Marc pulled her close, held out his arm and snapped a selfie. An ussie.

Alyssa glanced through the repeat shots. "Not bad. Mind if I post it to social media?"

"Sure."

"I have a lot of followers."

"Yeah? How many?" He didn't seem especially interested.

"Ten thousand, maybe more. It bounces around, and it's different across platforms."

Marc *hmmed*, his attention locked on some sort of control panel. His disinterest stung. Posting pictures to social media was her hobby, a way of maintaining some creative control in the face of her corporate job. Plus, the instant feedback of likes, comments, and retweets was an ego boost when it worked. Over time, she'd learned what images got a response, and Marc, being Marc, would undoubtedly be popular. The few images she'd posted of Zach had really taken off, though he hadn't exactly appreciated it.

"Is there anywhere to take a shower?" Might as well get out of the way and clean up if her presence wasn't useful up here.

"Yeah, opposite the kitchen below deck." He hardly looked up from whatever he was doing. Alyssa ignored her slighted pride. The last thing she wanted was him following her silly yoga-and-travel-themed Instagram pictures. He wouldn't, anyway.

Sure enough, tucked away in the little bathroom was a handheld shower. The only thing that could've felt better was Marc's body crammed into the little space with her. Hot water alone was damn good. The wet bandage peeled away from her heel. The puncture wound beneath had scabbed over and looked much better.

When she emerged, Alyssa's stomach flipped. A set of Marc's clothing lay on the banquette. She pulled them on. The faded beige shorts barely closed over her hips, while she had to tie a knot in the t-shirt to keep it from hanging like a bag. Marc was either very thoughtful, or he'd had a lot of practice with the morning after.

Jealousy gnawed at her as she finger-combed and braided her hair to keep it from getting snarled any worse. It was absurd. *You know how Marc operates; you were counting on it. Stop trying to make this mean something.*

When she came back up, Alyssa found coffee, fruit and toast on a small lipped table behind the captain's chair. She arched her back, then settled a few inches closer to him. He stretched one arm across her shoulders. It was blissful floating with Marc beneath the bright blue sky.

"I can't believe you live like this." Alyssa mentally face palmed.

Why can't you just talk to him like a normal person? He's always been nice to you—really nice, last night. You talk to strangers all the time at work without paralysis of the vocal chords.

She couldn't help it. Marc's inhumanly hot presence fried her neural networks and disconnected her tongue from her brain. Which was for the best, considering what nonsense came out of her mouth whenever she did get it to function within ten feet of him.

"It's great when it's like this. I'm out here most days. If the weather's good, I usually sail in the morning. In the afternoon, I work on my project house until about six, and then I get dinner somewhere and come back to the marina."

She breathed deep and tried again. *Just ask him a simple question. He's a person, not a god who's going to strike you dead if you say something dumb.* "How did you get into sailing?"

"College. I took a class for fun and decided to find a way to do this as much as I could for the rest of my life."

"Can I ask why you quit school, or is it a secret?" *There you go asking intrusive questions.* Maybe she should stick with awkward silence.

Marc didn't seem bothered by it. He just reached over to refill her cup with strong coffee. "I was bored. All I wanted to know was how to run a business the laziest way possible. Now I kick myself for not finishing, because there *is* no lazy way to run a business. Even real estate, which is supposed to be passive income, isn't very passive. Either it's easy, or everything is broken and you're fighting to get rid of a problem tenant." He shrugged. "I should've paid attention in marketing class, but it was full of girls and I was twenty years old. The prof didn't stand a chance."

Alyssa felt a stab of sympathy for the instructor. She wouldn't be surprised if Marc had singlehandedly brought the class grading curve down, not because he'd been such a terrible student, but because every student in the class with an eye for hot men would've been driven to distraction. "There's lots of marketing information online."

"Yeah, most of it hasn't worked. My tenants only want to hear from me when they need something fixed. They don't want a newsletter or emails. I don't have much turnover, but when I do, I post an ad in the local paper and on Craigslist. I get a lot of shitty applicants—no job, no credit history, bad references, and even outright scams. If I had a better website or ads it might make the process easier."

Well, now. This was a problem right in Alyssa's wheelhouse. "I could help you."

Marc shook his head. "You're too arty. I'll wind up with some abstract design, and no one'll know I'm trying to rent out an apartment."

"No, I'm not. Really! I used to have big notions about art, and I cringe to think about what I probably said to you the last time you talked to me. Which was, before yesterday, about six years ago?" *Not that I'm counting.* "But I work for an advertising agency, and I just got promoted to Lead Creative for Direct & Digital on a major client account. I can definitely help you."

He cocked his head and squinted at her. "What does that mean?"

She sighed. Her title sounded much better when she didn't have to explain its meaning. "I design junk mail and spam email for a living."

Marc threw back his head and laughed. "No fucking way."

Alyssa was so overjoyed that the conversation had shifted out of first gear, she didn't mind a little humor at her expense. "I know. I went to college with all these big ideas and yet ninety-nine percent of the work I do lands in the trash, unopened."

"Do you like advertising?" he asked skeptically.

Alyssa shrugged. "It pays okay. I work with a lot of talented people. If I could change one thing, though, it would be the hours. I'd love to have time to do something other than work, and more creative control." She stretched her arms wide. "This feels like a dream."

"It is when it's like this. Some days I just want to sell the properties and get a job I can stop thinking about at five every day. The grass is always greener, I guess."

"You wouldn't take over your dad's landscaping business?"

Marc laughed again. "No way. I grew up with dirt under my fingernails and getting up at the ass crack of dawn. Julian's not taking over either, since he's got his law practice. Dad will have to sell it when he's ready to retire. My plan has been to build enough of an income stream to let me sail around the world for a few years. Once the project house's permits are in place, I'll turn it over to a contractor and head out."

Alyssa gasped as a wave dipped the ship, grabbing Marc's arm and the rail behind the banquette seat. The roll of her stomach had nothing to do with the movement of the water. What was wrong with her? She understood the rules of a hookup even if she'd never played the game. Check emotions at the door. Play a better version of yourself. Don't overstay your welcome. Anticipate the end.

She was doing fine with rules two, three and four, but the first rule was proving problematic. Wanting him for so long had demolished her ability to keep any emotional distance. Marc's fingers clutched her arm, steadying her, and Alyssa suppressed the instinct to lean over and kiss him.

"I ought to let my family know I'm still alive. I disappeared last night."

She needed to go home and face up to the consequences of what she'd done, not tempting excuses to be alone with him.

"Oh, they know," Marc replied, kissing her forehead as he pulled her into his arms. "My mom texted me this morning saying she was worried about you. I told her you're with me. I'm sure they're planning the wedding already."

Alyssa buried her face in his shoulder. "Oh, fuck. This is going to be awkward."

"It doesn't have to be." He went quiet. "Listen, you said something yesterday about being here for the week. I'm not looking for a week."

Alyssa's heart sank. Great. He might have another girl lined up already.

Marc kissed her temple. "Aly, I don't want you thinking I do this with just anyone. I'd given that up ages ago."

She nodded, though didn't believe him any more than she believed in the Easter Bunny. His own mother had once commented that Marc treated girls like an all-you-can-eat buffet. Alyssa had seen plenty of women lining up to be brunch over the years, and she hadn't even been around that often.

"Flattery will get you anywhere with me," she replied flippantly, grinning. Marc was a genuinely considerate guy, the polar opposite of

Zach. She hadn't gotten to know him because she'd always been so intent on avoiding her hot neighbor.

Alyssa quit resisting her base instincts and kissed him in the sunshine as if they were the only two people in the world, her pale skin contrasting sharply with his dark tan. Probably ought to think about sunscreen, eventually.

His fingers threaded through her hair, setting it free to whip around her face. In response, Alyssa tugged his shirt over his head.

"No fair." He responded by pulling up the shirt he'd loaned her. Alyssa shrugged it aside. He cupped her breasts with his big hands. Then he took one in his mouth and nibbled gently on the tip. Alyssa sighed and curved against him.

When he thumbed open the button on the shorts he'd loaned her, she slid off his lap and kicked them off. Marc had pulled off his shirt and quickly discarded the rest of his clothes before rolling on a condom.

"I'll be gentle," he promised when she hesitated. Last night had been amazing, but she was feeling it today.

She nodded. Naked, Alyssa slid over him, her body extra-sensitive from the night before. Marc was as good as his word, moving slowly and focused on everything except where their bodies were joined. He let her set the pace. The more he teased and touched everything above her waist, the more her body could take. They found their pleasure with no audience but the sun, the sea, and the sky.

An hour later, Marc steered the sailboat into its slip at the marina. They held hands as they strolled to his truck. When she asked about it, he told her he'd caught a ride with his brother to his parents' house the day before.

Alyssa fidgeted with the shirt hem sticking out from the seatbelt. The loaner clothes were as good as a billboard for what she'd been doing and who she'd been with. Yet there was no point in trading them for her wrinkled dress, since last night wasn't exactly a secret. The knowledge didn't help her shoulders stay straight or calm her pounding heart as Marc parked on the street between their driveways, as though staking out a space in the middle of their families.

He took her hand. "We'll go in together. It's going to be okay."

"Yeah, I know." She squeezed his hand back. There was no reason for nerves. Yet she stepped out with an unshakable sense of foreboding.

A breeze coursed through the cab of the truck. Her dress fluttered like a captive butterfly on its hanger behind her. The screen door of her parents' house opened.

Her eyes narrowed at the man-shape. In a flash her stomach iced over. *No, it can't be.*

"What the fuck is this?" Zach exploded. The screen door jumped back on its hinges.

Alyssa cringed but stood her ground. "What are you doing here?"

"We were supposed to celebrate our engagement with your family this week, remember? I changed my ticket."

"I…" *Oh holy shit.*

6

Alyssa's better sense abruptly reasserted herself, and she was seriously pissed off. What had she been thinking, sleeping with another man less than a full day after her boyfriend had stood her up? Extreme.

"Who are you?" Marc snarled. His arm curled around her waist protectively. Her parents and her sister had filtered out of the house, and were watching this train wreck with blanched faces. Behind them, a door slapped closed from the direction of the De Lunas' house.

"Zach Kessler. Alyssa's fiancé."

The lie sliced through her shock and freed her voice. "I *never* said I would marry you, Zach."

"Yes, you did. I never had the chance to give you the ring, though. Two days ago, you were enraged when I was late for one dinner. I come all the way here to make peace, and what do I find? My girlfriend out with some other guy."

Hot shame rushed through Alyssa. Maybe she'd overreacted. She'd been hurt and upset that he'd left her hanging with no word for hours, especially after pressuring her into agreeing to get engaged in the first place. That didn't excuse going off with the first available guy, but she'd very definitively broken up with Zach, and he shouldn't be here now. The collision of her real life with Zach and her fantasy escape with Marc forced angry words past the tight line of her lips.

"Zach, I told you I never wanted to see you again. What part was unclear to you?"

"No, you told me to send your stuff, but you didn't say we were over."

"I totally did! I said I never wanted to see you again!"

"But you didn't mean it. I could tell. Don't you think I know when you're just angry, and when you really mean something?" He grinned. "I saw right through that. I know you were hurt. But we belong together, so I came all the way down here to get you."

What must Marc and her family think? He'd twisted everything around until she looked like the guilty party.

You were drinking. Maybe she hadn't been as clear as she'd thought.

Just like that, he had her questioning her own memories. He was so damn good at it, too. Zach stood there in his polo shirt and khaki shorts, a preppy stranger Alyssa never would've wanted to get to know, much less marry. Yet she didn't know how to get rid of him.

"What are you doing here?" She poked a shaking finger at her former boyfriend, though she couldn't bring herself to touch him.

"I figured the make-up sex would be great. Guess I won't be the one to find out." He shot Marc a glare. "Was it?"

"She wants you to go." Marc jerked his head at the rental car parked in the driveway. "Go."

Zach pulled out a car key. Slowly, he turned back, as if unable to resist getting the last word in. "Thought you had more class, Aly. Guess you had some fuck-the-gardener fantasy going on all this time."

Pure, white-hot fury burned through her as she clapped a hand over her slack mouth. Marc closed the distance in a few steps and replied for her. One muscled arm forward and slammed into Zach's jaw. His head snapped back and he went down hard, grass stains spreading over the ass of his new shorts as he rolled over. Blood and saliva streamed from Zach's mouth as he pushed himself upright and came at Marc with raised fists.

A riot of pure testosterone erupted across the lawn. Zach landed a few good punches. Alyssa stood paralyzed in horror.

"Wait! Stop it, both of you."

Alyssa's heart nearly stopped as her sister planted herself between the bloodied, brawling men. What the hell was Janelle up to? A glint of amusement shone in her green eyes.

Whatever it was, it could not be good.

"There's a better way to sort this out," Janelle continued as both men stumbled back, breathing hard and one heartbeat away from hammering one another again.

"Janelle, don't get involved." Alyssa's voice was harsh in her ears. In some grim sense, her sister was enjoying the spectacle. Betrayal knifed her.

"What do you have in mind?" Zach spat blood onto the lawn.

Her sister's green eyes glittered. "A contest. Like *The Bachelorette*."

"You watch too much TV, Janelle," Alyssa interjected.

Janelle tossed her head. "At least I got them to quit pummeling one another. Hear me out. For the next six days, you'll alternate dates with Zach and Marc. The winner gets to spend New Year's Eve with you."

Alyssa dropped her head into her fists and grabbed her hair. Could her love life careen off any more cliffs? First the engagement that didn't happen, followed by her questionable judgment in immediately sleeping with her neighbor, and now her sister's harebrained idea. Adults didn't do this crazy shit.

Zach and Marc were grown men. They wouldn't go along with it. Especially not Marc. She snorted a humorless laugh. Like he was going to fight for her?

What if he does?

Alyssa ruthlessly silenced the little voice that had gotten her into so much trouble and turned to her Marc with crossed her arms, too furious to acknowledge Zach. Her racing heart picked up even more speed at the sight of his scraped knuckles and loose fists at his waist He was ready to jump back into pounding her ex bloody. She was not into Neanderthals. *She wasn't.*

So why did Marc look hotter than ever?

"I'm in," Marc declared, his brown eyes flinty.

Alyssa gaped. Her mouth formed words without sound. *What the hell are you doing?* Yet part of her was thrilled. The same reckless part of her that couldn't think three seconds ahead and had barreled through yesterday like a teenager on a roller coaster ride. Her heart.

Marc fixed his attention on Zach. If he'd been a superhero, he would've obliterated her ex with a single hate-filled glare.

Zach touched his bloody lip, then checked the long red stains marring his plaid shirt and shorts. "No way you're going to win, Garden Boy."

Alyssa saw Marc's jaw tighten as the taunt landed with a blow. "Neither are you, Zach. Nothing you could do over the next few days could win me back. Especially after what you said to my…neighbor."

Though she and Marc were a little beyond chitchats over the fence now.

He's only doing this because Zach's acting like a complete asshole.

Marc had never had a girlfriend in his life, even if she wanted to hop from one serious relationship to another. *Which she didn't.*

Despite a liquid red stripe trickling over his chin onto his shirt, Zach managed to radiate arrogance. "Watch me."

"I do not agree to this!" Alyssa's hands were balled in tight fists as though she could pummel sense into everyone. "You are all insane. Every. One."

Who were these people? Her family? Her neighbors? How could any of them think this was a reasonable approach to resolving the unbelievably messy situation she'd put them in? She glared at Zach and Marc.

Zach's eyes flared with anger.

Marc's with something stronger.

"Alyssa, honey." Her mother's hand on her shoulder almost made her scream as if a spider had landed on her. "Janelle's idea is a little unorthodox, but think about it. You've gone from a long-term relationship to a…"

"They're called one-night stands, Mom." From the corner of her eye she saw Marc flinch, which sucked. She wasn't trying to hurt him, but if anyone should be used to hearing that term, it should be him.

At least her candor gave her the satisfaction of wiping the arrogance off Zach's face. Good. Her brain was back in control now, and her rational self had one hell of a mess to clean up.

Her mother closed her eyes. "I *know* what they're called. I can't believe I'm hearing this from you, Alyssa. I'd expect your sister to do something like this. Not you."

Guilt wormed its way through her anger. She'd made such a hash of things. Already stressed, her gut clenched harder.

If she'd been honest with her family about wanting to leave New York, about the job, and about the cracked foundation of her relationship with Zach, they'd know getting back together wasn't an option. But all they saw was the guy she'd been outwardly happy with for a couple of years, versus the one she'd leapt into bed with. The one who'd never been in a relationship in his life.

While she groped for words, Catherine turned to the two men seething with testosterone and hatred on her front lawn. Both were flexing their muscles, ready to resume beating the living crap out of one another, when her mother stepped between them. There was no denying that a not-very-modern part of Alyssa found this display of manly chest-beating a turn-on. Obnoxious, yes, but hot. She'd never admit it to another living soul, not even if her nails were pried off one by one.

"Marc, go to your house now. Zach, Alyssa's father is going to get you an ice pack. You should go back to your hotel to clean up. We're going to need some space to talk this through as a family."

"I can't believe you're making me do this." Zach accepted the ice pack and held it to his chin. "We've been together for two years, Aly. Doesn't that count for something?"

"I can't believe you dated this asshole." Marc glared at Zach, then at her. "What's the appeal?"

"A guaranteed million-dollar bonus is a hell of an aphrodisiac." Smirked Zach. "Bet you can't touch that with your dirty fingernails."

"Did you just imply I dated you for your *money*?" Alyssa gasp-shrieked. Oh, he was such a shit. Half the crap he'd bought her she neither wanted nor liked. She'd only accepted it to avoid a fight. She sure as hell hadn't asked for it. Maybe if she'd stood up to him before, she wouldn't be watching him brawl on her parents' lawn now.

Janelle stepped to her mother's side before they started swinging at one another again. "Enough. Since Marc was with Alyssa last night,

Zach gets tonight. It'll be a dinner date. Marc, you're taking her out tomorrow, so get planning. I'll be styling my sister—"

Alyssa groaned. Janelle shot her a *shut up* glare.

"You'll coordinate dates with me. For Aly, it'll be a surprise. No contact, no communication outside of the contest. That's a rule." Janelle kept talking, which at least kept Zach and Marc from one another's throats.

"Hold on. You're all assuming I agree to this madness. I don't," Alyssa said. Someone had to think with their brain. She'd fallen asleep on the job last night, but she was wide awake now and determined to shut this down. "No bachelorette, no contest. So, quit fighting. Zach, go home."

"Honey, let's get rid of the men and talk inside," her mother hissed, but it was too late.

"No problem, Aly, I'll happily kick your ex's ass from here back to New York just for being a racist shit heel." Marc lunged around Janelle, while Zach dodged to the other side of Catherine.

"That's what *you* think, Garden Boy."

Through fingers she watched her mother and sister try to hold two large, angry men apart. Up and down the street, neighbors popped out of their houses to see what the commotion was all about, like a ward of curious prairie dogs. Mrs. De Luna was among them. She began yelling at her son in Spanish. Alyssa wasn't fluent enough to catch more than a few choice descriptions. Marc's head jerked up at the sound, distracting him long enough for Zach to land a blow over Janelle's shoulder.

Oh, for chrissake. Alyssa marched over and grabbed a handful of Marc's shirt. "Get out of here."

He shrugged her off like a fly and huffily let his mother berate him into the house. Alyssa picked up the ice pack and handed it to Zach, and gave him a push toward the rental car in the driveway. "Get back on a plane and go *away*. Nobody asked you to come here."

"You did, Aly. At Halloween, when I hid the fake ring in the candy bucket at the parade in the West Village and said we should get engaged for real, remember?" The hurt in his voice shredded her remaining anger like tissue paper. "It was barely twenty-four hours,

Aly. Jesus. I wouldn't have wanted to marry you if I didn't love you."

Guilt well up through the ragged seams of her dignity. Maybe she'd been too hasty. Maybe she'd been more hurt than she'd wanted to believe, and last night had been more about revenge than rebound. Alyssa rubbed her forehead with her thumb and forefinger.

Or maybe she was giving in to avoid a fight. Again.

"Do the contest. Give me another chance. I'm going to prove how much I love you, and you'll see this guy's just a fuckboy. I know you were mad, but I can forgive whatever happened if you let me make it up to you."

He's right. Marc's a fuckboy. That was the entire point of sleeping with him last night. Yet being with Marc had been erotic than any sex she'd ever had with Zach.

Alyssa turned away, her cheeks on fire as she faced down her very recent ex while thinking about the wonderful night she'd spent with Marc. It made her pulse race and her breath shallow, and she wanted more.

"I'll consider it. Now get out of here before someone calls the cops. This is not the kind of spectacle that happens on our street." Alyssa gave him a little push. Touching him through the linen shirt was familiar, but she recoiled as if it had singed her fingertips. Finally, Zach turned and got in his car.

"Alyssa Carlisle, inside the house please." Her dad stood inside screen door, watching everything. Her mother and Janelle had already gone in.

They were sipping iced tea with lemon wedges in the living room, as if she hadn't turned their family into the after-Christmas community spectacle. Alyssa accepted a glass of tea from her dad and sat on the couch.

"I'm not doing the contest."

"Would it be so bad to take a few days evaluating your options from a calmer perspective?" Catherine replied, sipping her tea through a straw. "I can't take the excitement of two virile young men fighting over my eldest daughter. Mariana and I always thought you and Marc would make a good couple, if he ever settled down and if you ever came back to Florida long enough to talk to one another. Our instincts were on point, but this is not what we had in mind. It's not like you to act so impulsively."

Alyssa crunched an ice cube between her teeth. She wished there was some way to describe what was wrong with her relationship with Zach without sounding delusional. Maybe if she compromised—again—and went along with the scheme, they'd see it for themselves. Although that was probably too much to ask, considering Zach had spent several days here last summer and her family had been positively charmed. He could be very winning, when he wanted to be.

"I'll be out back. Sounds like you have this covered, Cathy." Her dad headed for the kitchen.

"Now you've scared off Dad," Janelle complained.

"I can't imagine why he'd want to sit here and listen to Mom describe our neighbor and my ex as 'virile' while you plot to force me into some cut-rate reality-TV knockoff." Alyssa stirred her tea with the straw, then set it down on the coffee table. "Maybe I'll join Dad out back."

"Do you have a better idea for cleaning up your mess?" Janelle glared.

Not if she wanted Zach contained so she could spend more time with Marc.

There was also her sudden guilt over the fact that Zach had come all this way to apologize, and she'd been out with another man. She had to contend with that. Yes, she was annoyed how straightforward *I don't want to see you ever again* had proven too subtle for Zach, but perhaps she'd been hasty in dumping him on the spot. He wouldn't have chased her to Florida if he didn't care about her. Whether it was enough to fix their relationship, Alyssa had her doubts, but going along with the contest would at least keep him away from Marc.

If it all went sideways, it wasn't as if she had to continue seeing either of them after the week was over. Her mom had a point. The contest was a balanced approach to spending time with both men and making a reasoned decision between her head and her heart. It wasn't as crazy as it sounded.

"Fine." She'd suffer through six dates, and when it was over she'd become a nun. "I can't believe I'm agreeing to this."

Janelle jumped out her chair and squeezed her. "It'll be great. You'll have fun. Promise."

Suddenly Alyssa's much needed vacation was in the hands of her impractical, surprisingly canny, fierce little sister. If only she could die on the spot and spare herself the continued humiliation of the next six days.

Speaking of which, Catherine got up and patted her shoulder. "Now that we've settled the contest issue, Aly, why don't you go next door and make things right with the De Lunas while Janelle arranges the details for tonight's date with Zach."

"I see you're on Team Zach," Alyssa sulked.

"I'm on Team Alyssa. Now go change out of Marc's clothes."

7

Years ago, when her parents had first begun talking about moving to Florida from their home in Ohio, Alyssa's father had brought home a whimsical cuckoo clock. Every hour on the hour, a tiny parrot leapt out of a colorful house and called the time in a speaking-parrot voice. The house was painted parroty colors, a mélange of yellow, red, blue, and green. It was, by far, the tackiest thing they owned.

Alyssa sat below the clock on a worn armchair, waiting for it to spring open. She felt marginally better wearing her own jeans and a t-shirt. Janelle claimed the earrings and necklace she'd given Alyssa for Christmas radiated positive energy. Since it was true she needed as much positive energy as she could get, Alyssa had put them on.

"Four o'clock," screeched the parrot. Marc's shorts and t-shirt, freshly laundered, were folded on the coffee table. She'd delayed going next door until they were clean, then rounded up to the hour. If only every mess was so easily tidied up as a bit of cotton. She gathered the pile of clothing into her leaden arms.

The bouquet of lilies and roses sat nearby on the coffee table, still beautiful. Alyssa ran her fingertip along a petal and wished she could go back in time, not that she would've done anything differently.

"Yes, dear?" At least it was Mrs. De Luna who answered.

"I came to apologize for the way Zach treated Marc today. I had no idea he was planning to come here. I never imagined he was capable of saying something so awful."

Yeah, you did. You thought he only said awful things to you. But outright racism was new. She'd never heard him say anything like that before.

"Please come in." Mrs. De Luna held the door open wide. Alyssa hesitated, but how could she refuse?

Marc's dad met her in the foyer. "This way, please."

The De Lunas, straight-backed and somber, sat across from her on the wicker sofa. Alyssa took one of the chairs facing them, perching the small pile of clothing on her knees like a scarlet letter A.

"Thank you for coming over. You do not owe me any apology. It wasn't you who said those words."

"But I'm the one who brought it into your life. If I hadn't…I swear Zach's never said anything like that in my presence before. Ever."

"Alyssa, do you think we have never been called names before?" Mr. De Luna's voice was soft, but there was steel in it. "There will always be circumstances in which people reach for the wrong tools to resolve disagreements. Your former boyfriend was threatened. His money had no power to stop you from leaving him, so he used the very last tools anyone should ever reach for to lash out at Marc. He wanted to drive a wedge between you and my son. He did so very effectively."

Alyssa dropped her eyes to her hands. "I made it easy for Zach to do. We…everything moved too quickly. With Marc." *Note to future self, next time you have a one-night stand, choose someone whose parents you aren't going to see socially.*

"Your mother told me you had broken up with your boyfriend and asked the family to dinner. We had an idea that you and Marc might suit, but you were always in New York. I thought you might talk, make a date. No one expected you to disappear together," Mrs. De Luna said sternly.

Alyssa was stung by a sudden longing for snowy Christmases. Maybe her family would come visit her in New York next year. "I don't think anyone expected it. I certainly didn't."

"I could not believe it when he said he was taking you sailing this morning," Mrs. De Luna continued. "None of us could. Marc never takes anyone sailing. It is his quiet time, his favorite way to be alone. He has never taken a girl out before. Your sister is outrageous. Get rid of the boyfriend and patch things up with Marc."

Alyssa swallowed. She'd hoped he'd be around so she could soothe his bruised ego, or if that didn't work, bully him into dropping the idea of this stupid contest.

Mrs. De Luna was grasping at a fantasy if she thought Marc had any interest in her beyond a hookup and a means of getting back at Zach. Well, she'd agreed to play along. "Do you have any ideas how to do that?"

"We were hoping you would." Mr. De Luna pushed his glasses up with one finger. Mrs. De Luna's face fell a little.

So much for finding an easy way out. "Can you tell me the address of his project house? The one he just bought?"

"That wreck? What do you call it—a boondoggle?"

"From how he describes it, boondoggle sounds like the right word." She smiled, and for this time it wasn't forced. Being around Zach's family had always set her teeth on edge. They bickered endlessly and let Zach off the hook for everything from hurtful jokes, to not cleaning up after meals, to outright drunken rudeness. As long as his star kept rising at the hedge fund, he was golden. The De Lunas *always* called their sons on their bad behavior, and if Marc had turned out to be the man-whore of Verona Harbor, it wasn't for parental laxity.

"He does spend a lot of time there trying to make it into a habitable property." Mrs. De Luna scribbled an address on a piece of paper. "He keeps some of his tools here in the garage, where he can lock them up. He usually comes by in the evening."

"For dinner," Mr. De Luna added with a ghost of a smile. "Sometimes he comes in the morning, too, if he needs tools."

"Thank you. I don't know what to do, but I'll try something." If he dropped out of the contest, so could she. But then she'd have to spend New Year's with Zach. It was worth trying, anyway.

She placed the clothes on the coffee table. "May I ask you to return these to him? I borrowed them. They're washed."

"Wouldn't you rather return them yourself?" asked Marc's mother.

She shook her head. "Yes, I would, but according to my sister's contest rules, I'm not allowed to see him outside of officially sanctioned dates."

Mrs. De Luna buried her face in her hands. "Young people are hopeless. In my day, we did not behave like this. We courted. This is not normal, but if Marc finally goes on an actual date, then you and your sister will have achieved something with this silly contest."

Yeah, well, she'd dated Zach as properly as could be, and look how that had turned out. Courtship had a new rule book. Somewhere. She'd never read it and doubted anyone else in her generation had either.

At least however things shook out with Marc, her parents wouldn't have to feel awkward around their neighbors.

Back at home in her bedroom, she booted up her work computer. She'd hoped not to have to use it but learned long ago never to go on vacation without it. This time, though, her mission was personal. She didn't open her email, though she did pop into each of her social media accounts out of habit. The picture she'd posted with Marc on the boat was getting buried under an avalanche of likes, comments, and retweets.

No wonder. In sunglasses, his hair ruffled by the wind, and wearing a life vest, he was gorgeous arm candy. She wished she was more like her online persona, the carefree fictional Aly who did yoga poses with a smile in fun locations.

She needed a strategy, a plan to see Marc as much as possible between now and when she left without Zach getting in the way. Last night hadn't exactly reassured her that he'd given up being the libertine of Verona Harbor, but she wouldn't mind a repeat or two of the amazing sex they'd had last night.

A knock at the door pulled her out of her work.

"Showtime, Aly. Green or silver?" Janelle appeared in the doorway bearing two tiny dresses as substantial as handkerchiefs.

But first she had to deal with her ex. He'd managed to spin the situation into one where she'd hurt him, not the other way around. With Zach, she was always in the wrong. Tonight would undoubtedly be more of the same. Alyssa popped one eyebrow. "Do you have a nun's habit?"

"Aly." Janelle lowered the dresses.

"I am not wearing either of those for a date with Zach." Alyssa pushed back her chair.

"Rule number one. You have to wear clothes the same level of sexy around both suitors."

Alyssa laughed. "Since when does my little sister use a word like 'suitors?'"

Both dresses smacked into her, the hangers bouncing off her shoulder as silk billowed around her face. "You have no idea how good you have it, Alyssa. There are two guys after you. One rich and ready to marry you. The other is an armful of hunky eye candy and judging from the way you walked up all glowy this morning, Marc knows what he's doing in the sack. I'd give my right arm to have those choices, and you don't even appreciate what you have."

"Janelle." What to say? Her sister radiated hostility, and it ripped her heart to shreds. "It's not fun being between the bone two alpha dogs are fighting over."

"I wouldn't know."

"Janie. What's going on?"

Her sister fumed for a few seconds, arms crossed and chin tucked as she leaned against the door frame. "You know why Ben dumped me?"

"He took a job in Texas." Ben was Janelle's boyfriend from college, the only man she'd ever seriously dated. But they'd been over for years, so why bring it up now?

"Yeah, but do you know why I didn't go with him?"

"Because you couldn't find a job. It's hard to find a job right after you graduate." Alyssa aimed for empathy, but Janelle shook her dark head.

"I did get a job offer. It was rescinded when the employer saw my credit report. I missed my first two student loan payments. I didn't have an income six months after graduating, and working at the coffee shop wasn't enough to cover both rent and the loans. I'm still working there, every morning before the work and every Sunday morning, and

I walk dogs in our apartment complex on the mornings I'm not slinging espresso." Her eyes shone with tears.

"Do you think I *want* to work in a warehouse filing customs paperwork? It was the only job I could get, and it pays twelve thousand dollars a year less than the one I could've had in Texas. With Ben. Who dumped me when he found out how much student debt I had. I'm stuck, Aly."

Guilt sucked at Alyssa. She might be treading water, but her sister sounded like she was drowning. She'd known Janelle had a lot of loans, but either Janie had been hiding the extent of her problems, or Alyssa had been too far away in New York to understand the full story. A mix of both, most likely.

Despite the scholarship she'd won, their parents had struggled to put both children through college after their father's early retirement. Janelle had attended a state school, worked two jobs, and taken out loans, yet her degree had landed her in a dead-end job after graduation. Clearly, she'd pinned her hopes on Alyssa's boyfriend bailing her out in some fashion. It explained her obsession with the engagement.

"I don't love Zach. I'm not going to marry him." Some sacrifices were too much to ask.

"Then why did you almost say yes?"

Alyssa shrugged helplessly. "Dating in New York is a shit show. When Zach started talking marriage last fall, I told him no. But then he threatened to break up with me, and I was scared of starting from scratch."

"Scared," Janelle echoed with a shake of her head. "Alyssa, you're a moron."

"You marry him, then." If Janelle was so determined to marry for money, she could deal with Zach's overbearing argumentativeness. Not that Alyssa would ever let Zach date her sister. She'd feed him his own balls if he tried it.

Why is Zach good enough for you, then?

Alyssa shushed the inner critic. No one wanted their ex dating their sister.

"I would. I'd prance down the aisle in the biggest, fluffiest princess gown I could find, with a rock on my finger the size of a golf ball, and

I'd pay off my loans and your loans, and I'd be happy and grateful even if he cheated on me a few years down the line. But I'll never meet a Zach because I hide out in a warehouse all day filing customs forms. I'll be there with the forklift driver guys staring down my shirt every day until I'm fifty years old, trying to pay off my student loans. On weekends, I'm too tired to go out because I still work at the coffee shop three years after I told them I was moving to Texas with Ben. Plus, I'm always broke."

Janelle's scowl cracked Alyssa's heart. Grown-up financial problems were turning her into a mercenary, and that skewed Alyssa's entire worldview.

"Janie, you know they'll stop looking by the time you turn thirty." Her joke fell flat. Janelle was right, though. Without Marc's dreamboat presence skewing her mind in the direction of hot hookups, her natural caution had reasserted itself with a vengeance.

So what if she didn't love-love Zach? He'd suffered a bad case of cold feet. He'd hurt her feelings. Right now, she couldn't forgive him for ruining her Christmas so cavalierly, but in the interest of avoiding remorse down the line she ought to see if they could work through their mutual betrayals.

Besides, no matter how she squinted, Marc wasn't boyfriend material. He was Hot Vacation Sex on a Stick, served with a side of No Regrets. Not that she was necessarily looking for a new boyfriend. But going back to New York, where her single life would telescope into twelve-hour days at the agency and collapsing into bed at her crappy apartment at night, wasn't appealing, either.

Zach wasn't perfect, but neither was she. The question was whether her life was better with him or without him, not if he was an ideal partner.

Before she closed the door completely, she had to talk things through with Zach. He'd said he was willing to forgive her night with Marc. She did want to repeat the experience, but in a few days the drama would be over, and she had to think to the future.

Alyssa bent to pick up the dresses. She held them against her body. "Okay, Janelle. I'll give Zach an honest chance to patch things up. You choose."

"Green dress. The beading will hold down the skirt on the way to the helicopter."

"The what?" Alyssa froze.

"Helicopter," Janelle replied grimly. "Zach's determined to win you back."

8

"You're home." Janelle clicked off the television.

Their mother sat up, her short dark hair tucked behind her ears as she peered over the arm of the couch. "How did it go?"

"Fine."

"Come on, Aly. Spill. I need a report for the contest." Janelle reached for a clipboard sitting on the coffee table.

Catherine frowned. "Janelle. Cut it out. This is all fun and games to you, but it's serious for Aly."

Janelle raised her chin stubbornly. Aly didn't have the energy to fight her. She kicked off the stiletto heels she'd worn for the evening and slumped on the couch next to her mom. In the end, she'd worn neither of Janelle's dress selections, opting for tailored trousers to keep her butt covered when the wind kicked up on the launch pad.

"Well, I've never been on a helicopter before." The chopper was classic Zach. He'd screwed up, so instead of trying to make it up to her in any meaningful way, he'd made a big splash by throwing money around. With the wind whipping her hair she'd remembered how she was just another problem to be solved with money. He'd been throwing the green stuff at her in the form of nice dates, fancy clothes, and expensive gifts ever since they'd met at her friend Becca's wedding.

"Me neither. What's it like?" Janelle settled in.

"Bumpy. A little scary. Very noisy. I was almost sick on the ride home." Not because of the ride, per se.

Janelle started to ask a question but Catherine cut her off. "How was dinner?"

"Very nice."

Janelle picked up her clipboard. "What did you order?"

"I assume you already know the name of the restaurant."

Her sister didn't look up from scribbling across her clipboard. "Of course I do. I helped Zach plan it."

"I ordered the Mahi Mahi, okay? One glass of wine. Sauvingnon blanc, if you must have all the details." She didn't mean to snap, but it had been an exhausting night.

"Five out of five for restaurant selection and food presentation. Great. Although he loses a few points for bringing you home half an hour late. Promptness shows respect for you and your family."

"At least something I taught you sunk in," Catherine interjected. "Aly, did you and Zach talk at all?"

Alyssa's stomach knotted. "Yes. He groveled quite convincingly."

For an hour, it had been impossible to remember why Zach hadn't made her happy in a long time. Maybe ever. He'd poured on the charm as he'd done in the early stages of their relationship, when they'd dated so properly even Mrs. De Luna would've approved. That was one thing in Zach's favor. She'd never worried he only wanted a fling.

Marc's put his hookup days behind him, her heart whispered.

Is that why he was so quick to take you back to his boat? Alyssa demanded of the credulous organ. It had no defense.

Yes, for the first hour, her brain had been fully convinced she should get back together with Zach. He'd messed up. She'd messed up. They were even.

Then he'd gone and ruined it.

"So is that where things stand? You'll try to work things out?" her mother asked. Janelle had stopped taking notes and watched her intently.

"No."

Her mother only nodded. Janelle's jaw dropped. "Why not, Aly?"

Alyssa's shoulder lifted and fell. "Zach proposed."

"Finally!" Janelle clapped her hands. "What did you say?"

"What do you think I said?" She let her head fall back against the couch cushion.

The long and hard discussion had built a tenuous bridge of trust over the canyon between them. She'd been ready to call off the contest and go home to New York with him the next morning. But then Zach had fallen right back into character the minute she'd made a conciliatory peep. Instead of building that bridge stronger and wider, he'd decided that all their problems could be solved with a diamond the size of the first joint of her ring finger, presented in Miami's best restaurant, in the best seat overlooking the ocean. Every single diner in the restaurant started banging silverware against the tables and chanting *say yes*.

No pressure or anything.

"I said no."

Janelle's stricken expression rivaled Zach's when he'd finally realized he couldn't embarrass her into accepting his gaudy ring. Alyssa wasn't selling out for a damned rock. She'd compromised enough, and nothing would change if she kept doing that. For the next few days, she was holding out for sex so good it made her eyes roll back in her head. Zach couldn't give her that.

"Truthfully, I promised him I'd think about it." The compromise position had given him enough of an out to back down from the unwelcome proposal. She *would* think about it. About all the reasons she should say yes, and all the reasons she was still going to say no.

Janelle slumped back in her chair. "Why didn't you say yes?"

The answer to that question was so complex, yet so simple. "Because I don't love him, Janie."

"You said you loved Zach before he backed out of proposing," Catherine pointed out.

"Right. You loved him until Marc crooked his finger at you. If that's the reason you turned down Zach, you're being dumb," Janelle echoed.

Maybe so. "Why are you so dead-set against Marc?"

"I'm not. He's a great neighbor. I'm one broken-down car away from financial ruin, and he fixes anything minor. Sometimes he doesn't even let me pay for the parts. But he's Marc."

"You're a long way from financial ruin, Janelle," Catherine scoffed. "You're doing it a bit too blue. Aly, I'll leave you to the full postmortem with your sister. I'm headed to bed. But if your heart's not in it, don't lead Zach on. You're not being kind by giving him hope where there is none."

Their mother kissed each of them on the forehead and went upstairs. Alyssa heard her mother's words, but she was preoccupied with wondering how honest Janelle had been about her student loan problem. Was she exaggerating, or was their mom oblivious, or was the truth somewhere between? Before she could consider it further, Janelle jumped back into her favorite topic.

"Remember how the first thing we saw when we moved here was a stream of cars cruising up and down the street, each one full of high school girls hanging out the window? And the time Crystal decided we were best friends in college so I'd bring her home for spring break, all so she could get with Marc?"

Alyssa smiled. "Yeah, I remember. You're still friends with her, right?"

"Yeah, sort of. I don't think it worked, not that Crystal would ever admit it. My point is, girls like Marc, and Marc likes girls." Janelle shrugged. "Except you. You never seemed to notice him. So why now?"

Janelle was wrong about her never noticing Marc, but she'd rather die than admit it. The man was a walking billboard for trouble. The difference was that after her disastrous Christmas Eve, she'd needed exactly his brand of botheration.

Alyssa wished she had her sister's talent for distillation. Janelle was sharp. She'd also spent time with Marc over the years. Janelle had never wasted a minute being shy around him. If he could help her fix her car, great. She accepted the hot guy next door for what he was, and went on with her life. As ridiculous as a reality-TV-inspired dating contest was, her sister might be the most pragmatic person Alyssa had ever met.

Which went a long way toward explaining why Janelle was so invested in getting her back together with Zach. From a purely practical perspective, there was no contest. Zach was wealthy, stable, and committed.

Marc was *Marc*. Commitment-phobe. Catnip to women. A good time at best. A broken heart at worst, if you were careless enough to imagine it meant anything.

Yet her heart wasn't sensible. It didn't want Zach. Hadn't wanted Zach from the get-go. Her head had ruled the relationship from start to finish. Only her heart had whispered it wasn't right, and she'd ruthlessly suppressed the little voice. Taped its mouth shut and locked it away so it couldn't cause trouble. That approach hadn't worked out very well either.

"Why now…I don't know. Because Zach makes me feel trapped. If I marry him, I'll stop pursing the things I want in life whenever they conflict with his job, which is all the time."

Tell her about how Zach lies. But maybe he wasn't lying. Maybe she was wrong more often than she thought she was. She hated how Zach made her second-guess herself.

"Didn't you just get a promotion? You wouldn't have gotten that if you hadn't worked for it."

"Yeah, but I didn't try applying for a bigger role at another company because Zach's hours are crazy and our schedules might conflict. My work seems less important because I can never earn what he does, but at the end of the day, he's just moving numbers around in Excel sheets. I'm trying to get people to buy things they don't need. Neither of us is saving the world. What happened on Christmas Eve clarified all the reasons I felt pressured to get engaged. I can't go back to pretending things were good between us. He needs to make big changes for me to consider taking him back, and I don't believe Zach is willing to make them, especially after tonight."

Janelle went pensive and silent. "Is that why you didn't move in with him?"

Alyssa huffed a laugh. "I guess. Although I basically did. He says he boxed up my stuff and sent it here before he left New York, to prove he'd listened to me. We'll see if it arrives in a few days."

"You weren't kidding when you said you'd broken up with him."

Alyssa's eyebrows popped up. "Didn't you hear me say that when I got off the plane?"

Janelle shrugged. "I heard you, big sis. I know you think I'm acting like a brat, but get out of your own head for a minute. For two years, you've been serious about Zach Kessler. You skipped Christmas Eve to get engaged to him because he had some special thing planned. We *always* do family stuff on Christmas Eve. It's the best part of the holiday. Then you show up and tell us it's over? And *then* you disappear with the one guy I'd have bet my life you've never looked at twice? You and Marc. My head's still spinning."

"Fair enough. All I'm saying is, money can create a power imbalance, and that's what Zach and I have." *Among other issues.*

"Maybe, but not having it is a sure way to sabotage a relationship." Janelle scraped her hair back and sighed. "I'd know."

"If Ben left you because of the job and the debt, then he wasn't a good partner. Or maybe you were both too young to be as serious as you were about one another." Alyssa's sister speared her with a gimlet glare, but she read more sadness than anger there. It was strange how Janelle was still so hung up on her ex, years after they'd broken up.

They sat together in awkward silence until Janelle spoke. "Hey, did you get a picture of the helicopter or the restaurant?"

"Don't I always?"

"Can I get a sneak peek before you post it?"

"Sure." Alyssa dug into her bag and handed over her phone. "It's a great view. Even with all the drama, I couldn't resist taking a few shots."

"You'd have gotten a ton of traffic if you'd said yes." Janelle flicked her thumb across the screen, smiling softly. "Although everyone would've been confused because you posted the picture with Marc a few days ago. How come you never posted pictures with Zach?"

Because Zach doesn't approve of my creative outlet. She'd let Marc into her digital space without thinking about it, though, and he'd accepted without hesitation. "There were a few."

"Not many. I follow all your social media accounts. Your life looks so glamorous."

"Janie, it's not my real life and you know it. My life's a lot like yours. I stare at a computer and sit in conference rooms all day thinking up catchy ways to sell stupid shit."

Her sister held out the phone. "You have me fooled. Besides, I've seen your conference rooms. They're nice. I sit in a windowless warehouse doing data entry and filing. No one ever asks me about my ideas on anything. In meetings, I'm only there to listen." She stood up. "Don't act so ungrateful for your life. It could be a lot worse."

True. But it wasn't working for her, either, on any level. No matter how much she hated it, Alyssa had to see the contest through. She had to be sure, and it was as good a framework as any. There had to be some way to reconcile her head and her heart.

MARC TIPPED UP HIS BOTTLE, wishing it was closer to finished. Times like this, the lack of a home where he could sulk in solitude was a real problem. He didn't want to be at his parents' house, with Alyssa and her family visible right over the fence. The *Escape* wasn't an option either, not with half the other live-aboard mariners giving him the wink and nod treatment, and the memories of their night together sharp enough to keep him semi-erect. So he'd come here, an old bar hangout, for a little space to strategize the bizarre situation with Alyssa.

Marc removed the four-page, double-sided rule list and smoothed it over the bar. There were so many typos that it was clear Janelle had tapped out reality-TV-inspired stream-of-consciousness contest parameters and hit print. It made him smile.

No cursing. Keep it to a mimimum, at least. Did that apply to Aly? Any time she dropped an f-bomb he wanted laugh and kiss the dirty word right out of her sweet mouth. Cursing was one thing she'd definitely picked up in New York.

No touching unless consent is explicit. It was a crime that this wasn't considered mandatory instruction in high school sex ed.

Say You'll Stay

No body-shaming. There was nothing to shame about Alyssa's body, if he'd been inclined.

Be home by curfew or loose points. A little high school, but it wouldn't be the worst thing in the world to take a few steps back and start fresh. Also, *loose* should've lost an o.

No contact utside of official dates. Sneaking aruond is GROUNDS FOR LOOSING THE CONTEST. The errors were cute. Janelle was cute. Sharp as a tack, cute as a button and a terrible speller.

If he'd been less cock-sure that one day Alyssa would come home for good, he'd have tried harder to get her to talk to him when curfews were still age-appropriate. Last summer, he'd been sucker-punched to discover he might've been overconfident about her coming back to Florida. But by then it'd been too late. Zach and Aly were serious; by fall they'd been talking marriage. His hands-off, approach-when-the-time-is-right strategy had backfired spectacularly. He'd moved out of his apartment and rented it to a tenant to accelerate his world trip departure date. The prospect of listening to his mother recount every detail of the wedding plans was too much.

Of course, he'd pounced at the first opportunity. Alyssa'd had every reason to think he'd be easy, and he had been. Way too easy. After all, he didn't have a lot of practice with turning down willing women. Besides, if he hadn't jumped at it, she might already have reconciled with Zach.

No regrets.

So yeah, he'd go along with Janelle's crazy-like-a-fox scheme to torture him and Zachole. At least one of them deserved the suffering, and he was going to make Alyssa see that he was good for something more than a one-night stand.

The prospect shouldn't make him nervous. It couldn't be a steep learning curve to go from casual to monogamous. It was sex with one person instead of a rotating cast. Right?

His plans to set sail into the sunset had screeched to a dead stop. He couldn't pull up anchor and leave Alyssa behind. He'd prevail. No way she was going back to the asshole who'd stood her up on Christmas Eve. He was better than Zachole. He'd win.

And then what? She goes back to New York while you set sail into the great unknown?

He'd figure out how to work in his adventure later. Marc finished the beer in one swallow. The bottle clanked hard against the wood countertop as he pushed back his bar stool. He had a date to plan.

9

Alyssa shifted her weight from one leg to the other and raised her arms. She held the yoga pose, then moved again, spreading her fingers across the beach towel spread out over her parents' patio. It had taken a little effort to move the table and chairs, but it was worth it. She needed all the centering she could get after the awful date with Zach the night before.

Downward-facing dog. *Breathe.* Warrior one. Warrior two. Triangle pose. Alyssa listened to the podcast playing softly from her cell phone. The sound of a truck engine roared over the woman's chant.

She took a few more breaths in tree pose until metal clanked against hard plastic, announcing Marc's return. Alyssa opened her eyes, walked to the fence and leaned against it. "Hey. Marc."

"Not interested, Aly. There's rules."

Alyssa tiptoed after him like a duckling following its mother, her scabbed heel burning against the sun-warmed pavement. Marc hefted the box into the bed with an ear-splitting crash. He opened the driver's side door and got in. The engine growled to life.

Alyssa yanked open the passenger side door and hopped in. She was going to say her piece, even if she had to shout.

"Why are you going along with this?" Alyssa crossed her arms.

"Why are you?"

"I asked first."

Marc reached over and took her chin in one broad palm. His gentle grip forced her to meet his eyes. "Because I'll do anything, including go along with your little sister's cracked contest, to make sure you don't go back to New York with Zachole. Anything."

A hot shiver tumbled through her, followed by a flare of anger. Alyssa jerked her head away. "So this is all about your pissing contest with my ex?"

"Not even remotely, Aly. This is all about you. Why you thought all I was good for was a one night stand. When I'm done with you, you're wonder how the hell you ever dated Zach. You're going to look at every guy that way." Then he leaned over and kissed her.

Alyssa stiffened, but met him more than halfway. Marc's tongue pushed past her shock and plumbed her hard. A second later he pulled away. She gasped as the air touched her damp lips. Wanted more.

"I'll quit if you do, Marc."

"Fat chance, Aly. Hope you brought something nice to wear on New Year's, because we're going out."

She stumbled getting out of the truck. Damn Marc De Luna. He was as good as his word. He'd already ruined her for other men. That wasn't supposed to happen. None of this was supposed to happen. Her plan for a vacation rebound was getting skewed six ways from Sunday.

THE WHIRRING BLADE should've been soothing. Marc adjusted his safety glasses and steadied a board. Two seconds later he stepped back threw it across the construction site. The image of Alyssa's butt in tiny short-shorts had superimposed over the otherwise ordinary two-by-four. He was going to saw his own finger off if he didn't get it together.

A knock at the door startled Marc back into reality. The architect he'd hired walked in through the hole where a door would eventually go. For now, there was only a large piece of plywood that Mark chained closed at night.

"I see we're going with the open floor plan," the guy commented as he eyed the remnants of the wall Marc demolished earlier. "I trust it wasn't structural?"

"You tell me. You're the architect."

"Just cool it with the sledgehammers for a while, okay?" Together they went over sketches, making changes to accommodate the missing wall. In a few days, Marc would have final blueprints and, once the permits were in place, a swarm of plumbers and electricians would descend upon the shell. By spring or early summer, the house would be a white box. All the structural components updated and prepared for him to take over and do the finishing touches. If he wanted to do them himself instead of paying someone.

He didn't.

Which meant, very soon he was going to be completely idle. He had reliable tenants, and his other rental properties were in good shape. It was the outcome he'd been working toward for years. It had been his plan ever since he'd taken his final year's tuition payment and summer savings to buy the first little house, instead of finishing his degree.

His parents had nearly disowned him. They were successful now, but while he was growing up they'd sacrificed vacations, driven aging cars, and kept living in their starter home even after they could've moved to upscale, nearby Naples, to save for his and Julian's educations. He'd thrown it in their faces, but he'd been confident it would work out, and it had. Sailing around the world had always been the plan.

Until Alyssa had shown up alone and unexpectedly single on Christmas.

It stung more than it should that she only saw him as a fling. He'd taken it for granted that when he wanted a girlfriend, all he'd have to do was say the word. Marc had always believed he was the one in control. Alyssa had exploded that myth.

This didn't feel like a choice. It was raw and compulsive and needy. Worst of all, unfamiliar. Guilt settled uneasily in his gut as he wondered how many women he'd left stewing in this toxic brew of lust and vulnerability. Probably not very many—his ego wasn't that out of control—but, suddenly, even one was too much.

He could still taste her on his lips. Maybe he was imagining it. Hell, he'd imagined all kinds of things over the years. But this felt real.

So did the hammer as it slammed down over his thumb.

A streak of Smurf-blue cursing echoed up the wood framing and plywood. At least he wasn't trying to sail while this distracted. God help him if Alyssa ever wore those damn short shorts on the boat. They'd sink and drown.

It was barely noon. He needed a lunch break anyway. Marc gathered up his tools and stowed them in the back of his truck. This time, nobody chased him down as he carted the heavy orange boxes. Disappointment dogged him as he locked his parents' garage.

Marc's feet detoured toward the fence gate, taking the rest of him. He pushed it open and mounted the step.

"Hi, Marc. Aly's not here."

"Any idea where she went, Janelle?" She could at least open the screen door.

"Out. What's it to you? You're not supposed to see her outside of contest dates."

"I need to coordinate with her about this evening." Janelle sure had a pissy attitude toward him all of a sudden. It was worrisome that she was running the show and had a clear preference for Zachole. Next time she needed her rust bucket car fixed, she could go pay someone else.

"You can coordinate with me. That's how it's supposed to work." She opened the screen door, but not to let him in. She stepped onto the stoop and let the door bang closed behind her.

"Zachole has her number, doesn't he?"

Janelle crossed her arms over her chest. "You know he does."

"In fairness, I should have Aly's, too."

"What if she doesn't want you to have it?"

"What if she does?" He was a younger sibling himself, but he hadn't been this mean to his brother's friends. Had he? Given he'd avoided his brother's infrequent boyfriends like the plague until Stephan, almost certainly not.

"Then she'll give it to you." Janelle smirked. Marc was suddenly glad he'd grown up without any sisters. If they were this much of a pain in the ass, he could certainly live without them.

"I have a better idea, Janelle. I'll leave my number for her. You can give it to her and let her decide what to do with it."

"Yeah. Okay." She didn't move.

"Will you let me in for a minute?" he demanded, exasperated.

"What, you want me to give you a piece of paper and a pen or something?" Janelle finally relented and held open the screen door. A gaudy parrot clock screeched one.

"Aren't you going to ask how Alyssa's date went last night?" Janelle reached for a pad of sticky notes and a pen.

"Nope." He scratched his number down, wincing at the pressure on his thumb. Between pounding Zachole's face and the hammer's revenge, his hand was pretty beat up.

"Zach proposed."

The pen skittered across the paper. Marc ripped off the top sheet and crumpled it. Stuck the yellow ball in his pocket and started over.

"Since I'm taking her out tonight, I'd guess she said no." That wiped her face clean of any momentary triumph. Marc held out the Post-It notes. "See she gets this."

"Sure."

"You really want Zachole to win this contest, don't you?"

"Yes." Janelle's stance was suddenly wary.

"Why?"

"Selfish reasons, partly. I don't have to tell you about those. Also because everyone up and down this block knows you're the biggest skirt chaser in Florida. I don't see you making Alyssa happy."

Janelle was a lot smarter than she let on. There was a canniness deep in her green eyes. She was hiding something, too, although she was the worst liar he'd ever met.

"Zachole isn't going to make your sister happy either."

"Maybe. Maybe not." She cocked her head. "He's a better bet than you are, though. I'm not going to let you discard my sister like you do to every other girl."

Her lack of confidence in him stung, a little bee sting of doubt venom swelling beneath his skin. "I wouldn't be playing your silly game if I wasn't serious about Aly, Janelle."

He chucked her under the chin. She jerked away.

"Why did you have to latch onto my sister? Why now?"

"It's the first time I've ever had a chance." Easy answer.

Janelle snorted. "Yeah, right. You hardly spoke to her the year she lived here. When she was home from college you ignored her."

"And vice versa." True, though, and it stung.

"It'd be easier to believe you were into Aly if you hadn't slept with half of Florida. You're direct. If you had a thing for her, why didn't you ask her out?"

Marc shrugged. "She was never single when she was home."

"Hm. I think there's more to it than you let on."

Maybe. He'd been fifteen when Julian had told him the truth about his sexuality. He'd reacted with all the maturity of an average teenager—not much. On some level, Marc had felt compelled to prove that he wasn't gay. The simplest way to accomplish that was to sleep with any girl who would have him.

Or maybe he'd been trying to provide cover. The De Lunas did not talk about sex. His behavior had forced the topic into conversation, made it all about him, and distracted anyone from commenting on Julian's perpetual lack of a girlfriend. Marc decided he liked the second explanation better; it was marginally more noble.

Janelle turned on her heel and headed up the stairs, hopefully to put the sticky note on Alyssa's desk.

Proposed. Marc didn't like the way that knowledge went down like an anchor in the pit of his stomach. He wasn't about to do something similar. If Alyssa wanted to get married bad enough, there was nothing to stop her from saying yes.

He'd better plan an evening 180 degrees different from Zach's date. In a few hours, he'd get to show Alyssa why he was the only one who deserved her attention. He'd better be damned convincing.

10

Alyssa stuck the sticky note to her phone so she wouldn't lose it. Adding the number to her contacts was inviting calamity. Besides, the disposable square of yellow paper with a barely legible phone number scrawled on it was the only tangible thing she had from Marc.

She pointed her dad's Toyota carefully into traffic. The navigation software on her phone told her to turn left, so she turned on her blinker and cautiously made the turn. The car behind her beeped. Alyssa's blood pressure shot up. She drove so rarely that whenever she got behind the wheel of a car she drove like an octogenarian. In Florida, actual octogenarians were the ones honking at her to get out of the way.

Marc's boondoggle house was easy to spot. Every other home was either neatly maintained or had been expanded and upgraded. The neighborhood was clearly on the upswing, and the project house stuck out as a crumbled wreck surrounded by plywood fencing.

No wonder his parents thought it was a mistake. The place was going to take a ton of money and work to make habitable. Still, Verona Harbor was a rapidly up-and-coming city, attracting families priced out of Naples with good schools, the harbor, and lots of parks.

She turned off the car and sat there. Marc's truck was parked in the driveway. Voices echoed from inside. He had company. Now what?

Well, she'd already put in the effort to have her ideas printed up and had driven all the way over here. The worst that could happen was a heaping spoonful of rejection and humiliation. No time like the present.

Alyssa leaned against the truck while she typed in the numbers of his phone.

I'm outside, if you have a few minutes. She hit send.

Seconds later her phone beeped. **Be there in five.**

Alyssa had to remind herself to start breathing again. After thirty seconds, the impulse to run back to the car and drive away unseen was almost uncontrollable.

Too late. Marc emerged from a plywood hole. Why hadn't she remembered to pack sunglasses so it would be less obvious that she couldn't keep her eyes off him?

Only she could make such a mess with a guy like this. Alyssa examined her feet to keep from staring at him.

"Hi," she said, glancing up.

"Hi."

Great conversation start. Almost as good as yesterday.

"Janelle said you stopped by." She brandished the phone, complete with the yellow sticky note.

"Contest rules. You're not supposed to be here." She wished he'd take off the sunglasses. His tone was bemused, but she couldn't tell what he really thought about her unsolicited appearance.

"Well, I am. I brought you something." Alyssa held out the over-sized plastic bag. He accepted it wordlessly and pulled out three large pieces of stiff paper.

"What's this?"

"They're brand boards. When we were, ah, on your boat, you mentioned you could use some help with your marketing presence. I went ahead and mocked some designs for you. It took a while yesterday to find a printer that could handle a presentation board as a walk-in." As in, it had taken all afternoon. She'd been grateful to get out of the house for a while.

Marc shuffled through the boards like an oversized deck of cards. "You're really good."

Alyssa shrugged. "There's two versions of this design. I chose colors that reminded me of your sailboat, with a serif font for a classic look. In this version, I used a sans-serif typeset. It'll read better in digital formats."

"What's the difference?"

Right. "See the little feet on the letters in the first version? That's a serif font. Sans-serif means the letters don't have those little feet. It's cleaner and more modern." A shy smile tried to creep across her lips. "I'm kind of a font geek."

Marc stared at the brand boards. "These are great. Thanks."

Her heart sank. He couldn't be too excited about them if all he did was put them back in the bag and set it on the ground. Marc turned to her. "How'd it go with Zach last night?"

"Fine." Alyssa didn't want to talk about it. She didn't want to talk at all. Not with Marc. That sentiment was exactly what had gotten her into this mess.

"I'm going to go." She turned away.

"How stiff is the competition?"

There is no competition. He didn't need to know that, though.

"He proposed." She'd thought nothing could top the humiliation of her almost-fiancé standing her up on Christmas Eve. She'd been wrong. So, so wrong.

"I heard." His expression below the shades turned impassive.

"I turned him down."

A ghost of a smile. "Heard that too."

"Surprised Janelle told you."

A real smile this time. "I'll see you tonight?"

"Whatever you worked out with my sister." She might've been a little too successful at feigning nonchalance. His jaw tightened as if she'd said something cruel.

She reached over and took his hand. His thumb was tinged blue and the knobs of his fingers still red from punching Zach. "Looks painful."

"It's not so bad." He withdrew. "I'll pick you up at seven."

Alyssa's heart cracked a little watching him retreat. Zach had hardly touched it, but she was already in deep where Marc was concerned. She couldn't tell him, though. Not now. Not ever. Not when he was leaving, and so was she.

MARC NEARLY MISSED the turn for his own driveway. He swerved just in time, overcorrected, and had to reverse the car. It was bad driving by any standard.

Going on a real date with Alyssa was like stepping into an alternate reality. One where he'd already slept with her, and her sister had laid out the dating ground rules after the fact. The whole situation was upside-down.

The porch light was on, but otherwise there was no indication anyone expected him. It wasn't too late to bail. He could turn around, park the car in Julian's garage, go home, and this whole mess would be finished. She'd go back to New York and date boring finance types; he'd stay here and wonder every year if she was coming home for Christmas alone or with a boyfriend. Eventually he would stop imagining Alyssa's short-shorts over every surface. It might take a thousand years, but he was a patient guy.

Her silhouette appeared in the door. The screen door cracked open and she stepped out, waving to someone behind her. She had dressed not to kill. Not badly; Alyssa was incapable of that. The clothes she'd chosen were casually elegant, a shimmery knee-length skirt paired with an oversized sweater that obscured any hint of curves.

It was a perfectly nice sweater. He wondered if she'd borrowed it from her mom. All he could see were her collar bones. They were very sexy clavicles. But everything south of that, from elbow to knee, was covered in at least two layers of fabric, floating around her body like a cloud. It was a far cry from the come-hither dress she'd worn on Christmas Day.

"Wow. Nice ride." Alyssa's eyes popped wide when she saw the BMW convertible parked in the driveway. She'd probably been expecting the truck.

"Julian's. It's on loan for the evening."

Alyssa tucked herself comfortably into the passenger seat, like she belonged in an expensive car. Then again, she had a knack for fitting in anywhere. On his boat. In Florida, doing yoga in the back yard on a sunny winter morning. In the cab of his beaten-down truck. In New York City, which he knew since he'd flipped through the pictures on her social media feeds looking for pictures of her date yesterday. It was the perfect way to torture himself, both now and after she went back.

They drove until the city fell away in the rearview mirror and the sky opened wide and dark above them.

"Where are we going?" she finally asked as he turned down a dark country road.

"Not to a restaurant."

"Then where?" He'd have had to be deaf not to hear the apprehension in her voice, even over the roar of the wind from the open car.

"The Everglades."

She was silent for a minute. "Why?"

He guided the car into an empty parking lot and killed the engine. "I'm tired of being around you in public, and there's no place private for us to go other than my boat. The point of this exercise is to talk, so let's talk."

"You're going to get a zero rating in the Food Quality category," she said nervously, tucking her hair behind her ear. The wind had whipped it into a tangle, like it had been on the boat. The sight drove a piling of desire right down his middle.

She'd *belonged* on the boat. With him. Just the two of them. They were silent for most of the drive.

Marc pulled a paper bag out of the back seat. "Hungry?"

"Not at all."

"Too bad. There's dessert if you want it." He carried the bag to a nearby picnic table, wishing they could go back to the easy familiarity of two nights ago. Alyssa followed him at a distance, as though he was going to do something horrible to her instead of give her a piece of chocolate cake. "So, we started off on the wrong foot, obviously."

Alyssa went still and silent. "I'm sorry you feel that way."

"Don't you?" He watched as she twitched the shimmery skirt over the picnic table bench. It settled around her legs like a cloud of stardust.

She placed her forearms on the table and leaned forward. Her hazel eyes were as intense as they had been three nights ago, when he had first touched her hip under her skirt. In the moment when it had been blindingly clear where things were headed, and neither of them had pulled back.

"I would not go back and change a single thing about that night, Marc. I want you to understand. I don't regret being with you. At all. I'd do everything again, and more, in a heartbeat." She glanced away over the sea of grass waving in the moonlight. "It's okay to tell me that you never want to see me again. You didn't have to bring me here."

What the hell was he supposed to say? His mouth was dry. His mind flashed through memories of her, like a runaway train of sensations, and images that he had been doing an excellent job of not remembering right up until she said the words *everything again, and more. In a heartbeat.*

Yes, now. Please and thank you.

Marc's distracted brain had hardly processed the second thing she said. Alyssa thought he'd brought her here to tell her he never wanted to see her again? What the hell was wrong with men in New York?

"That's not what I want," he choked out.

"No?" The hope and skepticism in her voice almost broke something in him. "Then what do you want?"

I want you all to myself. "To get to know you better. The way you talk about yourself, and your family talk about you, it's like they're describing someone completely different from the Alyssa I know. I feel like I don't know you at all."

She relaxed fractionally. "Well, you know the basics. I'm curious. What's your first memory of me?"

"The day you moved in."

"Really?" Alyssa sat back and crossed her arms.

Marc nodded, trying to remember what exactly it was that had drawn his attention. "You had a ponytail. You were cute, kind of quiet. You were…self-possessed. I don't think I would've dealt with it as well if my parents moved me my senior year of high school."

"I was relieved to move." She picked at the hem of her sweater.

"Why?"

She took a deep breath. "In Ohio I had a boyfriend. Just a high school thing. One day I caught him taking pictures of Janelle with his phone. Not okay pictures. She was thirteen years old. My dad flipped out, called his parents, and had the pictures destroyed. But the guy started harassing me at school. It got bad fast. Then Dad was offered an early retirement buyout, so he took it and we moved here. They were tired of the winters in Ohio, Janelle was starting high school the next year, and they wanted her to be able to focus without awful rumors dogging her. By the time we left, I had no friends to lose."

He shook his head. "That's sick. Did they call the cops?"

Her shoulder lifted and fell. "No. Everyone involved was a teenager. Kids, phones with cameras, and a whole lot of poor judgment didn't make it a crime. We moved, the problem went away, and nobody shovels the driveway anymore. It all worked out. What's your next memory?"

"Easy. The day you got your college acceptance."

"There was more than one."

The hint of pride in her voice made the corners of his mouth tick up. "The one in New York. Didn't you beat out hundreds of other applicants?"

Alyssa grinned. "The school admits about sixty-five students to the art program every year, out of thirteen hundred or more applicants. Nobody was more shocked than I was."

"I saw you check the mail, and then I heard you screaming." Impossible not to smile at the memory.

"My mom was screaming."

"Whoever it was, half the neighborhood heard it. When I saw you later, you were practically floating."

Alyssa grinned. It was strange and a little disheartening to realize that she didn't seem to know he'd witnessed the biggest turning points of her life.

"I was eighteen years old and headed to the best art school in New York City. That lucky break almost made up for all the bad things that had happened the previous year. I hadn't been happy like that in a long time."

Marc remembered it well. That was the moment when Alyssa had gone from the cute girl next door to beautiful, talented, and successful. Untouchable. Every year when she'd come home from the city, she'd been a little more polished, a bit more glamorous.

She wasn't untouchable now. He reached across the table and captured one manicured hand. Slim, elegant fingers curled around his. Marc ran his uninjured thumb over her palm. That simple gesture made her close her eyes with a little shiver. He wasn't offended when she let go.

"Was it everything you'd hoped?" he prompted.

Alyssa took a deep breath. "New York?" she asked, her mind clearly elsewhere.

"Yeah."

She shook her head. "Definitely not. I worked constantly that first year. I was so tired all the time. It was sink or swim. Which was a good thing, because otherwise I might have been totally crushed by the fact that you were off at college and having...a lot of fun with the girls. You think I didn't know that," she smiled, bumping his calf with her toe under the table.

Marc immediately shifted his leg closer so they were touching. He smirked right back at her, though her knowledge of his tomcat ways made him shift in his seat.

"I'm sure everyone knew about it. What about after college?" he asked, changing the topic back to her.

"I graduated, got a job, and four years later got a promotion. It was approved last week," she replied flatly.

"Congratulations."

"Thanks." The absence of enthusiasm in her voice bordered on bitterness. Weird. Alyssa was the least bitter person he knew. She had to like her work if she'd done a freebie project for him on her vacation. So, why the unhappiness?

Marc lifted himself to sit on the table and swung his legs to her side, propping his feet on the bench beside her. He didn't reach for her, though all he wanted to do was pull her close and make her come until she forgot all about bad jobs and bad boyfriends. Instead, he popped open the white cardboard box beside him.

"Cake?" he asked.

"What kind?"

Marc reached over and dipped his finger in the frosting. "Chocolate. Try some." He held out his hand, index finger coated with a thick layer of dark sugar almost invisible in the darkness, and watched Alyssa. Waited to see what she would do.

11

Marc was doing that eye fucking thing again. Watching her so intently that it was as if he had X-ray vision, only instead of seeing her bones, he saw her emotions in Technicolor.

His finger hovered inches from her lips. "Go on. Taste it."

Her eyes flicked involuntarily to his. The Everglades had burst into flames around them. An invisible boa constrictor had crawled out of the swamp to squeeze her tightly around the ribs.

Alyssa's lips parted. A warm puff of *no* escaped, but it was silent and conveyed no meaning. Marc's chocolate-laden finger touched her lower lip, the sweetly bitter scent mingling with fresh country air. Gently, he pressed his thumb into the gap between her lips until the confection touched her tongue. She moaned low in the back of her throat. Saliva flooded her mouth as she licked the frosting from his finger, sucking it deeper.

It was really good cake.

His entire body had gone still. Alyssa closed her eyes for a moment as his fingers brushed her cheek. She rolled her tongue over the first joint of his index finger, the frosting gone now, and tasted the salt of his skin. Alyssa tilted her chin up to graze the tip of his finger with her teeth.

Marc released a choked breath. The spell broke. Her eyelids popped open to find him watching her as if she had turned into the cake, and he was about to devour her. This time, she held his gaze until he was the one who broke contact. It required all her strength.

The moment passed. Then several more.

"What's your first memory of me?" Marc asked beside her, his knee hovering in her peripheral vision. If she'd moved him in any way with her little cake performance, it wasn't detectable in his voice. Alyssa leaned her head against his leg and stared up at the sky. It was easier to talk when they were touching.

"The day we moved in. Your mom came over to welcome us to the neighborhood. She mentioned you were in college, and I saw you later that evening taking out the trash. Since I was avoiding boys like the plague, I decided to work very hard at not running into you."

"You were the ghost next door." He threaded his fingers through her hair.

She smiled faintly into the dark. "There was a downside. It meant I was constantly aware of you." Marc traced the outline of her ear with his index finger. The one she'd licked clean of chocolate a few minutes before. A shiver stole over her as he brushed the hair away, exposing the nape of her neck to the night air.

"Maybe that explains why I sometimes felt like I was being watched. New question. What's your favorite memory of me?"

Alyssa sat up suddenly and shook her head. "I think you know what my favorite memory is." She stared up at the stars, grateful the low light hid the stain covering her cheeks.

"Before this week."

She just shook her head, embarrassed. "It's ridiculous. So high school. Maybe I'll tell you in the car."

"I'm holding you to it."

"No promises."

That was the problem. A few days from now she'd get back on the airplane and go back to the city, put her head down, and work her tail off. When she was home, she'd have plenty of time to sit around her minuscule apartment, reliving their night on the sailboat. In a few weeks or months, he'd leave on his great sailing adventure. Knowing

Marc, he'd find a girl in every port. All they had was this week, and it was flying by.

"Come here." Marc tugged her hand and nodded at the picnic table. Alyssa set one foot on the bench and stepped up to sit a few inches away from his side on the table top. He pointed up into the sky, where stars glittered like shattered glass shards. "See that bright star?"

His bicep bunched under the short sleeve of his t-shirt. Alyssa's eyes lingered on the line of his arm before she raised them skyward. "I see a lot of bright stars."

He glanced over his shoulder with an expression she couldn't read. Amusement and wariness, and something that was still cloaked in shadow. He leaned back on his arms and scooted over to settle one leg on either side of her.

The damned, invasive boa constrictor was back, and it had brought friends. The air went stale in her chest before she remembered to exhale.

Marc leaned her head back against his shoulder and pointed again into the night sky. "That one. See it?"

Suddenly, she did. One glowed more fiercely than the others. "Yes," she whispered.

"Polaris. The North Star."

"I remember it."

"Remember it?" Marc pulled away to look sideways at her. His hand fell to her thigh and stayed there, warm and welcome.

"There's no stars in New York. Not the celestial kind."

His chest tensed and relaxed against her back as he settled back. "Maybe you can't see them, but there are always stars." He brushed her hair aside. Alyssa turned fractionally, her lips hovering against his.

"No kissing," Marc's voice rumbled against her body, and his mouth brushed hers.

"Not you, too." She leaned forward to stand up. His arm snaked around her waist, pulling her back. Hard. Her heart hammered.

"I choose to interpret the rule as 'no kissing on the lips.' Everything else is fair game."

Alyssa's low pelvis clutched and released, sending a liquid sensation through her abdomen. His very hard erection pressed against her low back. She tilted her hips back fractionally and was rewarded with a hiss and an answering grind against her sacrum.

The hem of her linen sweater bunched in his palm until the air kissed her belly. Marc's fingers skimmed her ribs as his mouth dropped to her nape and traced a path to her ear. His teeth scraped over the lobe. She melted against him, her breath shallow in her chest.

Alyssa closed her eyes against the bright winking sky. Marc's hand flattened over her stomach. His thumb brushed the underside of her breast. She inhaled sharply and let her cheek fall against his hair as he made his way down her neck again.

Marc traced the contour of her bra with one palm. His breath was hard against her cheek as he pushed past the cup and found the tight bead of her nipple. He rolled it between his thumb and forefinger. Shockwaves of pleasure radiated outward, her other breast heavy and unbearably tight as it waited impatiently for its turn. Alyssa's mind blanked.

Instinctively, she moved to close the gap between their lips.

"No kissing," Marc reminded her, his voice rough, his arousal out of reach behind her. His lips resumed their progress over her shoulder, where her sweater had slipped down to bare her skin.

"Yes." Obediently, she turned her face heavenward.

His fingertips brushed her inner thigh. Instinctively she let widened her legs, to give him better access. Marc took full advantage, slowly stroking her with his thumb.

A breeze kicked up, fanning the embers of her overheated skin. Her skirt puddled over his jeans, leaving her open to the world.

He pushed aside her underwear and circled her sex with one finger. Everything south of her belly button and north of her knees tensed. Waiting.

The bastard left her suspended there, teasing, denying satisfaction.

"Why are you stopping?" she demanded hoarsely.

Marc's chuckle reverberated through her. The sensation came close to putting her over the edge.

"Do you want this?" he demanded, applying the slightest pressure to her clit.

"Yesss," she hissed, squirming.

"Inside you?"

"Yes. *Yes*." But he refused to give her what she wanted. Instead he ran his finger along her wet seam, touching her entrance too gently. Toying with her.

"Will you kiss me?"

"Of course! Marc, please."

"No kissing. Remember?"

"You're cruel," she complained in a hoarse whisper. "Fine. I promise I won't try to kiss you."

"Kiss me anywhere but on the mouth. And keep your eyes open."

What?

He must have a thing for watching her, or he wouldn't keep asking. Alyssa broke this latest rule the instant he dropped his lips to the opposite side of her neck, pinched her taut nipple, and slid two fingers of his other hand into her. Sensation crashed over her, roaring and cacophonous in the quiet night. She dropped her head against his shoulder and shifted wider. He took the invitation.

With a few long, slick thrusts of his fingers he found the sensitive spot deep inside her. A groan tore out of her as he pressed the heel of his palm against her tight nub and rhythmically stimulated her internally.

"Open your eyes," he ordered in a low growl.

The weight of million watchful celestial eyes bore down on her. They blurred and streaked across her vision as pleasure wracked her body. Marc's body was all around her, holding her as he wrung every ripple from her body. Watching her so intently that his flirty little game of eye contact was never going to feel like being eye fucked again because this was the real thing.

He'd watched her come in his arms.

She'd liked it. Needed it. Didn't want to live without it. And that was huge problem.

He withdrew his hand from her skirt and tugged her bra back into place. Kissed the curve of her shoulder as her breath slowed. In a few short days, she'd have to learn how to go without hot, blazing-stars sex indefinitely. Maybe forever.

Alyssa turned to Marc and pressed her lips softly against his cheek, the tip of her tongue sneaking past the barriers of her teeth to taste the stubble on his cheek.

"It's your turn," she breathed against his skin.

"Another time." He pushed back and stomped down the other side of the picnic table, leaving her bereft.

"Are you kidding me?" she demanded. "I could feel exactly how badly you want—"

Marc stopped in his tracks, his shoulders stiff. "It's after ten. You have a curfew."

Until he'd checked his watch, the evening had been proceeding perfectly well. Alyssa was so sick of people making up idiotic rules to control her behavior. She was a grown woman. If she wanted to stay out late and have mindless sex with her neighbor with every alligator in the Everglades for an audience, it was her business.

"I'm not going." She got down off the table but didn't move any closer. Instead, she crossed her arms and stood with her feet apart.

Marc turned, his lean and lethal silhouette backlit by the street lamp in the parking lot behind him. "Get in the car, Alyssa."

"No. I'm not ready to go home. I want to stay out. With you." Though his expression was shadowed she could feel him eye-strangling her. Eye fucking was better, but she'd gotten under his skin, which was sexy in a certain way. He did not get to be in control all the time.

"Come back here. We're not done." Crickets chirped. Whirring bugs filled the silence. She watched him struggle. Watched him lose. A thrill of triumph rocked her when he took the first step.

12

A week ago, if someone had told him he'd be staring down a pissed-off, thoroughly mussed Alyssa in a public park, Marc would've laughed and complimented the speaker on his or her imagination. Yet here they were.

As she stood there, defiant, his dick bucked against its denim prison. If they left now, they'd be home more or less on time. Any delay and he'd be in trouble with her family again. That mattered to him, if not to her.

The white cake box on the picnic table snagged his peripheral vision.

Marc stalked toward her. Alyssa's stance didn't change when he leaned over to pick it up.

"Forgot something," he murmured. He caught the scent of her hair and closed his eyes against a tidal surge of lust. He held the box in his right hand, leaving his left hand free to bat her hands away when she reached for his belt. Stymied, Alyssa reached up to wrap her arms around his neck. Her breasts flattened against his chest, and his lungs squeezed airlessly like a landed fish.

"No kissing," he whispered. Resistance was killing him by inches.

"You get one rule," she breathed, and then her lips were sliding over his cheek and the cake box fell to the table.

Not kissing her was the hardest thing he'd ever done. No wonder she'd kept trying. The forced passivity was maddening. She worked her way down his neck, each soft impression, each glide of her lips against his skin sending sparks shooting though his body. Her hands found their way under his shirt, and his stomach pulled back like an anemone. Her fingers followed the lines of muscle, and her breath hitched.

Marc put his hands around her waist and tugged her close against his body. Alyssa's chin tilted up. Their mouths were centimeters apart.

"No kissing," she whispered, turning away.

He'd never wanted anything as badly as he wanted to taste her.

Alyssa's hands found the buckle of his jeans. *Yes, yes, yes*, his body cheered.

"No," he rasped. "Stop."

She froze. No matter how badly she wanted to follow things to their logical conclusion, he knew she wouldn't continue without his consent. It was his last defense. If he let her push him one step further, he'd have her on her back and screaming into the night sky.

Yet there was one thing he wanted more than physical release with Alyssa. Marc wanted her to look at him and see a partner, not a hookup. He wanted them to be a couple, even if he was hazy on the details of how to make it happen. If that meant following a lot of stupid rules and disappointing everything south of his bellybutton for a while, so be it.

But disappointing Alyssa was shredding his resolve. Her shoulders pulled up near her ears as she stepped back. She raked her hands through her hair. The sweater she wore like a veil rose and fell with harsh breaths.

She reached for the cake box. "I'll be in the car."

Damn. He should have taken her to a hotel and given her everything she wanted instead of trying to be clever. But that was what guys who were just trying to get into a girl's pants did. He should know. It was the kind of thing he might've done, if he'd cared less about what happened between them after she went back to New York. His throat tightened and his erection finally began to calm down.

Right now, he couldn't see how this approach was winning him any points. Alyssa was determined to keep things casual. The thought deflated him.

He'd had enough no-strings sex to fill a lifetime. He was determined not to blow it with the girl he'd coveted for so long. But she wasn't making it easy.

THE STUPID CAKE box sat in her lap like a bomb, silence heavy and awkward between them. Alyssa was drowning in a depthless sea of mortification.

"Why did you tell me to stop?" she finally demanded when they pulled up at a stoplight.

"You deserve better."

"I'm not in the market for better. I'm on vacation. I'm looking for fun."

"Well, I'm not."

"Lucky me," she sulked. Her grip tightened on the box in her lap. "I've never known you to be serious with anyone. Why start now?"

He checked the rearview mirror and turned onto their street. Parked a few doors down and killed the engine. Turned in his seat to face her, all lean slouch against the fawn leather. "Because it's you, Alyssa."

"Ha." Still, the thought sent a jolt along her spine that almost made up for the park disaster this evening. She snorted. Leopards didn't change their spots, and men with a serious case of pussy affluenza didn't suddenly want relationships with their next-door neighbors. Especially when said neighbor lived in another city.

Or when the man in question was planning an open-ended sailing tour around the world in the not-too-distant future.

Alyssa hadn't made it to New York because she was stupid.

"What will you tell Janelle about tonight's date?" he asked softly.

"Not the truth." Alyssa opened the door and stepped onto the sidewalk, slamming the convertible door closed with her hip. She placed the bedraggled box on the seat.

"Look happy," he said, reaching for her fingers. The impulse to lift his finger to her mouth was almost as strong as the urge to pull away.

Her sister stayed on the porch clutching a clipboard to her chest. She made a decisive tick mark with a pen. "Well, you beat Zach for timeliness, Marc. You may have two minutes to say goodnight. Consider yourselves warned. One kiss, that's it."

"We won't need long," Alyssa reassured her. Janelle banged into the house with her clipboard, unappeased. Aly turned to face Marc. They stood inches apart, the evening breeze swirling her skirt around her thighs.

He placed one arm over each of her shoulders. "Let's consider this a do-over. When do you leave?"

She inhaled the scent of him, soap with a hint of sharp masculinity, and tucked it into her store of memories. "My flight is at 3:30 PM on New Year's Day out of Tampa."

Four days. Really, four nights and three days. "Tomorrow evening?"

Alyssa's face pulled as though she'd bitten into a lemon. "Nope. Tomorrow is Zach's date challenge."

He frowned. "Doesn't seem very fair."

Alyssa cocked her head and raised an eyebrow. "It's not about fairness. It's about convincing me to get back together with Zach. Surely you've picked up on this."

Judging from his expression, he had. "Is it working?"

"No. And it won't. Start planning New Years' Eve, because I am breaking. Every. Single. Rule."

Marc placed left hand at her waist, or where he thought it was under all the soft billowy fabric. "You heard your sister. One kiss."

"I'll give you a practice round." She smoothed her hair back.

Marc tilted her face to his with his right hand. He ran his thumb over her lips. "Don't need practice."

Of course, you don't. Alyssa closed her eyes. Marc placed his hands on either side of her face and brushed his lips across the tip of her nose. Her eyes flew open. A giggle bubbled up out of nowhere.

"That's it?"

"Call you tomorrow." He squeezed her hand and turned away.

THE NEXT MORNING, Alyssa sat on the swinging glider pretending to read a book while Janelle chattered at her. "I was thinking of going to grad school. For something practical, like accounting."

"Accounting. Really." Alyssa didn't glance up.

"I hear you can make a lot of money."

"You've always been terrible at math. Why not go to law school? You're good at arguing."

Janelle swatted her. It felt good to engage in normal sisterly bickering. They were interrupted by a UPS box truck rumbling up the street, followed closely by Marc's old red Ford. A burly man in brown shorts and a button-down shirt stacked three large cardboard boxes onto a hand cart and wheeled them up the driveway.

"Are you Alyssa Carlisle?"

She nodded.

"Sign here, please." The delivery driver held out an electronic pad for her to sign. Alyssa scrawled her name.

"What's all this? Extra Christmas presents?" Janelle asked.

"My stuff! I can't believe he actually sent it."

"Who?"

"Zach. It's all of my worldly possessions."

"Three boxes?" Marc had veered away from his parents' house and walked up their driveway. "Need a hand?"

They hauled the boxes up to her temporary bedroom. Alyssa fished a pair of scissors out of a drawer and sliced through the packing tape. She held out a dress. "He could've at least folded the clothes instead of dumping them into garbage bags. It'll cost a fortune to dry clean everything."

Janelle reached into a box and lifted out a plain brown shoebox with a fancy logo scrolled over the lid. Her green eyes went wide. "Whoa! You own a pair of Louboutins? Don't they cost, like, a thousand dollars?"

"It's not a garage sale."

Too late. Janelle had opened the lid and was trying on her favorite pair of patent leather open-toe heels. "Hey!"

"Oh. It says these were marked down to $298 at Barney's Warehouse sale."

"Yes, they were a great deal, thank you very much." She'd treated herself a few years ago, then Zach had proceeded to buy her more pairs at full, exorbitant retail price.

Marc groaned. "Tell me women don't spend three hundred dollars on one pair of shoes."

Alyssa shrugged. "When you only have space for a few pairs of shoes, you want love every single one."

"Oh, my God, there's two more boxes in here!"

"Janelle, get out of my stuff!" Alyssa lurched for the box but was hampered by the armful of dresses she was trying to untangle. Still wearing the first pair of shoes, her sister scooted out of reach. "At least let me unpack before you go picking through it."

"Check these out!" Janelle waved a glittery, feathered pair around.

"They look like a cross between a chicken and a disco ball," Marc commented dubiously.

"It's a twelve-hundred-dollar feathered disco ball to you."

"Janelle, you're being crass. Also, they've only been worn once, so don't get any ideas about borrowing them." She'd forgotten about them. On purpose. Wearing them killed her feet.

"Are you going to have room to store it all when you get back to New York?" Marc was leaning one broad shoulder against the door frame.

"No. I'll probably sell some of it." She slipped a suit jacket over a hanger. It was silly she had all this fancy clothing and couldn't afford a better apartment. Plus, there was someone who needed the little space a lot more than she did. Gina.

"Sell it? Why?"

"I'd rather have the money. Or give it to Janelle. I don't even like half of this stuff."

"Didn't you just get a promotion?" Marc's confusion was written on his face as he ripped open the two remaining boxes. "Why do you need to sell your stuff for money?"

"Honestly..." Alyssa poked her head into the hallway. Janelle had disappeared with an armful of clothes and was undoubtedly trying them on. "Don't say anything to my family. I'm thinking about turning down the promotion."

He stared at her. Not his usual flirty eye contact game.

Alyssa watched her sister's door. "Do you know how much more they're offering to pay me? Five hundred dollars. That's it."

"A month?"

"A *year*," she replied, shoving a skirt onto a hanger and banging it onto the rod. "HR says it's the difference between the top level of my current title's salary range and the lowest rung of the next tier up. My boss can't do anything. If I take it, I'll be responsible for two junior designers, so it's a lot more stress. I was so mad I told her I needed to think it over before signing the offer letter. I still haven't made a firm commitment."

"Why? You have talent. Lots of it. I have no idea what I'm supposed to do with a brand board, but I know great work when I see it. And you shouldn't pass up the career advancement just because of the money."

He reached for the stack of hangers in her hand and tossed them on top of the clothes yet to be hung in the guest bedroom closet, then he pulled her into his arms. Alyssa sighed. She wished she had someone in her corner like this all the time. Too bad it wasn't real. Marc was only on loan for a few days.

"Shh." The door down the hall had clicked open. Alyssa kissed him. Just to make sure his lips weren't free to say anything about her job situation. Really.

"Geez, get a room." Janelle breezed past, still wearing Alyssa's black patent Louboutins. She'd changed into a dress Alyssa recognized as one of hers and put on makeup.

"This *is* my room!" Alyssa yelled after her. "Or was, for a year."

"I can't tell if she looks like a badass entrepreneur or a high-class hooker," Marc commented wryly.

"Janelle, I need my shoes back."

"As soon as I get back from shopping!" Her sister minced down the hallway and took the stairs a little too fast, gripping the railing hard.

"Aren't you broke?"

"I'm using gift cards to hit the after Christmas sales, nosy." The front door slammed.

Alyssa's eyebrows lifted. "Pot, meet kettle."

"You know, it would be really nice to go somewhere where our families aren't completely up in our business all the time," Marc said casually.

"Like Alaska?" Alyssa slid her hand down the front of his shirt, the rise of his pectoral muscles hard beneath the soft texture of his shirt.

"Cold this time of year."

"There's always the boat," she mumbled hopefully.

A grin played over Marc's sexy lips. "Marinas are worse. I'm getting flak from everyone who lives aboard. I don't mind, but prepare for a lot of commentary on your next visit."

"Is no place safe?" she asked with mock horror. Lacking any immediate solutions to her problem, Alyssa rested her forehead against Marc's neck, his body warm and hard against hers, and the scent of his skin making her heart pick up speed. How could she possibly leave him?

His entire body tensed as if she'd telegraphed her deepest, darkest wish. "What if you didn't go back to New York?"

She lifted her head and forced a chuckle to cover the surge of longing. "Right. No thanks for the promotion, handing in my notice, I'll go live with my parents?"

"No. You shouldn't just quit. It's easier to find a job when you already have a job. What else can you negotiate?" He moved back, clearly determined to solve this for her. It was endearing, but a spark of irritation flared. It wasn't his problem. Marc was acting as if she should drop everything to come here and be...what? His fuck buddy for a few weeks? He kept hinting that he wanted something more, but he'd also been crystal clear that he intended to leave soon.

"What do you mean, what else? I tried for money." She let go of him and returned to sticking hangers into her clothes and clothes into the closet.

"Maybe you could get a work-remote arrangement and come here for long weekends. You'd keep your salary and your title long enough to find a job in Florida."

The instant her heart started down the runway for takeoff, caution clipped its wings. Walking away from her job now would be career suicide. Even if he meant it sincerely, Marc was *leaving on a sailboat adventure*. Pulling the plug on everything she'd worked toward for the sake of a few weeks with him was a worse proposal than even Zach's. Besides, quitting her job was a great way *not* to help Janelle.

"Working remotely won't work if I'm a supervisor. If I truly have so much talent and I'm not committed to staying in New York, I'd be a fool not to cast a wide net. See where my job search takes me. After all, in a few months, you're not going to be here."

The hitch in her voice caught her off guard. If she was honest with herself, the idea of leaving her job and being closer to her family, and to Marc, held more appeal than it should. "Besides, we're not a couple. You'll be back to the hookup scene as soon as your grudge match with Zach is over."

She tried to stuff the thought down into the back of her mind like a pair of socks with holes in the toes at the back of a dresser drawer.

His eyes glittered cold when she finally glanced up. Alyssa dropped her attention to the pale pink cashmere sweater dangling from her fingers. *Whoops*. She might've been a little harsher than she'd intended, but he couldn't actually believe this was going anywhere.

"Is that what you think of me?" he demanded. "I'm just some man-whore?"

Definitely too harsh. Qualifying her statement with *but you're a nice, fun man-whore, not the gross kind* probably wasn't going to fix it, either. Damn. She hadn't meant to hurt him. She'd been stating a fact, and she now wasn't quick enough to form an apology.

"Have fun with Zach tonight." His voice cleansed like rubbing alcohol on an open wound. Then he was gone.

13

"Tonight's date challenge is to enjoy one another's company without spending money. You are to spend no more than ten dollars over the course of at least two hours." Janelle held her clipboard close to her chest. She still hadn't taken off the Louboutins, which made her a stronger woman than Alyssa. Those heels made her calves cramp after a couple of hours.

Crickets chirped around them as she followed Zach to the white mustang. The night air was moist and soft on her skin, the humidity tugging little flyaway strands out of the braid she'd corralled her hair into. Best to remove any temptation for him to touch her; being here already felt like cheating on Marc.

It's not possible to cheat on a one night stand. It wasn't like they were committed. She'd said as much to his face only a few hours ago. She ought to be trying to fix things with Marc, not going on this stupid fake-date with Zach. But she'd promised her sister, and she'd see the contest through. Besides, Marc hadn't returned her phone call. He was truly pissed off. Only the stone in the pit of her stomach kept her anchored here in the car.

"I thought we'd drive around to see the Christmas lights." Zach's voice startled her out of her sulk.

"Sure." *Whatever you want.* She didn't have to argue about every little thing just to prove that she wasn't a pushover.

Twenty minutes later they were cruising down the streets of one of the wealthiest neighborhoods in Naples. The houses out the window of the car had ballooned from the modestly-sized postwar bungalows and ranches of her parents' neighborhood to giant barns with huge windows and three-car garages. Some were bedecked with tasteful light displays. Others had gone all-out, red-and-green strings winding over rooftops and down porches. A boat covered with twinkling strands sat in the driveway of one monstrous home.

"See the house with the sleigh and the reindeer?" Zach pointed across the street.

"Cute," Alyssa replied, trying to bring her attention back to the moment.

"Yeah, you think so? I could buy something like that. Your sister could live there." He tried to sound casual, but Aly heard the temptation in his voice. Like he was dangling a carrot. She gave him the side-eye, but said nothing.

"C'mon. Janelle would love it. And the way I see it, you kind of owe her."

"I—What?"

"Well, your parents mostly paid for you to go to college in New York, so your little sister's bogged down in debt. I could help with that. Seriously doubt Garden Boy could."

"Call him that again, and this date's over."

"I'm sure he calls me something just as adorable. You know I'm right. You love me, and I love you. So, what are we doing here? Let's just get a flight, and go home. We'll get you out of that apartment, and moved in with me. We need some time together, alone. That's all."

He reached for her hand. Aly stiffened. He was taking control, like he always did. If she wanted to break up with him, tonight was the night. This had nothing to do with Marc, and everything to do with her autonomy and independence.

"I'm surprised Janelle told you about the loans."

"She didn't. I guessed, from things you said over the past couple of years. See? I listen to you all the time."

"Yeah, for ways to manipulate me." She yanked her hand away. They drove to the end of the block and turned down another road, going nowhere. Zach went on as if she hadn't spoken.

"We don't have to get married right away. We can wait until you're ready. But I need to know that you feel the same way about me as I do you. I mean, sometimes you get a little frigid. Moving in together means we'd have more sex." He reached over to brush her cheek with one fingertip. "That's why I was so astounded that you'd been out with Garden Boy."

"This date is over," Alyssa declared through clenched teeth. "Take me home or I'm calling a cab."

"You can't mean that, babe. Think about the past two years. You're upset about the engagement, so let's cool it and take the next step together." They stopped at an intersection. Zach's tentacle—arm— pulled her closer. Alyssa lifted his elbow, ducked under his arm and opened the car door. A second later she was on the sidewalk, clutching her purse against her chest.

"Get back in the car, Aly."

"No." Instead, she turned and strode down the sidewalk. Thank goodness she'd worn flats. She'd left the passenger side door hanging open, and now she heard it slam behind her. Her palms were so sweaty that her bag slipped as she picked up the pace.

Zach trailed her slowly in the car. "This is stupid, Aly. Don't be dumb. Get in."

"No. I'm calling a cab."

"I won't let you do that. Come on. It's fine if you don't want to move in. Keep the apartment. Just stay over more often."

"No. I told you we were through on Christmas Eve. I shouldn't have to keep telling you. Go away." For the first time, a tremor of fear for her physical safety flashed through her mind.

She should've been honest with her family. This stupid contest was supposed to help clarify her choices, and boy, had it ever. Alyssa had never been clearer in her life about what she needed, and right now, that was a whole lot of distance from Zach Kessler. She pulled her phone out without breaking stride, but it took her two tries to open the app and request a cab. Three minutes. Then, she'd be out of Zach's reach. She kept walking. Zach tailed her in silence.

At last she spotted the driver, opened the car, and jumped into the back seat. Zach yelled one last time before she could get the door closed and locked.

"You said you'd give me an honest chance!"

I did. You blew it.

Alyssa kept looking behind the cab to see if Zach had followed her. The thought was terrifying. He'd never been violent before, and there was no reason to think he posed a physical threat, but suddenly she was reevaluating everything. She peered warily around before stepping out of the car in her parents' driveway. Her sister's shadow filled the porch. There was no sign of her ex.

Dread made her shiver despite the night air. What was she going to do about her sister? There had to be some way to help her. Janelle had taken the brunt of their parents' cheapness and even if he was a jerk, Zach was right about one thing: it wasn't fair to let her struggle alone.

"That was short." Janelle was still wearing the heels.

"I'm done with Zach. Contest over. Marc wins."

Janelle shrugged. "I'm glad."

"Really?" Alyssa crossed her arms at her sister.

"Yeah. Zach said a few things this week that were really off. When I called him on it, he'd either lie to my face or say I'd misunderstood him, when I knew I hadn't."

The hair on Alyssa's neck prickled. "What kinds of things?"

"Basically, that he'd help me with my loans if I helped him win you back. As if I'd sell my sister. He's also been dismissive of you. He made it sound like you were selfish for not marrying him to help me."

"Janie, that's exactly what you asked me to do."

Her sister hung her head. "Yeah, I believed you'd help me with my loans if you married him. I pushed you to do the contest, because I thought Zach was a good guy. A real catch, you know? Rich, good looking, generous, and crazy about you. But he was only manipulating me. He's been gaslighting us all along, hasn't he? What an asshole."

There was a word for Zach's behavior; she wasn't making it up. Relief coursed through Alyssa's body. The sensation was short-lived.

The white Mustang roared into the driveway. Zach stepped out, his hair mussed and his shirt wrinkled, his expression the picture of concern.

"Aly, I'm so glad you're safe. I was so worried when you took off. What's wrong with you?"

"Nothing's wrong with me, Zach." Alyssa tried to shove her sister behind her, but Janelle tried to do the same thing and they ended up side-by-side, a united front.

"You've lost the contest, Zach. Go away."

Alyssa wished she could tape her sister's mouth shut.

Zach ignored her. "Aly, don't be like this. You scared me tonight. It's not cool to jump out of someone's car. That's nuts."

"Why did she feel like she needed to?" Janelle interjected.

"I don't know," Zach shrugged. "I'd asked her to move in with me, as soon as we get back to New York, so we can put this week behind us."

"Is everything all right?" Catherine appeared at the screen door.

"Yes," Zach said hastily. "I was just saying goodnight."

"Mom, stay, please." Alyssa spoke over her shoulder, a command and a plea.

Catherine stepped onto the porch. Reinforced, Alyssa returned her attention to Zach and stepped off the porch. She had to make this *no* stick. "I got out of the car, Zach, because you never listen to what I say. You lie about me. You lie about me *to me*! I'd never, ever marry you. Not for any amount of money in the world."

Zach glanced away, then took two steps closer. "You don't mean, that, sweetie."

He grabbed her by the arm, slid his other arm around her waist and pulled her hard against his body. His mouth crashed down onto hers in a forced kiss that blocked her protest.

Alyssa tried to beat against his back with her free hand. Her fingers brushed the edge of his mobile phone sticking out of his back pocket. Clenching her teeth against the mouth assault, she forced herself to lean closer so she could pull it free.

Zach released her so suddenly that Alyssa nearly tumbled back onto her ass. Instead, she bumped into Janelle, who'd stepped off the porch to help. The entire incident couldn't have taken more than a few seconds.

"Get out of here before I call the cops," Janelle hissed.

"Janie, she has my phone. I'm not going until I get it back."

Alyssa retreated to the porch with her prize and wiped the taste of Zach's mouth away with the back of her hand. She unlocked the phone and quickly deleted her phone number and their text message thread. Somehow, Catherine had convinced Zach to get into his car. Alyssa strode over and tossed the phone onto the white leather of the passenger-side seat. "Don't call me. Don't email me. I've deleted my info. Contact me again, either here or in New York, and I'll get a restraining order. Do you fucking understand me?"

Zach's only response was to yank the car in reverse and accelerate backward without looking to see if she'd jumped out of the way in time to avoid being hit. The three women stared after the white car as Zach sped away.

"I take it you're on with Marc for New Year's," Catherine commented after a moment.

"Yeah." Alyssa pushed her hair back and grinned. "Yes, I am!"

"You might want to give Marc the good news." Janelle nodded, her shadow shifting. A car door slammed.

The growl of his truck's engine told her it was already too late. Alyssa's entire body jerked around in time to see it streak around the corner. She squeezed her eyes shut, her skin clammy despite the warm night.

"On second thought, I might be looking for a New Year's party to crash," Alyssa swiped hair out of her face, joy at her freedom from Zach instantly replaced by regret. Marc must've seen the awful kiss. Knowing Zach, he'd done it on purpose, to ruin her prospects with his rival.

"My car's parked on the street. If you hurry, you might catch him." Janelle held out a silver ring. Alyssa snatched it and sprinted to the old Volkswagen, turning the key twice to coax the engine to life.

But when she turned the corner, the street was empty.

14

The second whisky, glistening amber in the low light, sat untouched before Marc. Music throbbed, loud and distracting. Not his style, but so what?

"Don't be so glum. You can always come over to our side. *Lots* of men would be into you. Lots and lots and lots." The man speaking wore a tight t-shirt with a picture of a unicorn mounting another unicorn beneath a rainbow. Julian's arm draped affectionately over his shoulder.

"I'm considering it." Marc was used to this sort of banter from Stefan, Julian's boyfriend. He hadn't wanted to be around his own friends. Their solution was always the same: set him up with some Tinderella hookup on the spot. Ordering up easy sex was so simple, like getting pizza delivery, and time was he'd have hit it without a second thought. Not anymore.

"If you think women are dramatic, try dating men." His brother wasn't typically affectionate in public, but they were cozied up in the booth of a gay bar. Marc had invaded his space, so he was more relaxed than usual.

"Tits at twelve o'clock." Stefan nodded toward the door. "Not the usual fag hag here to shake it either."

Marc watched his brother's body freeze and unthaw in the space of a few seconds. It was all the warning he had before Alyssa materialized in his peripheral vision.

The whisky burned his esophagus all the way down.

"Hi Julian, apologies for chasing you down. Do you know where…" Her gaze fell on him like water hitting an open flame.

She'd come after him. If he could've throttled the sudden adrenaline rush running through him, he would've.

"You must be Aly," Stefan declared in a tone that told her everything about their topic of conversation for the past half hour. She blanched.

"Yes. A friend of the family." She stuck out one hand gamely. "And you are?"

"Stefan. A friend of Julian's." He reached over and pumped it once, Julian's arm bobbing where it still hung over a shoulder.

"A pleasure to meet you." Aly didn't bat an eyelash. "Great t-shirt."

He didn't want her casual acceptance of his brother to tug at the Gordian knot of his heart. Didn't want her to be here. Didn't want to care about her anymore.

But he did. It was bedrock, part of his foundation. He'd been waiting for her for so long, and he'd risked everything by leaping in without knowing how far he had to fall. Or how bad the landing could hurt. He'd kicked himself to hell and back, yet he couldn't put the mess all on her tab.

Aly was here. She must've been trying to find him for a while because a gay bar was the last place anyone would look.

"Buy the lady a drink, Marco," Stefan ordered. "We're headed out. Work tomorrow, not that you'd know anything about the office grind."

Julian scooted the length of the booth and waved over the waiter. "I'm staying at Stefan's tonight. The guest bedroom is yours if you want it. You know where to find the key."

Alyssa slid into the bench they'd exited. Not next to him. He was slouched against the wall, one leg propped up on the wood seat and taking up all the space. The waiter came back.

"What do you want?" Marc asked, his tone harsher than he'd intended. Until tonight, he'd believed he would win this contest. It gutted him to find that the closeness building between them might've been all coming from his side.

Alyssa blinked up at the waiter in the cool lights of the bar. "Whatever he's drinking."

Two whiskies appeared a few silent minutes later. She sipped hers and visibly repressed a shudder.

"Pour a little water in it."

Her pretty hands carefully tipped the water glass into her whisky. Despite the chipped polish on a couple of nails, her hands were elegant. The memory of her fingers barely closing around his cock sent a shudder through him. "Figured you'd be on your way back to New York by now."

"Still here." She drank again and managed not to sputter this time. "Zach's leaving. Alone."

"Yeah? One last goodbye kiss for old times' sake?"

"I know what it looked like. But that's not what it was. I didn't expect it. I didn't encourage it."

"You didn't think I was watching."

"True. It wouldn't have mattered. Like I said, I wasn't expecting it."

Okay. It didn't mean everything was smoothed over between them, not by a long shot.

"Do your parents know? About Julian?"

"No. So don't say anything for the next couple of days, or when you come back to visit next year."

She was silent for a beat. Her cheeks tinged pink, and she let the curtain of hair fall over half her face, hiding her expression. Marc wished she wasn't so sexy in a plain tank top and jeans. They hugged her curves in exactly the right places, a little vee of cleavage visible between the soft rounds of her breasts.

Aly shook her head, pushed her hair back and glanced up. "I'd never out him. I'd guessed, but until tonight I didn't know. You can't be assumptive about these things."

She reached for his hand where it cradled the whisky glass. Curled both hands around his. "You're making assumptions about me, and about what happened this evening. It's hard for me to talk about, but I want to tell you, if you'll listen."

Her touch was cool at first, warming slowly. Marc didn't pull away. Didn't encourage it either. Not until Alyssa's expression shuttered and she tried to let go. The instant their hands lost contact his skin cooled. He reached for her hand across the table and brought it to his mouth to kiss her knuckles. "I'm listening."

By the time she'd related the story of her relationship with Zach, his third whisky had disappeared. He'd better watch it or he'd be cabbing it back to Julian's. "That's fucked up."

"Yeah, well, it's over now. Finally." Alyssa withdrew, blowing a strand of hair out of her face. "Why didn't you ever talk to me, like a normal person? Like you are now? You were always such a flirt."

"I tried. How come you always ran away?"

"Because I was terrified of making an ass out of myself. You were *you*."

"What's that supposed to mean?"

"We've been over this. You don't need me to shine your ego to a high gloss." She shrugged and glanced around the edge of the high-backed booth. "There's an entire roomful of men who'd be happy to do that for you."

Yeah, but he was only interested in one person's opinion.

"It's not your looks as much as that...you're so damn confident. You decided college wasn't right for you so you went and made your own way. I admire you for that. Everyone in your family is successful because you go after what you want most." Weirdly, Aly meant it.

Successful. What a load of shit. He was lazy. He'd figured out that owning property could free him from a desk job, and he'd leapt at the opportunity. Because all he cared about was pleasure. Sailing. Sex. Anything he wanted.

But he'd never been able to entirely shut down the guilt nagging from the back of his mind. Aly's ambition had always appealed to him for this reason.

She sat up, blush receding. "And you had to go and look like movie star just to top it all off. How many women in their late teens or early twenties have the self-assurance to walk over and strike up a conversation? I didn't."

"Plenty of girls did."

But they hadn't. There'd only been enough conversation to smooth over the awkwardness of getting into bed with someone you'd just met. Banter made that process a little easier, and he'd perfected it. But it had been designed for short-term and impersonal, not for getting to know someone on any meaningful level. He'd never tried to talk to women he wanted to sleep with until this week.

He was the one who'd changed the rules. She'd been trying to play along. They'd confused the hell out of one another by switching sides of the hookup/relationship spectrum. It wasn't fair of him to be angry with her, not when he'd given her every reason to believe short-term sex was all he'd ever wanted. Maybe this would've turned out better if he'd picked a couple of girls to practice on before trying to click into a relationship with Alyssa and having no fucking clue what he was doing.

The question that Janelle's half-assed dating game had not resolved was whether they could get past the rocky start and find some way forward.

"I'm out after this one. Are you coming over?" The last sip of whisky didn't burn so much this time. It warmed his innards like a campfire in the dark.

She sat up straight with a sharp inhale. "I have to get Janelle's car back."

Lesson learned. Using sex to smooth over problems wasn't a winning strategy either. Good thing he was a quick study because Alyssa had a few things to teach him about intimacy.

Marc openly ogled her denim-clad ass on the way to their cars. There was so little time left to make her want to stay with him. He reached around Alyssa to open the door of Janelle's little white Volkswagen that was more rust than metal. The door stuck. Marc didn't force it. Instead he leaned against the body of the car and trapped Aly inches from his chest. The muscles in her long neck moved as she swallowed.

"No kissing, huh?" His voice sounded tight, the blood rushing through his veins in a tidal wave. Her mouth tilted up at the corners. All the blood in his body shot to his pelvic region.

"That was so last night."

It was the only invitation he needed. She tasted of whisky and woman, all silky strength and willing surrender. Aly opened, and he took everything she would give him, then demanded more. She moaned and offered everything he wanted.

Maybe there was some merit to his methods of smoothing over problems after all. His dick sure thought so.

"I'll make it worth your while. If you come with me."

"Coming is always worthwhile."

He grinned against her lips. Hardly the most risqué thing he'd ever heard from a woman, but coming from squeaky-clean Aly's lips it was downright pornographic. She had a dirty side he really wanted to get to know better. "I'll follow you."

"There's no need to go out of your way. I'll get a cab."

Damn. He wasn't drunk, but he didn't want to drive any farther than necessary. He yanked open the door of the car. Palmed her ass as she got in. She turned around and shot him a grin.

"I'll text you the address."

"See you in a bit."

But he didn't. He let himself into Julian's condo, tossed his few belongings into the guest bedroom he occasionally took advantage of when sleeping on the boat or at his parents' house were equally intolerable, and clicked on the TV to pass the time. A whole lot of it went by before he concluded Alyssa wasn't coming, worthwhile or not.

THE RUSTY VOLKSWAGEN wheezed up the street and conked out the instant she put it in park. Alyssa yanked the keys out of the ignition and grabbed her handbag.

Janelle was on the couch in the living room. Her Louboutin-clad feet were propped on the coffee table, which must mean their parents had gone to bed. Shoes on the furniture were grounds for disownment. Everything above the thigh was gray sweats and loose T-shirt.

Alyssa's new least-favorite show flicked across the TV. *The Bachelorette*. Her sister hit the pause button. A woman in a slinky dress froze mid-rose-twirl.

"Did you find him?"

"Eventually." Alyssa glared at the TV. "You should consider going out once in a while, instead of hanging around watching reruns."

"With what money?" Janelle clicked the TV back on. Her dark hair was tied up in a knot on top of her head, which made her appear fifteen and forty at the same time.

"Thanks for letting me borrow your car. I noticed it was low, so I filled up the tank."

"Great. Thank you. I was wondering if I'd be able to get to work tomorrow."

Alyssa plopped next to her and snatched the remote control. The TV blinked off. "Have you told Mom and Dad how bad your financial situation is?"

"They know. You turned it off at the good part." She made a half-hearted grab for the remote.

"Do they know in any detail? Maybe they'd help you out." Fat chance. Early retirement had flipped a switch in their father from frugal to downright miser. When the family's education savings had run out, he'd told them both to take out loans, over their mother's protests.

"You heard how dismissive Mom was. I'm managing."

Alyssa sat up. Janelle obviously didn't want to talk about it, and she couldn't force the issue. "I'm going out again."

"Meeting Marc?"

"Yeah."

"Mom and Dad won't be happy."

"I'm of age."

"You're here to see us, not shack up with some guy."

"Marc's not some guy."

Janelle scissored at the waist and put her feet on the floor at the same time she sat up straight. "Maybe not. I didn't think he'd fight this hard for you. Do you know where you're going?"

"Julian's apartment."

"I think that makes it worse." Janelle kicked off the heels and padded toward the kitchen. "Do you know where he lives? In *detail*?"

"Marc texted me the address." Although, come to think of it, she hadn't heard her phone go off. Alyssa followed her sister into the kitchen. Janelle took down two glasses and filled them with water from the refrigerator.

"He's *really* not just some guy for you, is he?"

"No. Yes." Alyssa ran her nail over the raised decorations on the glass. "He can't be more. He's got his big sailboat adventure soon, and he's been planning it for years. Plus, I'm leaving in two days. I want to enjoy the little time we have left." A rock-hard lump formed in her throat. There'd been a few too many honest moments to pretend this was short-term anymore. Janelle's ridiculous scheme had seen to that. But it was doomed, going nowhere. Temporary. They could try to keep it going long-distance, but it was postponing the inevitable. It was better to make a clean break.

Janelle observed her with catlike green eyes. "Better go find him then."

Yet the stiffness in her shoulders as she scooted off the counter stool and made for the stairs told Alyssa just how sad her sister was. She tackled Janelle with a hug from behind.

"Thank you. For intervening this week. Your methods are questionable, but the process helped." She'd never have regrets about not getting back together with Zach, for example.

Janelle embraced her arms. Her topknot tickled Alyssa's cheek as she leaned her head back. "Go call your cab."

But she couldn't. Alyssa's phone wasn't in her handbag. It wasn't in her pocket, or in Janelle's rustmobile. No one picked up when she called it from the house landline her mom insisted on maintaining even though everyone had mobiles.

Alyssa's heart picked up its pace as every place she searched turned up empty. *Fuck.* The word reverberated like an echo chamber inside her head. The parrot clock struck eleven. Alyssa bit back a scream and briefly considered smashing the thing into a thousand million pieces.

She called the bar. No one had turned in a mobile phone. Her fist smushed her lips hard against her teeth.

Sticky note.

Alyssa scrambled up the stairs and poked through the pockets of the clothes in her laundry hamper. The yellow square was still in the pocket of the jeans she'd been wearing when she went to find him at the boondoggle house. Triumphant, she punched the numbers into the landline.

It rang eight times before going to voicemail.

Shit, shit, shit.

"Marc I lost my phone. I don't know where I'm going. I can still get a cab if you call me back at this number with the address. Are you there? Call me."

Damn. It. Damnit all to hell. This was supposed to finally be their night, and she'd lost her damned, blasted, benighted, fucking phone. She was cursed. She had to be. It was the only explanation for luck this rotten.

15

Something hard dug into his arm. Marc rolled over and pulled out the remote control. The giant black television screen was dark and silent. He must've accidentally turned it off in his sleep. He tried to roll over on the soft couch cushions but his feet were trapped. He peered in the direction of his toes.

Blanket? The ugly afghan that Julian hid in the hall closet hadn't been there when he fell asleep. Someone was in the apartment with him. He hoped to hell it wasn't his brother. But how would Alyssa have gotten in?

He levered his body off the couch and stretched stiffly. Made his way to the guest bathroom and brushed his teeth. Checked his brother's room. It was still and silent.

Hope fluttered against his chest as he pushed the door to the guest bedroom open. A long lump under the blanket meant there was a person in the bed. Marc cracked the door wider. Hair sprawled across the pillow. A lot of it. He couldn't tell the color in the darkness, but it was definitely a female bed lump. Alyssa. He didn't care if she'd picked the lock, broken a window, or bashed in the door. The sight of her sent tingles through his entire body.

He pushed the covers aside and climbed into bed next to her.

Tugged her pliant body close. He'd never watched a woman sleep before. The even rise and fall of her breasts did something weird to his chest, like arousal but higher in his body, near his lungs.

He wished he could enjoy this fleeting sense of contentedness and welcome without ruminating over the end, but he lay there awake for a long time thinking about leaving. Her going back to New York. Him going anywhere, everywhere, just as he'd always dreamed. If only he could bottle this feeling and take it with him.

The solution was so blindingly obvious that he smacked his forehead with the hand that wasn't wrapped around Alyssa's sleeping body. It popped into his consciousness as a fully formed sentence. If it had been a sign, it would've been neon and flashing.

Take her with you.

Why not? They'd be completely insulated from their families. Unfettered, transoceanic sex on tap. Marc's dick leapt beneath the sheets, saluting the genius of this idea. She wasn't happy in her job. The money didn't sound good. Alyssa was talented enough to get work as a freelancer. Though she didn't know a mast from a tiller, she was used to living in small spaces. She'd jump at the chance. And this fragile feeling of homecoming would ride the high seas with him wherever he went.

WARM, hard legs tangled with hers as Alyssa tried to roll over. Her hair was plastered to her cheek. Raising one hand to brush it away, she accidentally smacked a rough chin.

Which explained the solid wall of slow-breathing man chest against her back, and the heavy weight of an arm over her stomach. Even on the edge of consciousness she recognized Marc's earthy scent. She pushed him over and flung her arm over him, trying to go back to sleep. It didn't work, so she nestled into the hollow of his body and ran her hand over his torso.

He cracked open one eye and peered at her between thick lashes. "Morning."

Alyssa wanted to lick the lazy smile off his face, but she was too busy enjoying where she was to move. They hadn't so much as kissed after leaving the car parking lot last night. Yet her body was as languid and relaxed as it had been the morning she'd woken on the *Escape*.

Ok. Not that relaxed. But considering she was waking up in a strange bed after breaking into a near stranger's home, she was darn comfortable.

"Hi."

Marc pulled her up and across his body. Alyssa dug her fingers through his thick hair just above his ears and kissed him thoroughly. Taking the time to taste his sleep on his lips, to let his chin scrape against hers. It made her inner thighs tense and release. She pulled her legs up, pinning him against the mattress with her knees pressed alongside his ribs. It put Marc's erect package into very close proximity to her totally-down-with-it clit.

"I could get used to waking up like this."

"Me too." Alyssa ground against him experimentally. His lazy grin sharpened into a leer as he tilted his hips in response. A moan escaped as she shuddered. Two thin layers of cotton separated them. His boxers and her underwear. They'd have to go, but she was too busy enjoying the friction of his erection against her sex to consider the logistics.

She put one palm on each muscular shoulder and pushed herself upright.

"Don't move," she ordered. Marc remained gratifyingly still as she crossed her arms, pulled the tank top over her head and tossed it aside. Naked but for a lacy pair of black underwear, Alyssa reached for his arms and pushed them high above his head.

"Like this?" she asked, grinding harder against him.

"You have no idea," he growled.

Oh, she had a pretty good idea, judging from the way his penis tried to jump straight through his boxers and into her vagina. Thwarted, Marc thrust against her again.

"Nice try," she panted, shifting. "Don't move, unless I need you to."

Alyssa took her time inching down Marc's body. The texture of his skin was a marvel, so fine and velvety, the hard muscle beneath a perfect counterpoint. Her tongue slipped out, unbidden, and she traced the line between his ribs all the way to his navel.

The thick bands of muscle crossing Marc's abdomen tightened as she paused to lick the center of his stomach, then casually continued her exploration down the trail leading to the waistband of his boxer briefs. The waistband was tented enough for her to play peek-a-boo with his cock.

She peered through the annoying mass of her hair. If he didn't like it so much she'd consider cutting it short. Marc was watching her with hooded eyes so dark and hot it made her blood thrum in her veins. His arms were still propped on the pillow. A man who could take orders was a rare gem. She'd never tried giving orders before. She'd never tried a lot of things.

More intriguing was the considerable lump covered by one thin layer of fabric resting just between her breasts. She hooked her fingers into the elastic and inched it down. Marc writhed.

"No movement," she chided, inching the blue shorts down until the tip of his penis emerged. Marc's body stilled instantly, until she licked the drop of liquid seeping from the head. Then his taut hips bucked beneath her, trying to gain entry.

Alyssa *tsked* and took the opportunity to slide his underwear down over his hips.

"I'm going to get you back for this."

She sat up, her mouth turning up at the corners though she was trying hard not to smile. "I can't wait. This time, however, I want to play boss."

"I'm yours to command," he rasped.

Alyssa dispensed of his shorts and folded her torso back down over his body. Daily yoga had several advantages in the sack—flexibility, and the ability to hold awkward positions for a long time. With his thick thighs trapped between hers, Marc couldn't have gotten up if he wanted to. His arms were on the pillows. The sight of the fine hair under his arms made her pelvis pulse. It was an odd thing to find exciting, but it was earthy, masculine, and it totally turned her on.

Alyssa hovered above Marc's erection and cupped her breasts. Rubbed them over the solid length of him. She grinned as he fisted the pillows. She taunted him a little longer before placing her hands on the bed and moving back a few inches to take the tip of his cock into her mouth. She clutched his hips as he desperately tried not to thrust. Then she tortured him by flicking her tongue over the vein that led to the tip.

"Fuck. Alyssa. Stop. Don't stop. I—"

She wasn't done with him, so she sat up and extended her body upward along the length of his. He panted against her cheek, his chest rising hard against her breasts with every breath. Marc abandoned following orders, hooked his fingers into her underwear, and pushed them down to her thighs. Alyssa reached down and managed to kick them off without kneeing him in a very sensitive place. She kissed him hard and wet as she pulled her legs up into the same position she'd started from. Then she returned her hands to Marc's wrists and pushed them up beside his ears. "Do you have a condom? I don't."

Marc stared at her in disbelief as he clapped both hands over his face.

"What's wrong?"

"I don't have one either. Julian probably does, but I don't want to go through his cabinets."

Understandable. He and his brother were closer than she'd realized, but there were still boundaries. Alyssa shrugged and lay down next to him, one hand propping up her head.

"I'm on birth control." She hesitated before saying it, unsure whether she wanted to have sex with him without a condom. He'd played the field for so long.

He let go of his face and rolled up and over, pushing her backward onto the bed. He kissed her hard, then gently as his body began to relax. "I've never done it without a condom before."

"Not once?" Marc was full of surprises.

"No. An underappreciated advantage of a gay older brother is on demand access to lectures on how to have safe sex and horror stories about what happens if you don't. When I discovered girls, Julian laid down the law."

"I'm dying to know what he told you," Alyssa muttered around his mouth, tilting her pelvis upward against him.

"The basics. Learn when and how to put a condom on and do that every time. Get tested regularly. Communicate with your partner. Don't lie if there's a problem, and have fun."

"You've done that to the letter?"

"Every time. Especially the fun part."

Marc nuzzled his way down her neck, his lips tracing a lazy path along her clavicle, a slow burn trailing over her skin like the wake from a boat.

"I had my annual a few weeks ago, and I got an IUD so I don't have to think about birth control. Everything checked out." She'd requested it in part because she hadn't entirely trusted Zach not to sabotage her pill supply if he decided he wanted kids after the wedding. The new equipment was still untested.

She'd never seen him hesitate before. Alyssa answered the question in his eyes with her body, pinning his hands back to the pillow. Sliding over him was so easy. The warm, wet friction of his body sliding into hers was the same, but better. Closer. She was on top, nominally in control. But somehow, within a few strokes, Marc had taken over. He matched her pace. When she curved her spine to take him deeper, he groaned and complied. And then she let go of his hands and propped herself up on her elbows, her face buried in his shoulder as he hooked his forearms around the backs of her knees and plunged hard and deep.

Alyssa writhed helplessly as he fucked her in a frenzy, dragging animal gasps from her as he hit every over-sensitized nerve. The orgasm hit her hard and fast. She sat up and cried out, jamming herself down over him as she worked out days of frustration and denial on his body.

His muscles stiffened beneath hers, and she glanced down to find wonder in Marc's eyes as he came inside her.

"Fuck," he gasped when he could breathe again.

"Yeah, that's one word for it." Alyssa tried to collapse over his chest, but he pushed her to the side and withdrew. *Huh.*

She was a first for Marc in one very crude sense. The knowledge sat uncomfortably in her stomach like a half-digested meal. She'd had sex with exactly three people, all in college or after, and all in the context of relationships. Clearly Marc had learned a lot about how to please women, but he'd held himself back on some level. It was a strange time to be going outside his comfort zone.

Given he'd already violated his ingrained sexual norms once, they may as well keep going. He didn't need a lot of encouragement. She gave it anyway, just in case he had any doubts. They made out for a long time, kissing hard, exploring softly. Tasting one another's skin.

"You have gorgeous breasts," he murmured, palming one, and watching her reaction. One rosy tip glistened. "Perfect. I could do this all day."

"I'm not going anywhere." She squirmed against him, hoping he'd go back to what he'd been doing.

"Oh. Yes, we are."

"We're what?"

"Going somewhere," he replied, kissing his way over to the other breast. "I get one more date with you."

"You can't be serious. You've won. Contest over. We could stay here, right?" Alyssa suggested hopefully.

Marc shook his head. "Julian throws a party every New Year. There's a balcony overlooking the harbor with a great view of the fireworks."

"I know all about the balcony." Alyssa sighed.

"You do?" Marc's amber eyes peered keenly at her between the twin rises of her boobs.

"How do you think I got in last night?" She stretched upward, a little pleased with herself.

"It's two stories up! You're not Spiderman."

"No. But I'm also not afraid of heights. It wasn't hard, honestly."

"Why didn't you come by last night? I mean earlier." His eyes searched hers.

"I wanted to. I lost my phone at the bar."

Marc put his head down and inched up her body. "Damn. I can't believe you did that."

"Me neither. I'm usually more responsible." She rolled back onto the pillow. It hadn't been her finest moment. It had been a rough evening, and she'd been a little scattered. Standing up Marc, even accidentally, wasn't an option. She wasn't going to think about why it had been so important. Her head wasn't ready to go there yet.

He put his hands on either side of her face. "I mean you risking your neck."

Alyssa kissed him. "It wasn't the first thing I tried. I searched everywhere for a key, but I couldn't find one. I rang the buzzer until I was afraid I'd wake up the neighbors. When you didn't answer, I checked the mailboxes to figure out which one was Julian's apartment. It was a simple a process of elimination to figure out which balcony was his. I'm not sure what I would've done if the door had been locked though."

"Mmm. I'll have to tell Julian how easy it is to break in." He resumed kissing her, lazily, then more intently, fully erect now.

Alyssa shifted her hips until he bumped against her entrance. Though he was on top, it was easy to press herself down over his head by tilting her pelvis.

She watched as Marc's eyes glazed. His shoulders tensed under her forearms. His hips flexed, and he thrust slowly, clearly reveling in the sensation of flesh on flesh. It touched her in a way she knew she couldn't afford. They had tonight. They had tomorrow. Then, it was over.

She *shooed* away the sad thoughts. There was plenty of time to process all the pain still to come while back in New York.

16

Janelle hung up the phone and sat back. "Marc says to wear something nice. He has a specific request for a certain pair of disco chicken shoes." Despite her general crankiness where Marc was concerned, Janelle's green eyes crinkled at the corners with amusement. The contest was over, but he'd planned something fun, so Alyssa and Marc were keeping the date.

"Any idea where we're going?"

"Normal rules. It's a surprise. I can tell you to wear your hair up and bring a bathing suit."

Alyssa's nose wrinkled. "I didn't bring a suit."

"I have one you can borrow. It's a bikini."

Alyssa wrinkled her nose. "I'm not ready for a bikini in December."

Janelle rolled her eyes. "You look great, Aly. Nothing we can do about the lack of a tan, but at least you won't have awkward lines."

Swimwear settled, Janelle set to work curling and pinning her hair up off her neck. Tonight, she'd opted for a backless dress made modest with a white cardigan. Other than the ridiculous heels that shortened her steps and added five inches to her height, she could've been headed to church service. The bikini was rolled up and tucked into her handbag.

"Showtime." Janelle grinned as the BMW's headlights turned into their driveway. Marc stepped out and slammed the door behind as if he'd owned it forever instead of borrowing it from his brother.

A sudden attack of nerves struck Alyssa as she tottered out onto the porch. The shoes were ostentatious—fine for Manhattan, but Florida was a less fussy scene.

"You look great." Marc reached for her free hand and pulled her close enough to buss on the cheek. The heels put her nearly on eye level, a scant inch between the tops of their heads. No wonder he'd asked her to wear the damn shoes.

"WHERE ARE WE GOING?" Aly finally asked as he steered the car onto the highway.

"Villa Havana." He knew how taking her to a hotel sounded, and he couldn't resist a quick check of her reaction: startled, a bit wary. "My mom's cousin owns it. We redid the landscaping after the last hurricane swept through, in time to salvage an expensive wedding. His son's a friend of mine. I'm calling in a favor."

Maybe requesting the shoes had been a mistake. But he loved what they did to her legs, the way they angled her ass out into two perfectly clutchable rounds, and put her light hazel eyes almost even with his. His dick was certain that not booking a hotel room was an oversight, a grievous error. Waking up with her this morning had been amazing. He wanted that again, all the time.

She thought she couldn't trust him. He was desperate to find some way to prove otherwise, which was the whole reason they were here tonight. He pulled up and handed the keys to the valet.

"Are you sure this date's not going to cost more than ten dollars?" Alyssa asked him with a sidelong, questioning glance.

"Immigrants' kids are resourceful. Two bucks for the valet, eight dollars to spare." He took her elbow. "Can I buy you a drink?"

"Oh come on, that's over budget and you know it." Alyssa tucked his arm closer to her body, slowing him down as she tripped along in those absurd shoes. People looked up curiously as she went by. No, as *they* went by as a couple.

"We have an open bar and free use of the roof deck all night."

"Roof deck?" She stopped before a long, gleaming wooden bar backed by a huge mirror and teardrop-shaped blue lights. "I've heard of this place. Isn't it famous?"

Marc nodded and flagged the bartender. Aly shrugged out of the demure white cardigan, and he sank onto a leather bar stool.

Holy shit. Her entire back was bare from waist to neck.

She set her handbag and sweater on the chair next to her and leaned onto the bar over crossed arms. The outline of her unfettered breast pressed soft and plump against one toned bicep. If they hadn't had an audience, he'd take her right against the bar. Aly shifted her weight into one leg. Marc caught her gaze and ran his hand along the inside of her bent knee.

The bartender interrupted to take their order. Alyssa ordered as he stroked her leg higher, out of sight of the rest of the room. His thumb rested in the crook of her knee between strokes.

"On the house." The bartender winked. Aly's shook her head, but she was smiling.

"Roof deck's this way." Marc left a tip, picked up his drink and her sweater. She trailed him to the elevators, glancing around the grand hotel that lived up to its name. The air conditioning had pulled her nipples into hard beads beneath the red fabric.

Weird, since the cooling system didn't seem to be working for him. He tipped his drink up to his mouth and wondered if they'd make it as far as the roof deck before he pinned her to the nearest hard surface.

"You're really something," she declared as the numbers climbed higher.

"What the hell's that supposed to mean?"

"It means…" she trailed off, lips closing over the rim of her cocktail glass, "I can't figure out how you were hiding in plain sight all this time."

"I wasn't in plain sight, unless you had a telescope all the way back in New York."

The elevator pinged open. Marc steadied her over a treacherous marble floor and leaned against the bar of a storm door. Three steps down and they were outside on the patio.

Alyssa's laughter cut off as she sucked in a breath. "Oh my God. This is beautiful. How did you know I have a thing for roof decks?"

I didn't, but I do now. "It's spectacular, isn't it? You can see all the way to the bay, to Fort Meyer, and out into the ocean. There's also pool and a hot tub."

"Hot tub. Really?"

The damned woman gave him a sly smile over her shoulder.

"I might use it. I'm still sore from sledgehammering my house. You don't have to though." Marc's cheeks went warm. What was it about Alyssa Carlisle that made him as nervous as a teenage virgin?

She traced her way slowly down another flight of steps, taking in the elegant roof deck. Marc followed at a distance, watching her more than his surroundings, needing her attention.

"How about a picture for your fans?"

She turned and leaned against the wall. "Fans. Ha. You're funny."

He pulled out his phone as she leaned forward against the concrete rail and let her curls touch her shoulder. Snapped a series of pictures he'd send to her later. "Don't you have thousands of followers?"

"Yeah. I didn't think you'd heard me when I told you." She changed position, adopting a friendly pose, like a friend you'd want to go out on the town with.

"I peeked to see if you'd posted anything from your dates with Zach. Have you ever considered monetizing it?" Her posture went stiff. Marc lowered the phone and walked over to her. "You seem to enjoy doing this a lot more than you like designing junk mail."

Then he ran his palm down her back, tangling in the beads dangling between her shoulder blades. He wrapped the beads around his hand once, twice, until the necklace pulled up hard against the hollow of her neck. Not enough to choke her. A little taste of his strength. Alyssa's eyes flared.

"I do like it," she whispered, and Marc wasn't sure whether she was talking about her hobby or the pressure at her throat, or both.

"Do you want me to let go?"

"No, I want you to kiss me."

He inhaled, but the air that entered his lungs was filled with the perfume of her skin. He pulled gently on the jewelry, and she bent willingly toward him. He started with the vein that leapt beneath her skin, pressing kisses along her strong, elegant neck, along her collar bone. Marc released his grip on the necklace, and Alyssa gasped. One red strap fell down her shoulder. He traced its path with one finger, then pulled it up over her shoulder.

"I'm getting in the pool." He had to cool off. His body was on fire, every nerve aflame. He sensed her watching him as he unbuttoned his shirt and removed it, draping it over a chair. Then he did the same with his pants. Beneath them he wore a bathing suit tenting out embarrassingly. Hence the sudden need for a dip.

The cool water was a good antidote. Not perfect. His erection didn't subside immediately, but the water helped. In another world—one where his parents hadn't been running a business, one where they'd been more familiar with American school sports—he might've been a competitive swimmer. He cut across the pool to Alyssa and pulled himself out of the water. "You brought a suit, right?"

"Yeeees." She drew out the word, eyes riveted on him, which didn't help his problem in the least. "But I'm not wearing it. I'll need a place to change."

"There's tents beneath the statue of the dolphin," he said, pointing across the roof. There was a shower back there, too.

She glanced over. "Back in a minute. Meet you at the hot tub."

It was impossible to hide her amazement that Marc had given her this rooftop experience for nothing. Where Zach had floundered, trying to figure out how to spend a few hours together without falling back on his money crutch, Marc approached the challenge with a sense of adventure.

Alyssa padded back out to the pool area. It was also impossible to feel bold when her swim top was headed for her bellybutton. Her B-cup-at-best boobs weren't up to the task of filling out Janelle's green strapless bikini top. The cool night air wafted gently over her skin.

Marc sat on the edge of the hot tub, his rugged form outlined in black, lower legs in the bubbly cauldron. "Hey."

Alyssa held her top as she stepped into the frothy water. She couldn't remember the last time she'd been in one. Her body warmed quickly, surrounded by countless bubbles. This was much more in line with the hot vacation fling she'd needed.

"Feel better now?" she asked, kicking one foot forward, then the other. Blue light from below turned her body into a shadow.

"Now that you're here, I do." He slid into the water. It came up to his mid-chest. He sank lower, but kept his distance.

Clouds hid the stars above them. "I wanted to ask you, Marc..." Alyssa licked her lips, her cheeks warming, and not from the hot water. "How do you use the stars to navigate? We didn't get very far into your explanation before we were..."

"Distracted?" His voice was smooth with a little edge to it, like the whisky she hadn't finished at the bar last night.

She nodded, the curls pinned to her head dipping into the water and dripping down her neck. The jets caught the loose top like a wind catching a kite. Alyssa yanked it up over her floating boobs. It promptly began slipping again.

Oh, the hell with it. She couldn't be the first woman to go topless on this roof deck, and the bubbles would conceal her nudity from any security cameras.

"You use a nocturnal. Now you can use GPS, but when I was getting my captain's license, I learned how to navigate the old-fashioned way in case the equipment malfunctions."

"What if you get lost or the ship sinks? How are you not terrified by the idea of sailing across the ocean alone?" Alyssa kicked her feet in unison, like a mermaid.

"I always figured I'd have company."

"Oh." Of course he'd have company. The female variety. This was Marc.

Yet he said he'd stopped playing the field after last summer. It would've been around the time she'd first brought Zach home to meet her family. She believed him now, or she wanted to.

He pushed off the wall and came to rest beside her. The water whirled around his pectorals, his nipples just out of sight. "What's 'oh?'"

"Nothing. I have another question." She kicked her foot out again. His shot out and hooked around her ankle.

"Ask anything you want."

"How do you see this working?" The words came hard, though she spoke them softly. "Us, I mean. After I go back. You've hinted at that a few times."

"Do you have to go back? I assumed the details will sort themselves out."

Not a good answer. "I either have to make the job I have work for me or find a new one."

"Why have a job at all?"

"Because I'm not independently wealthy like you are, Marc." She splashed him.

"I think of it as being retired before thirty." He splashed her right back. "So what? Your biggest expense is probably rent, right?"

"Yes."

"I have nine apartments to choose from."

"I though you owned four properties?"

"I do. One is a four-unit rental and another is a duplex. There's the project house, which will have four bedrooms and a studio apartment in the back when it's done, and the single-family."

"I—" Alyssa reached behind her back. The green bikini top drifted to the bottom of the pool and covered one of the lights briefly before disappearing. She'd find it later. "Now I want to ask you rude questions about how you financed it all."

"Slowly. Julian and my parents invested early. I just finished paying them off and refinanced the last property into a loan that doesn't require a cosigner. Now I'm free to plan my sailing trip, or I will be as soon as the new house gets permits." A confused expression crossed his face as he reached down and pulled up her bikini top. "Are you naked?"

She grinned. "Maybe."

"You're trouble." The fabric strip hit the concrete with a wet plop. Then Marc reached over and pulled her onto his lap.

"Aly. Wow." He ran his hands up her back and over her naked breasts, then up over her chest and around her neck to pull her in close. His mouth demanded she open, and she didn't pretend to resist. Alyssa pressed her tongue forward to kiss him deeply while arching her back.

The deck below flooded with light as the door swung open to admit a more people to their rooftop paradise. They froze. Then, Alyssa scooted off Marc's lap and pulled him in front of her. The top splashed into the water as she tried to feel how it went on. It was astounding how such a simple device could be both complicated and ineffective at its job. Marc took her legs and wrapped them around his waist.

"I thought you'd reserved the deck for us," she whispered in his ear as she tried to stifle a giggle. What an embarrassing situation.

"I got us access. I didn't shut down the whole deck. Play it cool," Marc whispered, tickling her trapped feet. Alyssa stuck the bathing suit under her bottom and relaxed against his broad back.

Five older women in thick white spa robes brought their wine glasses to the side of the hot tub. One discarded her robe and stuck her feet in the pool. "Mind if we join you?"

"Not at all," Alyssa assured them, running her hands over Marc's muscular chest. She caught one of the women give him an appreciative once-over and winked. The woman smirked and turned back to her friends.

The past week with Marc had pushed her far beyond her comfort zone. She'd never had a one-night stand; been on a sailboat—much less had sex on one; climbed a balcony to break into someone's apartment; sat topless in a rooftop hot tub; or been on a helicopter before. Yes, the last one had been with Zach, but he wouldn't have felt the need to impress her if she hadn't moved on so quickly to Marc.

But the hardest barrier she'd crashed through was intangible. She'd held her ground when Zach pleaded and cajoled and groveled. He couldn't buy her heart with closets full of luxury goods, fancy vacations, and a social status she cared nothing about. This week, she'd stopped listening only to her head and started listening to her heart. It was telling her to trust Marc. Maybe they could wing it and the details would take care of themselves. But his impromptu offer was exactly what she didn't want. However generous, she couldn't accept being dependent on anyone.

She needed her job if she was with Marc, for the same reason that she'd needed it with Zach. She wanted a partner, not a savior. He'd asked her to abandon her responsibilities, and that was something she'd never do.

17

Marc sensed Aly brooding against his back. Her hands were busy exploring his chest, which was making the prospect of getting out of this cauldron ever more difficult. He caught her hand in his as she traced one finger up and down the indentations of his abdominal muscles. It tickled. Pulling her forward, he murmured, "Let's get out of here."

"Okay." Her arms disappeared, though his arousal was here to stay. It didn't help that her tits rubbed across his back as she tried to get the bikini top on without attracting the notice of the older women. What a pickle.

"Can you hold it together in the back long enough to get out?"

"Think so." Her skin glistened in the low light. Moisture from the pool curled the fine tendrils around her face.

He got out first to retrieve a thick towel from the nearby stand, holding it out for Alyssa as she stepped out of the water like a nymph. Marc shook his dripping head. She was turning him into a pathetic, love-struck fool. He didn't mind a bit.

If it hadn't been for their audience, he'd have joined Aly as she rinsed off in the rooftop shower. By the time they were dressed and headed back down to the lobby, he'd mostly regained control over his body.

The elevators closed behind them. "How much time do we have left?"

Marc didn't need to check his phone again. "A little less than half an hour."

She took one very sure step forward. "This is a hotel."

"Yes. It is." Another step. A third and she leaned in, her breath against his skin. Soft lips closed over his. Damn, he loved these shoes. Anything that put their faces this close together was all the fashion he needed.

"We ought to be able to find a room somewhere."

His hand landed on her low back. Fine. It was the top of her exquisite ass. Who was he kidding? His thumb traced the indentations of her spine while his fingers splayed over the round muscles below.

"No sex on dates," he growled.

"You get one rule. What's it going to be? Punctuality? Or no sex?" She licked her way down his throat. Marc was suddenly lightheaded as the blood in his body hightailed to parts south.

The elevator stopped with a *ding* sound. The door opened to the lobby. Alyssa stepped back and leaned against the opposite wall with a smirk.

Marc leaned over and smashed a button on the console.

"I'd been hoping not to use this." He pulled a plastic key card out of his back pocket. His cousin had handed it to him with a grin. *In case of emergency.* The only reason he'd taken it was to avoid being rude. He'd flinched at the insinuation embedded in the offer, but he'd damn well earned his reputation, and the room was about to come in handy. His entire body tingled with anticipation.

"You are a fucking boy scout, Marc. Always prepared." Alyssa's smirk widened into a grin.

This woman was too much. He loved seeing her let go of her reserve, and watching her push her own boundaries did weird things to his stomach. He'd heard the term butterflies, but he'd never felt them before. His were prehistoric giants. Maybe everyone's were.

The door *dinged* open again. He trailed her gorgeous legs into the carpeted hallway. She glanced at her phone. When they'd finally peeled themselves out of bed that morning, Marc had taken her back to the bar, where she'd found it stuck between the bench and the seat of the booth.

His hands shook as he slammed the plastic card into the slot. He'd be lucky to last five minutes. "How do you want this?"

"Like you did with the necklace. Hard. Fast, obviously, as we're short on time." She tossed her sweater and bag onto a chair.

"Rough, you mean." Bullshit. Whatever Aly had read or watched, she didn't have any real idea what she was asking for.

"Yes." She swallowed.

If she was asking for it, she wanted to try. "Take your hair down."

Alyssa reached up to comply. A long, fat tail, dark from the pool, tumbled down her back. He raked his fingers through the cool strands, separating her hair into damp tendrils. The necklace dangled below, near the curve of her waist. A large mirror stretched along the wall above a heavy wood bureau.

Marc gathered her hair and the necklace into a single long strand. Then he wound them around his palm until the jeweled knot at the front pressed into the base of her throat and her hair tightened against her scalp. "Too hard?"

She shook her head, a fractional movement. Her eyes followed him, uncertain.

"Tell me if you want to stop. At any point."

She nodded a little. The muscles in her neck softened.

Marc took her arm and bent it uncomfortably behind her back until she gasped. "Walk to the dresser."

Alyssa stumbled forward. Having her completely under his power made him drunk with lust. He tugged her hair, pushed her forward, and bent her over the dresser. He let go of her arm in time for her to catch herself against the glossy wood.

He pulled her head up. "You were naughty tonight. Wearing this dress with no bra. Going topless in the pool."

Aly's eyes were dark. Her lips curved up. "You liked it."

"I *loved* it." He kicked her feet apart and ground against her so she could feel exactly how much he'd enjoyed her risqué tease. "Pull your dress down."

He pulled on her hair hard enough to make her lean back against his chest. Aly's attention riveted on his reflection in the mirror. Slowly she tugged the red fabric down over her breasts. One taut nipple appeared. The other popped out of its prison.

The longer he stared, the harder his cock tried to escape his trousers. He let it out, fumbling awkwardly with his left hand, the right still wrapped in her hair with the beads biting into his palm.

"Touch them."

Aly traced the outline on one areola with a painted nail. He nudged her legs wider apart and ran his hand up her thigh. "Harder."

She cupped her breasts like an offering. Marc shoved the skirt over her hips and reached for the vee at the shadowed crest. Found only skin and a small nest of soft hair.

"You were really naughty tonight." His voice sounded like gravel.

"Terrible," she agreed, unapologetic.

"I should punish you."

"I deserve it."

Did she fucking ever. But they only had a few minutes, and he wasn't letting her out of this room without a satisfactory resolution. Instead, Marc rubbed the tip of his penis along her sex. Back and forth.

"Inside," she begged, squirming hotly against him. "Please."

He yanked her hair, not hard enough to hurt but enough so she felt it. "Who won the contest, Aly?"

"You, Marc." Her breath a gasp, a whimper.

"Me. That's right. I own you."

"Nobody owns me."

"You're going to give yourself to me, aren't you? You're mine because I won you."

"There was never any competition. It was always you," she panted, grinding against him as he slid the head of his cock up and down her sex.

"Say it again," he ground out.

"I always wanted you, Marc."

He rewarded her with the tip of his dick. Aly gasped and tried to tilt pelvis backwards, but the angle was wrong and he slipped out. Her frustrated gasp nearly made him come. He took his cock away and pulled her tight against his body. "Say my name louder."

"Fuck me, *Marc*."

He did as he was asked. She was so slick that he slid all the way home with a single thrust, taking every inch. He locked his hands around her hips and slammed hard and fast, like she said she wanted it. But he wasn't going over the edge without her.

"Show me your treasure," he ground out, his breath hot against her ear. "I want to see your clit."

He pushed her against the edge of the desk. The heels put her at the perfect height to shove her hips forward. Alyssa's hand trembled as she reached down to part her groomed sex. The nails of her other hand dug through the cotton of his shirt and left grooves deep in his skin beneath.

God *damn*. She was so pink and glistening, the pale nub glistening at the apex of her bright sex. Below, the underside of his cock was barely visible where it intruded into her rosy core. The rude sight wrenched him. It was base. Animalistic. Explosively hot. "Touch yourself."

Aly moaned and frantically complied.

Oblivion beckoned. Marc took her with long, deep strokes, until her back locked, and she screamed his name as he followed her.

THE BACK of her left hand accidentally brushed Marc's as they exited the elevator. Instinctively, she curled her fingers around his. Alyssa was back in the white cardigan and fully dressed, still shaking from the massive orgasm that had rocked her five whole minutes ago.

Happy, though. Especially when he locked his hand around hers. Who would've thought she'd be holding hands, out on a date with Marc De Luna?

Alyssa idly watched the palm trees sway in the night breeze as they waited for the valet to return with Julian's car.

"Something nice for the lady?" A street vendor carrying a white bucket with individually wrapped roses approached a nearby couple, who shooed him away.

"I'll take one." Alyssa fished in her clutch for money, the plastic bag holding Janelle's wet swimsuit squishing coldly. She gave the man her money and chose the biggest red rose in the tub.

When she turned, Marc was holding the BMW door open. "What's that?"

"For you." She stepped in like the lady she most certainly hadn't been tonight and relaxed against the leather seat.

"Really."

"Janelle was watching *The Bachelorette*. The winner gets a rose, right? You won the contest. This is your rose."

He shot her a bemused glance as he steered the car into the street. "You mean you've never seen it?"

"No, I don't watch much TV."

"I've never seen it either."

"You're joking."

"Dead serious."

Alyssa burst into laughter. "So neither of us had any idea what we were getting into."

"I had an idea." He grinned. "But no, this is not how I expected to spend the week. Lucky for you I can rearrange my schedule on a whim."

"Truth." She twirled the flower stem between two fingers. "Could you get away for another hotel adventure?"

"You liked that?"

"I did. Very much."

They were still kissing when Janelle banged open the front door and sighed. "Hello, this is very uncomfortable for your audience. How about you get out of the car, Aly, and we'll call that your goodnight kiss?"

Marc held her close an extra beat. "Next time, I'm not playing around."

Alyssa felt her eyes go wide and her cheeks flame. "That was playing?"

He opened the car door for her and helped her stand up, laughter crinkling the corners of his eyes. "Foreplay. I'll try anything twice, so ask for anything you want. Now go talk to your sister while I plan our New Year's."

18

Alyssa heard the wolf whistle and shot the offender an irritated glare. She was still working her way through her first paper cup of hot coffee, and she was never in the mood for obnoxious catcalls. Though she'd been warned it might happen.

Alyssa followed the numbers past a flock of pelicans to the *Escape*'s slip. Marc waved. He took the small bag she had packed and dropped it on the deck before reaching over to help her jump across the choppy strip of water between the *Escape* and the pier.

"Morning, gorgeous." The kiss he gave her more than made up for the lack of caffeine and the catcalls combined.

"I'll stow this downstairs—"

"It's called below deck."

"I see we're starting the sailing lesson right away." Alyssa grinned. "Okay, I'll take it *below deck*. I'm also going to top off my coffee before we jump into sails and ropes and knots."

"When you come up again, you can put on this little number." He dangled some sort of blue ropey thing from two fingers. It didn't look like a life vest.

"Uh..." She held it up for closer examination. "I brought something better. For later."

He grinned at her. "This is an inflatable life vest. So you don't have to wear the orange one."

"Well, then." She climbed down the steep ladder into the cabin, pulled on a rash guard, and ditched the loose linen beach pants she was wearing over her yoga shorts. They'd work as makeshift swimwear for one trip. She buckled the life vest around her body, her sunglasses falling off her head onto the floor in the process. Marc hadn't told her where they were going, though she knew it was about a two-hour journey up the coast. They could drive it in less time, but sailing was more fun. More to the point, by midafternoon, she'd have mastered the difference between an anchor and a wind instrument.

Once they were cruising over the open water at speed, sailing was just as exhilarating as it had been the first time.

"Here, take the wheel."

"Me?" Alyssa scooched into the captain's seat. Marc's warm palm slid along the curve of her rear as he moved by her to fiddle with a rope wound around a cleat. She grinned at her recently gained knowledge. Steering was fun.

"Where am I supposed to go?" The boat dipped hard to one side as she spoke.

"Just try to keep the ship upright. Bonus points if you can track that lighthouse."

Later, Marc made her untie some ropes and take down the sail. Wherever their destination was, they were arriving. He expertly steered their vessel down a row of canals bordered by homes, turning down one canal and then another. The big boat barely fit into the dock. Alyssa boasted many new vocabulary words after today.

"Welcome to Saint James City, just off the San Carlos Bay and the Pine Island Aquatic Preserve. It's a step up from a marina, and, best of all, it's ours for tonight."

"We get a house? Without neighbors?" Maybe Christmas wasn't over yet.

"Don't get used to it. A couple at the marina rent it out on Airbnb, but they had a cancelation." He looped one arm around her waist and kissed her neck.

Heat surged in her belly as his palm glided over her hip. Alyssa's stomach chose that moment to growl ferociously.

Marc chuckled. "We'd better feed you. Unfortunately, there won't be any food here, so we'll have to go out." He unlocked the front door to a bright little cottage. The walls and floors gleamed white. Blue print curtains hung over the windows.

"This is adorable." Alyssa walked around slowly, trying hard not to imagine a part-time life here with Marc. No boss. No stress. No…

Not happening. Work would follow her even if she did manage to get away every few weekends, and in between she'd wonder who else Marc was screwing. That was more stress than anyone needed. This was only a vacation mirage. "I'll go clean up."

LISTENING to the shower run over Alyssa's naked body was killing Marc. He'd nearly died when she had shown up in his favorite little shorts that hugged her curves and left little to the imagination. Every time he managed to get ahold of himself all it took was one glance at her ass, and he snapped to attention faster than an Army cadet.

Only a few hours had passed since he'd been inside her, but if anything, his desire for her had grown. He was voracious for her touch. It was better than anything he'd imagined all those years. She stepped out of the shower, her body cocooned in a towel. "Your turn."

Marc stepped into the shower and took care of business. He pulled on clean clothes and opened the door to discover Alyssa standing at the window. She turned and gave him a knowing little smile over her shoulder.

"Ready?" she asked, reaching for the door.

Marc's mouth went dry. Her dress hugged her hips and her ass, then draped loosely from the waist on up. Best of all, Alyssa tottered on the ridiculous five-inch feathered and sequined heels.

"Can you wear those shoes all the time?" he asked, crossing the room. His hands slid over her hips.

Alyssa ground naughtily against him. "There's a strict three-hour limit. After that my feet hurt."

"I can do a lot in three hours."

"You can do a lot in twenty minutes." She giggled, pressing the door latch open. His forearm slammed it closed before she had opened it more than an inch.

"We should order in." His lips grazed the nape of her neck. Alyssa bent her head and moaned. He took the invitation she offered, sliding his hand under her skirt. With one quick motion, he shoved it up around her waist to reveal her lacy underwear. Not a thong. More coverage, but it was cut to display the perfect mounds of her ass like a picture frame.

He could not get her naked fast enough. When his fingers found her, she was already wet. Mark dropped to his knees. Slowly, he kissed his way across her thighs, toward the pretty curls between them. Parting her, he swirled his tongue over the delicate little nub hidden there.

Alyssa's moan quickly became more urgent. He added a gentle fuel to the fire of her excitement by sliding his fingers inside her. Her body pulsed around him.

Leaving him in the exactly the same predicament as before. Hard and aching and needing release.

Marc stood up and tugged down her skirt. "I should've just joined you in the shower."

"Next time." Alyssa tugged the dress over her head and tossed it aside. She wasn't wearing a bra.

As much as he loved her butt, she was one gorgeous total package. The sight of her naked and unfastening the belt of his jeans was a movie he would be playing in his mind for years to come. The lady would not be denied. He kicked his jeans across the kitchen floor. Marc backed up until his bare rear end hit the kitchen counter, which he suddenly, desperately grasped with white-knuckled intensity as Alyssa's lips closed around his cock. The mere sight of her half-closed eyes and long tresses at his waist was erotic enough to make him come. He dug his fingers into the fine thread of her hair.

"If you don't stop now, it's over," he said between clenched teeth.

Alyssa glanced up. Her naughty leer hit him straight in the gut.

She wouldn't.

To his astonishment, she did. She tightened her fingers around his shaft and licked the top of his head. Marc's hips flexed involuntarily. Her warm mouth opened and sucked just enough to push him over the edge as she ran her palm over his shaft, pumping him dry.

His fist was filled with the silk of her hair. Not holding it tight, only touching the threads like a lifeline as the world telescoped back out. His limbs slowly released, a drugged contentment stealing through his body.

He could not give this up. He had to make her stay. Alyssa pushed herself up, wiping at a stray glob with a kitchen towel. "I'm not fit for public view again. Guess we'll have to stay in. It's hard to get a table on New Year's anyway."

"We need food." He rummaged through the cabinets and thrust a stack of menus at her with one shaking hand. Alyssa shuffled through them while he went to clean up.

"Steakhouse takeout?"

Marc eyed her skeptically. "Shouldn't we just go out if we're going to order fancy?"

"The other logos look like food poisoning on a platter." She'd shimmied back into her dress, which was falling off one shoulder.

He barked a laugh. "You don't eat the logos, silly."

"I know. But I like to think the design is indicative of the final product."

It was as good an approach to selecting a restaurant as any. "Maybe we should go out after all. Those shoes are too nice to keep in here."

"They're not really made for walking. But sure, if you want to go out, I'll get ready again." She sauntered back toward the bedroom, a little smile playing over her lips.

She didn't make it very far, and they didn't go out for dinner either.

LATER, Marc switched on the motor and drove them back out into the bay, where a hundred boats bobbed as dark shadows against the gray horizon. Fireworks cracked and popped all around them. The real show had yet to begin.

Marc lowered the anchor. Neither of them bothered with life jackets, since they weren't going anywhere except the deck or below deck.

He disappeared below and returned with a bottle of champagne and two plastic flutes. It fizzed a little in the starlight as they clinked glasses.

"Quick selfie," she demanded, holding out her phone. The sky flashed green and yellow, purple and red. Gold rained down from the heavens.

"Sure." Marc took the phone from her and reached out with his long arm, capturing the first fireworks behind them. "This is going out to ten thousand people, right?"

"More or less. Depends on the day. I don't keep track."

He turned and kissed her full on the mouth. Alyssa kissed him back as the flash burst again and again. He put down the phone and hauled her onto his lap. A sharp thunderclap of rockets exploding brought their heads up.

"Happy New Year," he whispered.

"You too."

Marc's warm palms slid her skirt higher. Already, she wanted him again. Would never stop wanting him like this. It was a huge problem she couldn't bring herself to face. Not yet. Cinderella hadn't felt this dread as the clock ticked down to goodbye with her prince. "When are you leaving?"

"As soon as the new house is permitted, I'll give notice on the slip at the marina."

She nodded against his shoulder. A shiver wracked her body.

"I want you to go with me."

Alyssa sat up. Couldn't stop the sharp bark of laughter escaping her lips. Saw the flash of raw pain in Marc's eyes and shook her head as though to take it back. "Don't be ridiculous. I have responsibilities. I have a job. A lease. I can't pack up and run off on a whim."

He knew that. Didn't he? He didn't live a normal adult life. Maybe he didn't understand why she couldn't drop everything.

"I'll wait. How long do you need to wind things down?"

He was serious. Alyssa shoved away from him. Her bare feet hit the deck so hard the shock reverberated up her spine. "I can't go with you, Marc. It's crazy of you to ask."

"Why?" he demanded, his tone low and hurt.

"Because sailing is your dream. Not mine. I have obligations." Her sister, for one. She wasn't sure how to help Janelle yet, but she'd find a way. Quitting her job would mean turning her back on family. She'd never do that, and Marc had no right to ask it of her, either.

"Okay. I'll cancel the trip if you look for a job here."

"Marc, I don't want you to resent me for making you give up your dreams. Besides, I'd never ask you to do that." Alyssa placed her hand on his arm. "The timing's off."

"It's never going to be the right time unless one of us compromises. There'll always be barriers, Aly, unless we decide to stop letting them get in our way."

He was right, and he was wrong. There wasn't a choice to be made. Not for her. "This was never meant to extend beyond tonight."

His jaw had turned concrete, and his eyes blazed.

Marc was dangling something that, under any other circumstances, she'd jump at. But the prospect of a long-distance relationship with a man whose history with women was checkered at best was way too much, way too soon, no matter how good he was in bed. What if she left her job and it didn't work out with Marc, only to find herself unemployed and living with her parents a few weeks later? She'd be in a worse spot than her little sister was. She hadn't shaken free of Zach only to latch onto the next available guy the minute he asked, even if the guy was Marc.

Especially if the guy was Marc.

At least she was going home tomorrow. Back to her big ambitions, her tiny apartment, and the city where she was an invisible cog in an uncaring machine. Until then, she was stuck on this boat or in the not-much-bigger house. She was alone with Marc and all his wounded pride. Well, tough. It wasn't fair of him to go and change the rules. Caring about him didn't mean anything had fundamentally changed. Their lives still only intersected over the fence separating their parents' houses.

"This was *supposed to be fun*." Alyssa's voice carried on the wind, louder than she'd intended. She snatched up her champagne glass and downed the contents.

"Fun," he spat, pushing a button to pull up the anchor. "That's all you wanted from me, all those years?"

No. "Yes."

"The last week hasn't changed your mind?"

Yes. "No."

She hadn't been thinking beyond this week. All her goals in relation to Marc had terminated at New Year's. Had she changed her mind? About who Marc was, yes. Absolutely. About his interest in a relationship? Not at all. One minute he was fighting for her and the next he couldn't get her naked fast enough. He'd been sending mixed messages at best. Her heart said one thing. Her head, in full control of her mouth, the opposite.

HE SHOULD'VE SEEN this coming.

He hadn't changed her mind. Putting up with her sister's demented contest scheme and standing back while she finished things with her ex had been tough. Hell, he'd trusted her enough to abandon everything he knew about safe sex. That had been a big moment, and he knew she understood what it meant to him. Marc knew, *knew* in his bones, that what they had could last. He needed to find out how far it could take them.

Yet she'd laughed in his face when he'd asked her to go with him. It was supposed to be *fun*.

"Yeah. Chasing after a girl who hardly noticed me for years, only to find out I'm nothing but her toy, is a fine way to spend Christmas week. Next time, buy a fucking vibrator."

She'd refilled her champagne glass and was sitting on the banquette staring out at the passing houses. Most were brightly lit. Music pumped loud, carrying over the water, mocking the tension between them.

"I'm sorry." Sullen. What the fuck did Aly have to sulk about?

"Me too." He cut the engine and hopped onto the dock, grateful for the cover of night and the chance to focus on tying the boat down.

He reached out to help her across the gap. She ignored his outstretched hand and landed gracefully on the wood deck.

Marc snatched his hand back as if she'd slapped it. Undoubtedly, if he went back to the cabin with her, they'd end up having aggressive, hot sex. Part of him—the usual part—was enthusiastic about the prospect. Somewhere north of his belt, though, his heart hammered as though it were trying to smash itself against his ribs.

He was sick and tired of her writing him off as *fun*. He was far too invested in her to keep having mind-blowing sex and then simply walk away. For him, *everything* had changed this week. "Go ahead. I'll be up in a minute."

She hesitated, then went inside. But he didn't follow her. He'd sleep on the *Escape* before enduring another minute of this charade.

19

"What in the name of Christ did you do last night?"

Alyssa's head pounded with every terse syllable. She was cold. Her neck had cramped from sleeping at an odd angle on the couch. What *had* she done?

Oh, right. She was mad at him for inviting her to go with him on his sail-around-the-world folly. Peering up at Marc's dark eyes, she croaked, "You didn't come back."

"I didn't want to see you." His jaw hardened.

Sass kicked in where humility would've played better. "Yeah, I can tell."

He almost said something, stopped himself, and shoved a coffee mug at her. "You'll feel better if you drink this. I'll go pack your stuff."

Alyssa took one whiff of the coffee and set it down untouched. "No, I'll do it. Just take care of yourself."

Ugh. Champagne. Always a bad idea. She must've made off with most of the bottle. She almost knocked over the half-empty container sitting next to the couch she'd fallen asleep on as she stood up. Dumping the flat, sweet liquid down the sink made her gag. Then she crammed her belongings into her bag, too nauseous to process a pang of regret at the sight of the shoes they'd had so much fun with the night before.

Fun. Such a loaded word now.

Alyssa locked herself in the shower and vomited endlessly. Then she scrubbed it down with bleach and scrounged in the cabinets for painkillers. Nothing. Of course. Just her luck.

Dressed and packed, she stumbled back out to the *Escape*. Marc took her bag and helped her onto the boat, the brief contact searing through the haze of hangover. As soon as he let go, his expression went distant. Polite.

Neighborly.

His were shaded behind sunglasses. "Here. You might need these."

The sight of two little pills in the palm of his hand squeezed a few drops of saltwater from her dry tear ducts. "Thanks."

"I'll get us home in time for your flight. Why don't you go sleep?" The compassion in his voice stung worse than being stood up for your Christmas Eve engagement.

Alyssa knew she was useless for any kind of sailing lesson. What was the point, since she was headed back to New York? She nodded once, took her mug of cold coffee, and went down to the cabin. There, she crawled into the berth and burrowed into the sheets still smelling of his presence. She cried into them as quietly as she could until the painkillers kicked in and unconsciousness drifted over her like a blanket of snow.

Upon waking, the headache was gone and she'd rejoined the land of the living. She washed up in the little bathroom and went up to find Marc steering them toward the marina in the distance. Alyssa stood there watching the place creep closer faster than she'd ever imagined a boat could go, trying to find the right words.

"I'm sorry," she finally said. Fail. Completely insufficient.

He was quiet for a long minute. The motor purred gently behind them. "For what?"

"That I can't say yes. That I hurt you. It was a weird week, but a good one." Alyssa exhaled for what might be the first time since the last firework had blinked out the night before.

They tied down the boat. Marc retrieved her bag from the cabin.

And suddenly they were out of time. Alyssa's mother waved from her car parked at the marina gates.

"Did you have a fun night together?" she asked as innocently as possible for a mother who had no illusions about what her daughter and neighbor's son had been up to.

"Definitely," replied Marc, as easily as if nothing bad had happened. Alyssa glanced at him sidelong and found the strain at the corners of his mouth and the tight line of his shoulder. Wordlessly, she nodded her agreement. It had been fun. Right up until he'd asked her to drop everything and run off with him, as if her life didn't matter.

Alyssa accepted her bag and tried to project as much cheer as she could muster.

"Let me know when you're home safe." They stood there awkwardly, two feet and a million miles apart.

"Be careful out there sailing," Alyssa whispered. She reached for his hand and squeezed it.

Marc pulled her into a stiff hug. Alyssa burrowed her face into his shoulder, pressing all the words she didn't know how to say into the force of her arms around him. She leaned up and kissed his jaw, tension thick between them, hating this goodbye. Reluctantly, Alyssa broke the embrace and turned toward her mother's car.

Then she was off to the airport, reversing the trip she'd made on arrival, no happier and more confused than ever.

"What'd you do last night?" Janelle hung over the seat.

"Quit prying, Janie."

"It's okay mom. We had dinner and watched the fireworks from the harbor. It was beautiful. Then I slept in the house and Marc stayed on the boat. We agreed to end it."

"You did *what?*" Her mother and sister gasped in unison.

Alyssa shrugged. "It's Marc. You know how he is."

Janelle flopped back against the seat. "All that effort for nothing?"

"Maybe next time you'll keep your nose out of my rebound business," Alyssa grumped.

Catherine side-eyed her. "I'm surprised, Aly. I was certain Marc had grown out of his womanizing."

Alyssa flinched. "He has. I think he really has. We didn't want to do long-distance, and I'm just out of a relationship. It's the wrong time, that's all."

Her lungs didn't start drawing air again until she'd made it through security. The boots hanging off her shoulder bag literally kicked her ass every step to the gate, where she discovered her plane was delayed. Finally, alone among strangers, Alyssa watched the sun set over the tarmac and stopped pretending that she hadn't just walked away from everything she'd been looking for.

She didn't text that night, though Marc nearly drained his phone's battery checking it. To keep busy, he went through the ship cabin tossing every unnecessary item into a plastic garbage bag. Though he didn't have much stuff, he'd managed to fill it most of the way. On the table was a list of items he'd need before he sailed off into the sunset. Provisions. Warm clothes. A better first-aid kit.

Alyssa.

Marc tossed the remaining box of condoms into the garbage bag. He wasn't stocking up on those either. A minute later he took them out again. Maybe Stephan and Julian would want them, but what was the protocol for giving away condoms? Besides, he ought to hang onto at least one, even if he was off women permanently. He might feel differently a few months and continents from now. The torn black box sat on the table, a monument to indecision.

The minute the permits came through on the project house, he was out of here. Marc didn't know where he'd land, but he knew he wasn't coming back to Florida. Once the project house was finished, he'd sell it, take his profits and go live in a cheap country. Maybe find a girl to shack up with and get over Alyssa. If there was any getting over Alyssa. Right now, he wondered how he was still walking around when she'd packed his heart with her to take back to New York like some gruesome trophy.

His phone beeped. Marc lunged for it.

Stephan and I are going out for a drink. Come with us. We're dying to hear how your New Year went.

Julian. Not Alyssa.

No. I don't want a drink, he typed.

Yes, you do, dumbass. Too late, the text was already flying out into space. All he wanted to know was that she was home safely, and then he'd be done with her.

Still hungover?

No seas gilipollas. **It was terrible. Everything fell apart with Alyssa. I want to be alone.** Marc knew he wasn't hiding anything. Might as well get it over with.

Stephan typing now. We're coming over. With Scotch.

Joder. Marc's Spanish didn't extend much beyond curse words. His parents hadn't encouraged it. **You're not very literate for a lawyer. A-L-O-N-E. By myself.**

Stephan isn't an attorney. He's a mouthy –

You love my mouth.

I don't care who's got the phone now. I didn't need to know that, Marc shot back, irritated but half desperate for company. He'd take the needling, meddling kind if he had to. Before he could put it on silent, the phone beeped once more. He turned it over, heart picking up speed thinking it might be from Miss New York.

We'll be there in ten.

Alyssa should've been home hours ago. Was a final text message too much to ask?

THE ELEVATOR WAS out of service. Again. Alyssa wondered if the landlord had bothered getting it repaired over the holiday week, or if it had been broken the entire time. It was after midnight when she hauled her wheeled suitcase through the door of her apartment, gray snow dripping as it melted over the scuffed wood floor. She set her boots in the hallway to dry off, and hung her coat on the back of the door.

The apartment smelled different. Not bad. Only different. It didn't smell like hers. Or maybe it had always smelled musty with a tinge of iron, like water left to boil for too long.

The keys she'd given Gina lay on the desk that also served as a table. The walls she'd painted French blue, yellow, and white as a student to brighten up the drab space looked childish now, with dark smudges creeping up the wall behind the couch next to the window. The tiny IKEA couch sagged pathetically in the center.

She'd thought she was done crying, but tears welled up and her cold nose turned warm and runny. Alyssa grabbed a tissue. She opened her suitcase and unpacked her belongings. She wished she was stowing them on Marc's boat instead of in her apartment.

The knock on her door startled her so badly, Alyssa's tears dried mid-snivel. She swiped them away and cracked it open with the chain across the gap. A short, balding man with glasses over sadly hopeful brown eyes stared at her, confused. "Is Gina here?"

"Who are you?" Alyssa was too drained to care about rudeness. Nobody with manners knocked on someone's door after one in the morning, not unless you were…

Making noise.

"Vernon. I live downstairs. I heard someone walking around, and I thought Gina might've come back." He turned to go.

"Hey." Alyssa closed the door long enough to remove the chain. "I'm Alyssa. I've lived here for six years. Why didn't you ever come up before?"

Vernon shrugged. "You never came downstairs, either."

"Fair enough," Aly replied. No, she'd been locked in a battle of mutual annoyance with this harmless crank. Instead of reaching out to him to solve the problem, she'd retreated into her own misery. It was the same thing she was doing now with Marc, like a hermit crab trying to jam its body into a shell that no longer fit. One thing she loved about Marc was how he kept searching until he found solutions for his problems, no matter how unorthodox. They didn't have to be perfect, only better than the alternative.

Loved. Shit. She loved him. Stupid heart.

Speaking of hermits, Vernon shuffled and made a *hrumph* noise, bringing her back to reality. "If you see her, would you give her my phone number? I didn't have a chance to before she left."

"I will. Good to finally meet you, Vernon." Alyssa nearly slammed the door in her haste to get to her phone, only to drop it again. She couldn't text him in the middle of the night. Tomorrow was plenty soon to reach out to Marc. After she figured out what to tell Dana, her boss, to do with the crappy promotion she couldn't accept.

I'm back in New York.

Marc wished she'd called, that she hadn't waited until Monday afternoon to let him know she was safe, that he wasn't reduced to texting a thumbs-up emoji as his response. His stomach roiled like the time when he was thirteen and his older cousin had dared him to drink an entire bottle of Tabasco sauce.

Can you come to the city this Friday morning through Monday afternoon?

He stared at the glowing screen in his palm until it went black. Then he tapped the button to turn on the screen again. The message was still there. It said exactly what he thought he'd read. His thumb glided over the screen, deleted misspelled words, and tried again.

Give me one reason to.

You'll try anything twice.

The words made his stomach flare like an oil rig. He'd said those very words to her. Now she was throwing them back in his face.

Or not. The phone buzzed in his hand.

I want another chance. A do-over.

The first time he'd gone sailing, when the wind had whipped the sail full of wind and the ship had leapt forward beneath his feet so fast he nearly lost his balance, Marc had felt as weightless and breathless as an astronaut. The idea that something as elemental and common as air and water could, when harnessed, send him soaring over the waves had been the closest emotion he'd ever experienced to falling in love. Until now.

This sensation was a lot worse. Sailing was exhilarating. This was more akin to being dropped out of an airplane without a parachute, like imminent, excruciating death.

Let's talk tonight, he sent back, unsure what to think, how to feel. She wanted another chance, and the idea was as heady as inhaling helium. Yet if he hadn't convinced her that he was crazy about her over the past week, what had changed her mind now?

ALYSSA TAPPED the Skype icon on the first beep. "Hi."

"Hi. No video?"

"I look awful. My plane was massively delayed last night, and I only finished working twenty minutes ago. I'm beat."

"Turn on the video, Alyssa. I want to see you."

She gave in, mostly because she wanted to see him too. Marc had already seen her hungover; tired couldn't be any worse. His face pixelated into view on the computer screen.

"I miss you. I'm so sorry. Is the offer still open?" *Don't cry don't cry. Jesus. Do. Not. Start. Bawling. Pull up those big girl pants, Aly.*

He didn't respond for a long time. "Not sure."

"You kind of sprung it on me." Her eyes were hot and her lashes were damp, but she was determined to keep it together.

Marc stared at her a bit mournfully. His expression told her exactly how hard he'd taken her refusal. He was always easygoing, borderline flippant. Serious was not Marc's style. "If you'd been paying attention for the last week, it shouldn't have come as a surprise."

"Well, it did. I told you how bad things were with Zach, and how hard it was to end things with him, even though it had been over in any meaningful sense for a long time. You were asking me to jump immediately into another relationship, and I couldn't. I'd worry about what you were doing, if it's long distance."

"Back to the man-whore problem." He sighed. "I'd given it up, you know."

"I'm glad you made an exception for me."

"That wasn't thought out, and you know it."

"On either side. All I'm saying is, it's a fast track from where we started a week ago to 'quit your job and sail around the world with me.' You caught me completely off-guard. I wanted to enjoy New

Year's with you and suddenly you were asking me to change my whole life."

The hours she'd spent waiting for her delayed plane had given her the distance she needed to start processing events. Part of the problem was that he didn't know how to send signals that didn't read *one night stand*.

Agreeing to that silly competition had been the only declaration he knew how to make. Yes, he'd said a few things that strongly suggested he'd wanted more, but when she'd asked him for details he'd been evasive. She'd thought it was pillow talk, until the boat. It was Marc, after all. Convenient, sexy, boy next door. She'd pigeonholed him and refused to budge.

But that wasn't Marc as she'd come to know him. He was independent, hardworking, and inventive. She'd been half in love with him before they'd exchanged half a dozen words years ago. Sleeping with him had never been about Zach. It had always been about going after what she'd wanted all along. Somewhere between Tampa and New York, Alyssa had realized that she didn't need to make a choice between her head and her heart. She needed them working together.

With help from Dana, her boss, she'd started down the path toward a solution today. Now she had to show Marc that she was serious about making it work with him before sitting him in a conference room and pitching her big idea. He'd endured enough craziness over the past week. They both had.

"What do you have in mind, Aly?"

"I'm working on an idea, that's why I need you here this weekend. I meant it when I said I can't run off on a whim. Is the offer still open? Or am I burning bridges at work for nothing?"

A long pause. Thanks to the miracles of video technology, she could watch him rub his jaw as he struggled to answer her question. She'd burned him bad, but she had big plans to make it up to him this weekend. If everything lined up as she hoped it would. She was a walking a high wire with no net.

"The offer's still open." He almost said something more and stopped himself.

"What?" Aly sat up straighter, wishing she'd worn something more flattering than yoga pants and a loose top.

"The permits on the project house came through today."

"What does that mean?"

"I'm shipping out soon, Aly. If you want to go with me, I need to know. I don't think I can go back to being friendly over the fence. I can't watch you go about your life as if being together meant nothing, because it's meant everything to me."

Alyssa sucked in a breath. If her idea didn't work, she was going to have to make a very tough decision. "A few more days won't deprive you of checking off your number one bucket list item."

The taste of panic rose in her throat. Did she sound too desperate? Too dismissive? She couldn't compromise on helping her sister, and she needed time.

"You know I'd do anything for you, Aly."

Despite Marc's resignation, she inhaled with relief.

"I would for you too, Marc. I know I didn't show you that. But I'm going to. Come to New York and you'll see."

"Like I said, anything for you, Aly. Get some rest. We'll talk again later."

THEY FINALLY CONNECTED AGAIN on Wednesday evening. Alyssa had recovered from her flight. This time, her hair hung straight around her face as if she'd blown it dry, and she wore lipstick the color of bricks and blood. Maybe she was trying to torture him. Or maybe she'd been as busy with work as she'd claimed. "How's the frigid tundra?"

"You're about to find out," she winked. "Bring your warmest coat. Don't pack light. It's in the low thirties all week."

"I don't know if I own one." He relaxed fractionally. At least one of them was feeling upbeat about this visit. The forced passivity of not knowing what would happen on Friday was driving him crazy. How the hell had Alyssa dealt with the suspense of her date week? It sucked lemons.

"You need to get one, then. Unless Julian has one you can borrow?"

Good call. "Where are you?"

"In my apartment."

"Can I have a tour?"

A giggle, the sound making his skin go warm. "Sure. It'll take thirty seconds. Here's the kitchen, such as it is. Note the stove small enough to fit in a dollhouse and the dorm room refrigerator. The living room, complete with two-seater couch that's seen better days. The desk doubles as a dining table. Behind this wall is the bed. Across from the bed is my one and only closet, and on the other side of the bed is the bathroom. Ta-da!"

"Wow. It almost makes my boat look spacious."

"Yes, it does. So. For Friday, bring business clothes. It doesn't have to be a suit—jeans and a sweater are fine."

"That's what you call business clothes?" Bullshit. Alyssa was always put together. He never had to dress up, but if she wanted him to do so for the occasion, he wasn't going to disappoint.

"It's advertising." She shrugged.

Oh, so she wanted to show him her office. Made sense. Jeans and sweaters were practical for freezing weather. Occasionally, Florida temperatures would drop into the thirties, so he owned a few warm clothes.

"So, Friday morning," Aly continued, "there will be a black cab driver at the airport to meet you. Don't go with anyone who isn't holding a sign with your name. You're flying into LaGuardia. It's a confusing place, but it's the closest airport."

"You're not picking me up?"

"I have to be at work. You're going directly to my office, so come dressed to meet my boss."

"Does this have something to do with quitting your job?"

"Sort of. I have a proposal for you."

"Sounds serious."

"It is. You'll find out about it on Friday morning."

"Why can't you tell me now?"

"Remember when you asked what else I could negotiate for, since I wasn't getting a raise?"

"Yeah. So? I figured you'd ask for a remote work option, to buy time to find a new job here."

"While you sail around the world without me? No way. I'm working on a proposal that, if it works out, will benefit the clients, the agency, me, and you. I'm going for broke. This week is all about negotiating what we'll present to you on Friday. If you agree to the plan, we're lining up client meetings for Monday."

"Do I have any choice in liking the idea?"

"Depends on how badly you want me to go sailing with you." She grinned wickedly. "That's why we're meeting Friday. If there's anything you aren't comfortable with, we can work through the weekend to change the pitch."

"I didn't think this was a working trip."

"That's an incentive for agreement. The sooner we wrap up, the sooner we can...play."

"What are you wearing?"

"That's an abrupt change of subject." She smirked.

"Don't be coy. I want to see you."

The camera crept lower. Alyssa was lounging on her bed in a lacy bra and his favorite shorts.

"Isn't it freezing in New York?"

"Yep. But the landlord blasts the heat. Sometimes I have to open the window. Or sit around in skimpy clothes. Or both." Her smirk widened into a grin.

"Can you change the ticket so I can come earlier?" It was so good to banter. He'd been on edge for days wondering what she was up to, where things were headed. Marc had had a lot of time to think about their last conversation, and in retrospect, he'd been kind of a jerk. Aly was right. He'd only considered his own desires.

At least she was giving him a heads-up on what to expect. He hadn't been kind enough to do that to her. He'd blurted out his fondest wish and it had burned when she didn't immediately accept. He still had a lot of ground to make up in the relationship department, though he was learning as fast as he could. He'd been trying out the word *girlfriend* since she'd left. Saying it was starting to feel natural.

"Ha. My employer is already suspicious this is a tax-deductible booty call."

"It had better be." He was rewarded with another giggle. The pixelated video call facsimile of the sound sent tremors through his body.

"You're getting a hotel room," she informed him. The camera bobbed as she shifted positions.

"Mmm. Too bad. I wanted to see your apartment."

"This palace of luxury? I already gave you the grand tour." She waved one hand in an elegant gesture and nearly knocked over a glass of water sitting on a shelf above the bed.

"It's bigger than a boat. You know what else is bigger than a boat?"

"Your ego?"

Marc laughed. "No, I have you to keep that in check."

Alyssa chuckled too. "I have to get back to work."

"Work? It's after nine."

"I have to prepare for a meeting first thing in the morning. You have no idea how many hoops I'm jumping through to pull this off."

Marc disconnected, humbled by whatever Aly was up to. He tried to remember if he'd ever seen snow. As a child, maybe. The idea of snow was a little exciting, but cold wasn't. He could live with it though. The wind at sea could cut right through you.

The rest of the week passed so slowly that finding himself strapped into an airplane seat on an early flight out of Tampa on Friday morning was surreal. He carried his coat and sweater, his t-shirt damp at the pits and the small of his back as he lugged Julian's weekender bag to the gate. He felt ridiculous wearing pressed wool trousers and t-shirt in the warm morning air, but most of the other passengers at the gate looked as overheated and overdressed as he was.

Landing at LaGuardia gave Marc the sick feeling the aircraft was about to crash into the water. He sure as hell hoped Chesley Sullenberger was flying this plane, or his clone.

It was as if he'd landed in an alternate reality. The airport was an unbelievably dingy, run-down hole packed with bodies seething around him. It smelled of bleach and damp wool. Marc couldn't decide whether to follow the signs or the people, but since both were headed roughly the same direction, he let the crowd push and pull him along until he spotted a sign for Ground Transportation.

Carried outside by sheer momentum, he inhaled and watched his breath crystalize in the cold air. Everything was gray, dirty, and cacophonous. Vehicles of every description honked and thrust and flowed in a river of metal and angst.

A man of Middle Eastern descent held out a sign. Marc's name was written on it in neat capital letters. "Are you waiting for me?"

"Mr. De Luna?"

"Yes."

"This way." No introduction. No hello. This was another world, and a brusque one.

Skyscrapers weren't a new sight. He'd spent plenty of time in Tampa and Miami. Yet the scale and closeness and downright shabbiness of the city he glimpsed out the car window astounded him for the next forty minutes. It was nothing like he'd expected. New York was dirty and gritty, and he couldn't figure out how Alyssa had lived here for almost ten years without losing her mind.

The car stopped before a glass building indistinguishable from any other of the hundreds of buildings he'd passed in the past hour. The exterior bore a name. He recognized it as Aly's employer. The car stopped. Marc stepped out onto the street.

"Watch it!" A cyclist sped by, spraying gray slush on his not-warm-enough pants. Who the fuck rode a bicycle in snow?

A veritable mountain of the stuff stood between him and the revolving gold door. Marc planted one foot into a crevice and launched himself over it. A woman in a black coat and sunglasses staring at her phone sidestepped him without looking up. A guy in a bright red coat didn't move away in time.

"Sorry," they both muttered as Marc's bag swung into the human obstacle.

"Tourons," another passerby muttered.

Marc shook his head. Some sort of mashup of *tourist* and *morons*?

The advertising agency gleamed across a sidewalk like a game of Frogger. So many people raced by that all he could do was count on them to move around him. Miraculously, they did. Then he pushed through the doors into the foyer and approached the long white lacquered desk and security guards in black suits. It was a goddamned triumph over adversity, if he did say so himself.

"Security will let you through the gate. Take the elevator to twenty-two. There will be someone to meet you."

Good. It would be all he could do not to pin Alyssa against the nearest wall.

20

The doors *pinged* open. An attractive woman with brown hair, glasses, and tall boots stood waiting for him. He swallowed disappointment as anticipation cranked a notch higher.

"You must be Marc."

"I am."

"Dana Larsen. I'm Alyssa's boss. I've heard a lot about you." She held out her hand. It was warm and firm and impersonal as he pumped it twice and let go.

"All good, I hope."

She smiled. He guessed she was around forty, though she could have been anywhere between thirty-five and fifty. "I trust Alyssa's judgment. I wouldn't have promoted her otherwise. Turns out she had other plans. You are a part of those plans."

Dana opened a glass conference room door and held it with a knowing smile. "I can see why."

Alyssa sat across a round table, hair blown flat most of the way with a perfect blonde curl hanging right above her breast. Marc's heart flipped in his chest and followed that stunt with a series of cartwheels. She wore a close-cut blazer over a tight-fitting black top. Stark gold earrings decorated her lobes. A silk scarf with a pink and gray pattern wound around her neck. Her lips were painted the same color from their video chat a few days before. It was better in person. He could think of several of his body parts the color would look great on too. His mouth. His finger. His cock.

Her red lips moved. "Hi, Marc. Thanks for joining us."

This was her world. It was sleek. It was hard. It was cold. She was completely at home. He was captivated. Suddenly, his sailing obsession didn't seem cool or fun or even interesting. He'd asked her to abandon everything she knew, everything she'd worked toward, without understanding what he'd asked her to give up.

No wonder she'd laughed. Selfishness had a place, but it wasn't center stage in a relationship. He'd fucked up, but he was here now. Listening. "Hi, Aly."

"Marc, Alyssa tells me you're planning to sail around the world. The client we work on is a major player in the travel and hospitality category and looking for an interesting way to promote the brand on social media. The target audience is affluent, culturally literate, and seeks adventure, whether vicariously or in person. We believe we can convince our client to sponsor your journey."

Alyssa clicked on a large flat screen mounted to the wall to his left. An image popped up. It was similar to the brand boards she'd given him, but it had been adapted to feature the *Escape* instead of his rental properties.

"Alyssa has a social media presence with over ten thousand followers. That alone is enough to merit a fee, but we believe she can do better with the right campaign support. The concept we're proposing to you is this: Aly will pitch a sponsorship opportunity to the client on Monday. If the client accepts, we plan to approach all of our agency's other clients in the category."

"What does a sponsorship mean, exactly?" Marc eyed Alyssa as she glanced up at the screen and clicked a button on the laptop before her. This was a version of her he didn't know. Professional. Polished. Intimidating.

"It means we'll take over your social media presence in exchange for fifty thousand dollars for the first six months. We want to use your profile to build an audience amongst affluent males ages 25 to 50. We'd need access to all of your Facebook, Twitter, and Instagram accounts, the ability to create new profiles on platforms you're not already on, and strict adherence to guidelines agreed upon in a contract. No reposting political screeds from your aunt, for example."

Marc glanced at Alyssa, unbelieving. "What if I want more money?"

Dana didn't bat an eyelash. "We might be able to accommodate you. It would be easier if you already had a substantial following, but we can leverage whatever you have. If we get the sponsorship approved, there's additional opportunity with other clients for product placement and click revenue. Fifty is the minimum we are proposing for budgeting purposes."

Marc's ass ground against the chair as he fought not to fidget. This was too weird. Fifty thousand dollars of basically free money. "What's Aly's role?"

Alyssa clicked her laptop. The picture on the screen changed. He recognized several of the pictures she'd taken with him, but others were unfamiliar. "You know I have a small base of users across several social media sites. The primary platform is Instagram. I agree to expand my followers to one hundred thousand within three months. If I hit a million followers within a year, I have the option of selling the Instagram account to the highest-bidding client, a sale to be negotiated through the agency."

"How much is that worth?" Marc asked skeptically.

"Recent sales of Instagram accounts of that size have netted into the six figures."

Marc sat back in his seat. "You have got to be kidding. All that for taking a few pictures and posting them online?"

Alyssa leaned forward, her forearms crossed flat on the conference table. "All that for a lot of pictures carefully composed, edited, and posted at regular intervals for maximum impact. It's work. It's not a free ride."

"How are you going to increase your followers over tenfold in three months?" he demanded. This was too weird to be real.

"I can answer." Dana took over the laptop. "We'll start with a contest. Every existing follower and all new followers for 30 days will be entered into a drawing to win a two-week trip anywhere they want to go. Alyssa will highlight their journey to her social media accounts. We'll have a full PR campaign, all major media outlets covered. We're bound to get some buzz. A hundred thousand followers in three months is a conservative goal. A million followers isn't unrealistic, *if* Alyssa keeps up the momentum. The key to success will be frequent, high-quality posts from exotic locations. Your job is to provide the locations, Marc."

"Dana wants to pitch this project to the agency's clients in the travel & hospitality, sporting goods, apparel, and beverages category. We may have to wear branded clothes or pose with specific beverages from time to time."

"Product placement." He hated product placement, but he'd find a way to live with it if it meant Alyssa came with him. "Okay. What else?"

"We need you to develop a travel plan. It doesn't have to be overly specific. A list of places you intend to visit is all we need. We'll have Studio mock up a slide for Monday with stock images of each location."

Marc nodded. He could rattle off twenty destinations off the top of his head. Cuba, for starters. He'd love to see his family's country and meet the relatives that still lived there. Travel had opened up, but who knew how long it would last? "Can you help us arrange visas?"

"We can ask HR. They arrange the international visas for employees," Dana replied, jotting a note. The screen blinked dark behind them. Marc thought of his father's cramped office with its dual-screen desktop for inventory and schedule management and papers neatly stacked on every surface. This was a completely different world. If he'd known business could be like this, he might've been more committed to his education.

"Delightful to meet you, Marc. Alyssa will take you to lunch. I'll join you if I can get away. We'll regroup this afternoon with the strategist and the creative working on the proposal. Bring any questions you think of between now and then." The women stood up, so he did, too.

Alyssa leaned forward to push a printout across the table. He was treated to a glimpse of cleavage that kick started his libido's engine. All-business Aly was even sexier than the down-home version.

"Here's a copy of the deck. We can go over it at lunch." When she looked up, her red lips had quirked up at the corners. She knew damn well he'd peeked.

"I have another meeting in five, and we're using this room. Alyssa, will you show our guest around the office?"

"My pleasure."

If her word choice wasn't bad enough, Marc almost groaned at the sight of the high heeled black shoes as she picked up her laptop and stepped out from behind the conference table. The top turned out to be a dress, a clingy one he suspected she'd worn on purpose to torture him.

He held the door for her so he could get a better view as she walked by.

"You're a gentleman too," Dana commented. "Alyssa's a lucky girl."

He agreed with Dana. Aly rolled her eyes at him as she passed by, not buying her boss's comment. He followed her down a hallway to a room lined with windows and long tables with computers sitting on them. People sat at each station, some young, some middle-aged, dressed in business casual or hipster sloth. Alyssa went to the middle of the row and set down her laptop. Then she removed her jacket and placed it on the back of her chair. The dress hugged her body. His fingers tingled with anticipation.

Marc deposited his bag beneath her desk and trailed after his girlfriend, the silly word that made his body flash hot. Curiosity made him hang on her every syllable as she narrated their way, though his gaze kept returning to her ass. He couldn't wait to find out what she was wearing under the clingy skirt. She led him down an empty hall lined by glass walled conference rooms. A few were occupied.

"And here is our view of Central Park. If you're interested in seeing the city on this trip and not just undressing me with your eyes across conference tables."

Marc forced his gaze upward to find Alyssa and watched him. One eyebrow arched higher than the other. He glanced at the fishbowl rooms. "It's been a few days."

"I know. I'll make it up to you later," she grinned. "Don't worry, those rooms are soundproof. Go on, check out the deck."

He shifted his attention to the window. Beyond it was a snow-crusted roof deck, and beyond the glass railing stretched Central Park, neatly bordered by tall buildings. "Wow."

She wasn't immune to the view either. "It's closed for the season, or I'd take you outside. The city looks a lot better from twenty stories high."

"Why?"

"You can't see how dirty it is from up here." Alyssa bit her bright lower lip. The sight of her white teeth against the crimson made Marc's balls tighten.

"Seen enough?"

Not even close. "Of your office? I'll be seeing it again later, right?"

"If you agree to the plan. You can walk away any time." They returned to her desk. She let him hold her coat while she shrugged into it. She changed her shoes for boots, much to his disappointment, and collected a sleek black handbag from her desk.

Did he agree?

In the bright white elevator, she leaned against the opposite wall. "What's your reaction so far?"

"I wasn't thinking there would be an audience of a hundred thousand people." Sailing was his world. He didn't want to share it. He didn't want to share Alyssa either. Not with a job, not with strangers on the Internet. He wanted her all to himself. If she'd thrown this plan at him back in Florida he'd have told her she was out of her mind.

A week ago, he'd believed relationships were no more complicated than two people deciding not to have sex with anyone else. Maybe monogamy technically entailed sex with one person, but to keep that person around you had to figure out what made them tick. Sometimes you had to give up what you wanted to get something you needed more.

Alyssa liked her work. He loved her for her ambition, even when it had carried her here, to this drab, cold city beyond his reach. He couldn't deny her an opportunity to stretch her potential.

"Is that a no?" she asked into the long silence.

"It's a maybe." It was the best answer he could give. For now. At least he hadn't laughed.

ALYSSA SIGHED, her lungs pressed upward in her chest by a giant ball of stress seething like the surface of the sun. The elevator door slid silently open.

Alyssa stuck her arm through Marc's, guiding him expertly through the crowded sidewalk. "This way."

Marc yawned in the cold bright light.

"The first six months I lived here, I napped every day. Like a toddler." Alyssa vowed to get them each a glass of wine ASAP.

"I can see why." He rubbed his jaw.

"You get used to it after a while."

"Speaking of naps, can we check into the hotel yet?"

We. Alyssa's body went hot inside her jacket. "Not until after two."

He frowned. "I want to know how you went from a crappy promotion to this plan."

"Dana agreed HR was being pedantic about the money. You asked me last week what else I could negotiate. I hadn't been thinking beyond the next rung on the promotion ladder. I spent some time imagining my dream job. The first requirement was something that let me travel with you. The second was an income that lets me help my sister with her debt problem. The third piece was how I could have more creative control. On Monday, I asked for a half hour with Dana and told her I wasn't taking the promotion. I told her what I needed, and we brainstormed from there. I would never have done something like this if it weren't for you, Marc. In fact, I credit you with the idea of monetizing my social media following."

They separated momentarily to leap over a mountain of slush. As much as she'd missed him, the past week had given her the space she needed to finally process her crazy vacation. If Marc didn't say yes, she couldn't go with him now. Their relationship would have to be long-distance until she'd helped Janelle. She might be able to do that soon, if Dana's instincts about the value of her social media accounts were on point.

She knew she was asking a lot. There were plenty of reasons for him to say no. But she wasn't going to flake out on everything she'd worked toward simply because he'd given her the best orgasms of her life. She couldn't be a full partner to him if she was dependent on his largess. That was part of what had messed up her relationship with Zach, and she wasn't making the same mistake with Marc. She loved him too much to let that happen.

"I guess that's a compliment?" he asked as they rejoined on the other side of the street.

"It is." No matter what happened between now and Monday, he'd given her the push she needed to chart a new course. Marc was her Polaris, her North Star. "I tried to keep you out of it, but Dana thinks the clients will be interested in the couple angle because it opens up more target audiences."

"If we do this, I want to be in it all the way. For one thing, I had no idea there was that much money in snapping selfies. Maybe I'll give up real estate. Speaking of which, what about your apartment?"

Predictably, he'd hit the roof when she'd told him about impulsively loaning her apartment to a homeless woman.

"I spoke with Gina. She needs to resubmit paperwork with the new address, which might take months, but the voucher should cover most of the rent and it will help her get on her feet while she finds a job. We're talking with the landlord, but it looks like it'll work out. In the meantime, I've got a place to stay until I wrap things up here." Alyssa turned and put her gloved hand on his arm. "I'm glad you want to be involved in the project. I want it to be something we do together. Both the social media and the sailing."

Marc looked away. He tucked her hand into his elbow. "You've been busy."

Alyssa nodded. Fatigue weighed her body like a layer of mud. She'd pushed hard this week. She wouldn't get much rest over the weekend, either, judging from the way Marc was devouring her with his eyes. Good.

The cold, dry air scraped her cheeks until they were raw. Yet the Christmas lights still hanging over the streets and in the shop windows somehow made the city feel warmer, full of twinkling magic if you dared turn your attention away from the filthy slush at your feet. She'd miss New York. Parts of it.

On a whim, she tugged Marc's hand. "Let's see if the tree is still up at Rockefeller. It's only a block out of our way."

The huge tree rose before them in all its gaudy glory, tinsel still winking with cheerful strands of lights and decorated with giant ornaments. They leaned against the rail watching skaters milling on the ice rink below. Their breath steamed in companionable silence. Her phone beeped.

"Dana's not joining us for lunch." Inane. Yet she didn't want to ask him again whether he would go along with her plan. Alyssa knew he was turning the idea over. It wasn't fair to pressure him, no matter how badly she wanted his answer.

"Maybe we could check into the hotel early."

"Worth a try."

"And our next meeting with Dana is at three?" He wasn't watching the skaters any more.

Aly smiled, staring at the tree for as long as she could before she succumbed to temptation and met his eye sidelong. "Yep."

"Good. I can't wait to get you out of business not-so-casual." Marc held her gaze until the intensity became too much. This time, she had to break eye contact.

"Since you plan to join us at three, is that a yes?" *Please say yes.*

Marc shifted and faced her. Alyssa pushed herself up from the wall and looked up at him and wished she was still wearing her heels so their mouths would be a few inches closer.

"You know it is. All I ask is that you cabin off space for us to be alone. I'm tired of seeing you in public. I want to take you somewhere secluded and not come up for air for weeks. But if I have to share a little bit of you with a hundred thousand people to get that, I'm all in."

Alyssa grinned up at him. Her breath steamed and curled in the cold air. "Thank you."

"Excuse me. You take our picture?"

Alyssa turned, ready to snarl at the perfectly nice foreign woman holding out a camera.

"Sure." Marc took the camera. The woman and her family posed, the camera clicked, and the moment was over.

"You want picture?"

Marc turned to her. "Start things off right?"

"Sure." Alyssa guarded their territory in a prime spot with a view of the tree as Marc set up the camera. When he joined her, she didn't cheese it up for the camera. Instead she kissed him the way she'd wanted to when he'd shown up that morning. Slow. Lingering. Deep.

The tourists took photos until there was nothing more to photograph, waiting awkwardly for them to finish. A breathless Marc retrieved his camera. Alyssa reached up to rub her lipstick away with her thumb. She surely looked a mess. Her toes were frozen, her cheeks numb, and she could hardly feel her fingers or ears, but it didn't matter. Her heart was warm enough to revive it all.

"WHAT ARE WE DOING THIS EVENING?" Marc asked as they rode the elevator up to the hotel room. Indeed, there had been a room available for early check-in. How convenient.

"We could stay in." She flashed a grin at him, then trailed a fingernail down his chest, trailing a wake of ripples down his abdomen. "New Yorkers tend to be homebodies. We don't go out much."

"Does that mean your apartment?" This environment was so foreign to him. He didn't understand the appeal. His girlfriend was no hothouse flower if she could thrive in this barren place. If he'd held any lingering doubts about her ability to sail with him, they'd been obliterated today.

Girlfriend. He was still trying that word on for size and liking the way it sounded better and better.

The elevator *pinged* open. Alyssa made a face. "No. My neighbor complains about every imaginary noise. I can tiptoe in socks and he's calling me."

"We should give him something to complain about as a parting gift." Beneath her wind-chapped cheeks, he could see he'd made her blush.

Alyssa inserted the key card into the door and held it open. They had an hour until the meeting. More than enough time to get reacquainted.

He dropped his bag on the floor as the door slammed behind them.

All that and more. In a heartbeat. He'd follow this feeling with her anywhere it led. To the ends of the earth. And back again.

End

AUTHOR'S NOTE

While I've tried to represent Cuban-American life in Florida accurately, readers interested in a more authentic voice will find it in the works of Andie J. Christopher: https://andiejchristopher.com. She's terrific.

A few years ago, I had the pleasure of staying at Le Pavillon in New Orleans. I knew I wanted to use the beautiful roof deck in a story, so I've brought the hotel to Florida for Alyssa and Marc (and you) to enjoy. Pictures at www.lepavillon.com.

Homelessness is a significant problem in the U.S. For those who find Gina's subplot a stretch, I was inspired by the story of a Washington, D.C., couple, Rachel and Erik Cox, who chose to forfeit Christmas gifts and help a homeless stranger obtain an apartment. Read more at http://bit.ly/2y6Vhlm. 10% of the proceeds from this book will benefit the National Coalition for the Homeless.

Enjoyed this book?
Leave a review on Goodreads, or with your favorite eBook retailer.
Sign up for my newsletter for sneak peeks, excerpts, and and new titles from Carrie Lomax.

ACKNOWLEDGMENTS

I am profoundly grateful to fellow Maryland Romance Writers Association members Ingrid Hahn, M.C. Vaughan, and Mona Shroff for feedback, insights and general hand-holding. You are all amazing writers and friends. Emma Prince, without your encouragement this book would still languish on my hard drive. Anya Kagan at Touchstone Editing provided editorial guidance and much-needed wisdom; without her insights, this book would still be a hot mess. To Margaret Bates for quick-turnaround proofreading—you are a lifesaver. Liz Durano, thank you for the support, cover and teasers! All errors are my own.

Last but far from least, to my husband and family for tolerating my side gig despite a messy house, embarrassing PTA conversations and a constant supply of microwave dinners. The next books are for you.

ABOUT THE AUTHOR

Carrie Lomax grew up in the Midwest before moving to New York City for 15 years. She lives in Maryland with two budding readers and her real-life romantic hero.

www.carrielomax.com

SAY YOU NEED ME
CHAPTER ONE

Janelle Carlisle's phone beeped, waking her long enough to squint up at the bright, warm Florida sun. Even in March, she could sunbathe by the apartment complex pool. With one hand, she pushed up her cheap sunglasses to read the message.

Happy Birthday! Crystal's in town. We're taking you out.

Crystal was more her roommate, Rachel's, friend. Janelle had taken over Crystal's room when she'd gone to law school.

It's not until tomorrow, she texted back.

Besides her ambivalence to both her birthday and toward Crystal, Janelle had only the sixteen dollars she'd earned in tips from her second job at the coffee shop to last her until Friday, when her paycheck hit. Drinks were out of budget, birthday be damned. She relaxed onto the chair. Her phone made another noise. Janelle sighed and dragged herself up.

Nobody goes out on Sundays. Are you really going to mark turning twenty-five by staying home to watch *The Bachelorette* **for the millionth time?**

A second, impatient beep. **Seriously, what's the appeal?**

The fantasy of having hot, successful men compete for a woman's attention. *Duh.* Was it so strange to enjoy the idea of sitting in the power seat for a while? Of having a little romance?

It wasn't as if she hadn't seen every episode of every season, at least twice.

Only if you're buying. My car's done for, she texted back.

Thursday, the Volkswagen rust bucket almost as old as she was had developed a sickening clanking sound, then ground to a halt two blocks from home. Friday she'd cadged a ride to work, and this morning Janelle had swallowed hard at the bad news: she needed a new set of wheels, STAT.

Come to think of it, Janelle could really use a birthday drink or two. Even if it was charity.

If you MENTION money this evening I will personally pour a drink over your head. Come out with us. Make out with some random guy just because you're single and you can, FFS. Pick you up in an hour?

Well, okay then. Time to get off the chair and into makeup and actual clothes. Janelle lay there for another ten minutes trying to summon the energy.

Tomorrow was her twenty-fifth birthday. Only another fifty more to get through, before she could legit give up trying to get somewhere in life and die in peace.

Although they were friends, Crystal was not one of Janelle's favorite people. Her confidence bugged Janelle for reasons she didn't like to articulate.

"How's law school?" Rachel asked as the waitress delivered their margaritas.

"Great. I love the professors, and the students are really dedicated. I'm planning to go into public service."

"Careful you don't wind up like me," Janelle's tone came out waspish where she meant to be flippant. She gripped the slippery stem of the margarita glass hard enough to snap it. Catching herself, she eased off. *Quit with the jealousy.*

Crystal didn't bring out the best in Janelle. Law school was the inevitable place for someone like Crystal, who made a habit of asking annoyingly incisive questions. She was the kind of person who skated right past barriers, then gave them a good kick just to watch them topple over.

"In what way?" Crystal turned wide brown eyes toward her. She'd dyed her hair blonde, though a half-inch of dark roots showed through. Curvy, smart, and adventurous, Crystal had been notorious for sleeping around in college. She'd had a lot of friends but not many close ones. Rachel was one of the few.

"Mired in debt." Janelle sucked the dregs of her margarita through her straw. Her life had peaked in college. She'd had a great boyfriend named Ben, and she'd been confident her psychology degree would get her a decent-paying job after school—though she was vague on what it might be.

Then her parents had run out of tuition money and offered her the option of moving home for three years to finish school. In love with Ben, she'd opted to move off-campus and pick up another job, instead. Her grades had suffered, and she'd ended up taking out too many loans.

In three years since graduating she'd chipped away almost a third of her debt, but the payments still took almost half her monthly income. Rent was another third, leaving her with a few hundred dollars to cover utilities, gas, food, and incidentals. Forget getting ahead. Janelle was barely hanging on.

"Want another?" Rachel asked, indicating her empty glass.

"Sure. It's not as if I'm not driving," Janelle deadpanned.

"Why aren't you driving?" Crystal asked, her thin, red-painted lips wrapped around a straw.

"Car broke down. The White Knight finally gave up the ghost." Janelle slurped the last of her margarita before the waitress could whisk it away.

"The gleaming steed lays down its life." Rachel clutched her heart, giggled, and reached across the table to dip a chip in salsa.

"The only thing gleaming on that car was the bumper I had replaced," Janelle said ruefully.

"You should get a sugar daddy. I have one." Crystal continued sucking her neon green drink, brown eyes bouncing between Janelle and Rachel, assessing their response.

The astonished laughter burst out of Janelle in a hot rush. "Funny, Crystal."

"You have a what?" Aghast, Rachel nearly knocked over her new drink.

"A sugar daddy. An older man who pays some of my law school bills and housing expenses in exchange for sex." A knowing, worldly smile played over Crystal's lips. "Georgetown's expensive."

The sentence hung there, a bomb gone off in the middle of their margaritas.

"You're a prostitute," Janelle said flatly.

"No. I have an arrangement. Sort of like a mistress in the nineteenth century."

Rachel's mouth hung open. Janelle snorted dismissively. "Lucky you. Those arrangements always worked out so well. It's all fun and games until things go south and you're stuck with an illegitimate kid and no way to get a job."

Undeterred, Crystal kept smiling. "I'll have a job, and a good one. The modern miracle of birth control almost guarantees I won't get pregnant. It's not the Victorian era. It's not prostitution. It's a mutually beneficial system that allows bright young women like myself to exploit rich older men for their money."

"It's sex for money," Janelle replied flatly. "Call a spade a spade."

"I'm not a prostitute," Crystal insisted. "It's more akin to having a rich boyfriend who pays for everything with a specific agreement up front. Like a prenup. The arrangement only lasts for as long as both parties want it to. It's one-hundred-percent about consent."

"It's exploitative." Janelle's fingers were relaxed around the stem of her glass. This was simple, easy. Sex for money was bad. How clear-cut could it get?

"Don't be so judgmental, Janie. It's a fair exchange between equals. Didn't your sister have a rich boyfriend in New York?"

More to the point: How had Crystal known?

Rachel's gaze dropped guiltily to her lap. Janelle shot her a glare. They'd be discussing her loose lips later.

"Yeah, Alyssa had a boyfriend. They broke up right before she and Marc got together." As in, literally the evening before. That hadn't gone over so well. Janelle liked to think she'd had a hand in helping them work it out in the end, even though she'd been cheering for Alyssa's ex at the time.

"How is what I'm doing any different from your sister dating a rich guy?" Crystal demanded, calmly placing her crossed forearms on the table.

"I need another margarita if we're going to continue this conversation," Rachel interjected, summoning the waiter.

"It's...she...Alyssa loved Zach, for a while. What about you, Crystal? Are you in love with your sugar daddy?"

"No. But I am faithful to him." Crystal smiled. "It's monogamous, at least on my part."

"On his part?"

She shrugged. "It's not part of the deal. He's married."

"Okay, this is too gross, Crystal. I can't believe you'd do that." Rachel looked sick, but she quickly drained the third huge margarita anyway. "It's wrong."

"Why not? I didn't make his wife any promises. If he wants to cheat, that's his business." She leaned against the vinyl booth.

"Rachel, eat some more chips. Let's get another round of appetizers." Janelle tried to flag a passing waiter, and failed.

"I'm going to head out in a few minutes." Crystal pulled out her phone, the latest Apple model.

"How's the sex?" Janelle blurted.

"Not bad, honestly," Crystal barely glanced up. "You should consider it, Janelle. You could find a really good protector with that rack of yours."

Eww. *Eww.*

No.

"Send me the info. I'm curious." Only curious. She'd never do something so morally compromised. Rachel's eyelids were hovering half-open, and a stab of worry hit Janelle. "Maybe we should skip the appetizers and head home."

"Sure," Rachel slurred. "Or shots."

Crystal reached over and moved a strand of hair over Rachel's shoulder. "No shots for you, Rach. You never could drink worth a damn. I've got the bill. I'll charge it to Barry's credit card."

"Thanks, Crys." Janelle suddenly remembered why she liked Crystal enough to be casual friends. She could be very generous. Although, apparently, someone else was paying. A stranger she'd never met. One who cheated on his wife. It was hard to summon much outrage about a couple of birthday margaritas in the grand scheme of things, but it left a queasy feeling in the pit of her stomach that had nothing to do with tequila.

Janelle focused on helping Rachel out of the booth. Her part in the Crystal/Barry/Barry's wife mess was incidental. They all abandoned the table, Crystal and Janelle on either side of Rachel, supporting their drunk friend.

"I don't think she's going to make it home," Janelle said worriedly.

"Are you okay to drive?" Crystal asked.

"Not really, no." Never a big drinker, two margaritas were the upper limit of Janelle's tolerance, and she'd had three. "We'll get a car service and come pick her car up in the morning."

"Okay. Be safe. I'll go let the restaurant know she's leaving it overnight." Crystal unwound herself from Rachel, who lurched against a lamp post.

Then she gave Janelle a warm, if awkward, hug. "Happy birthday."

"Thanks, Crys."

"Oh, hey, I meant to tell you. I heard Ben's getting married."

It was as though Crystal had raked claws across her face. "My Ben?"

"He hasn't been yours in a few years, right?"

Now Janelle knew how birds and mice felt when cats toyed with them. Her body felt disengaged, almost paralyzed. She swallowed. Janelle ought to be happy to know someone she'd cared about—still cared about—was in love. If she were truly a good person, she wouldn't feel the hot sting of jealousy. But she did. "No. He hasn't. Who's the lucky girl?"

Crystal shrugged, nonchalant about the bomb she'd dropped. "Some Texas blonde. You know the type. Big hair. Blue eyes."

"Thanks for drinks," Janelle replied tightly, suddenly hating every blonde-haired woman in the Lone Star State with a raw, unreasonable passion. The driver pulled up, sparing her from further humiliation. Janelle tugged the seat belt over her friend's petite body and clicked it into place.

"Oh, Janie, I meant to tell you earlier. I got distracted by Crystal's sugar buddy news." Rachel slumped against her shoulder, a fine sweat breaking out over her pale forehead. Her skin practically glowed, she avoided the sun carefully.

"Sugar daddy," Janelle corrected automatically. "Can you believe she'd do something like that?"

"Crystal? Yeah, I can. Listen. I forgot to tell you. I'm moving out."

The car swerved. Janelle's stomach heaved as though she might vomit half-digested margarita all over the upholstery. "When?"

"At the end of the month. Caleb wants me to move in with him. He says he wants to get engaged, and so do I. It doesn't make sense for me to renew the lease. Do you think you can find someone to take it over?"

For the past two years, Rachel had been the sole lease holder on their apartment. Janelle paid her cash for her share of the rent and utilities. Her friends' lives were progressing normally. Jobs. Careers. Starting families. She was flailing in quicksand, and now they were all leaving her behind.

"I'll try." Janelle pushed her friend upright. On Friday, she'd received a check from her sister, Alyssa, with a note: *Hang in there. More to come. Enjoy your birthday.*

If she'd saved it, she might've had enough for a deposit on a new apartment. Or a down payment on a car. Instead, Janelle's heart had swelled up like a desiccated sponge dropped into a bucket of gratitude, and in a fit of determination she'd sent the entire amount directly to her student loan servicer this morning. If Rachel had told her sooner, she'd have planned differently.

Given a do-over, Janelle would've done a whole lot of differently. Trying to be responsible had gotten her nothing but too much debt, a dead-end job, a broken-down car, and no way to rent an apartment of her own. She was slipping backward. If she didn't stop the fall, her entire future would be buried under an avalanche of debt and regrets.

Something in her life had to change. It had to change now. Today. Tonight. Maybe Crystal's unexpected visit was a sign.

After she hauled her roommate upstairs, dumped Rachel into her bed, and set a glass of water and two painkillers on the nightstand beside it, Janelle checked her email.

Crystal had sent her a link. Janelle clicked it. She was twenty-five years old—almost—and broke as fuck, with no hope of escape unless she took a big risk. A huge risk.

The screen popped up. Janelle shook her head and closed it. *No way. I deserve better than some gross, old guy cheating on his wife.*

Yet maybe Crystal was right. Being good wasn't getting her anywhere. Maybe it was time to try being bad. What better day to commit to a big change than on her birthday?

CHAPTER TWO

He shouldn't be here.

The red carpet and gold chandelier recalled another world, another lifetime. One that beckoned with the thrum of muted excitement, even now. He could go back. If he wanted to. Poker was mostly math and patience. But he wasn't that person anymore. Six years ago, everything had changed here in the banquet hall of the Astoria Casino Hotel. His life had crashed down from the high only this palace of chance could give.

He was here to pay his respects. To remind himself why he needed to stick to his chosen course. He had find out whether his old life still had any power over him.

It did.

Trent Mason ran one hand over the back of a red velvet chair. The soft fabric slipped beneath his palm like a lover's back.

Six years ago, he'd lost millions. Professional poker was a game of probability, not money. It didn't matter whether you were up or down at any given moment until you bet wrong and lost. Everything he'd built had been vaporized in a flash of inattention and bad luck. A few weeks before, everything else that mattered had been vaporized, too. He'd been twenty-three, and left with nothing.

Chapter Two

Trent walked around the first floor, though he knew that if security caught him on the premises he'd be arrested on the spot. He was counting on the six intervening years to have wrought personnel changes and faded memories. He wasn't here to make trouble. Only to pay tribute. In a few minutes, he'd move on.

Indignant-woman noises punctuated his reminiscence. Garbled words, spoken in a low hiss, then louder, reached his ears. Security guards appeared from shadows and swarmed toward the elegant lobby.

"Let go of me! I need my things. You can't just toss me out with —*oof.*" A flash of long leg, obscured high at the thigh by a flash of jade green appeared at the center of a cluster of security guards.

Time for him to go. Damsels in distress were usually up to no good in this town. He knew from crushing experience. Whatever heart he'd had left had been smashed, stomped, and blown to pieces when Penelope betrayed him.

Bad Penny. A name he'd rather forget. One imprinted indelibly on his soul.

Penelope, whom he'd met in this very casino. She'd been far away from this luxury, or faux luxury, when she'd nearly died. It might've been a kinder fate than the heroin that had eaten her from the inside out.

At least he'd escaped. He was sworn off rescuing Vegas damsels, for life.

"Can I at least get my stuff?" The angry woman pulled futilely against the burly guards. Her gold high heels threatened to rip holes in the carpeting.

She didn't stand a chance. Trent relived the helpless feeling for a moment. Then he took one last look at the elegant light fixture and the glittery gold lights and plush red velvet of the Astoria, tossed his suit jacket over his shoulder, and headed for the door.

Sunglasses topped the bridge of his nose even before he made it to the first set of darkly tinted automatic doors, but he ducked his head as the security guards returned into the building. Just in case.

They passed him without a second glance.

"Send someone upstairs and get her boyfriend to pack her bag. I'll

Chapter Two

take it out to her if she's still there."

She was. The skimpy strapless dress looked cheap and trashy in the broad light of day. Her bare shoulders shook. Crying, probably.

No tan lines.

The expanse of smooth, evenly tanned skin between the bright fabric and the thick dark hair between her shoulder blades *would* be the first thing he noticed. The sight made his cock perk up.

Down, boy.

Trent glanced at his watch. Quarter to noon. The conference sessions that had broken fifteen minutes ago wouldn't resume for more than an hour yet. He ought to find out where the attendees were clustering for lunch and try to make some business contacts. It was the only reason he'd come back to this town. Otherwise, he was content to never set foot in Las Vegas again for as long as he lived.

She wobbled a few steps away, then stopped as though unsure where to go. Trent sighed. He could at least let her know she'd get her belongings back if she hung around. "You all right?"

The girl stiffened as though he'd smacked her. A loud sniff. Then she raked back her mane of dark hair and rubbed beneath her eyes, a gesture that turned the dark smudges of mascara into huge circles. Like Elizabeth Taylor as Cleopatra, minus the poise.

"Fine." She glanced over her shoulder as though trying to figure out the best way to run if he attacked her in the middle of the street at high noon. The sun was at its zenith in the sky, the air hot and unforgiving.

Then Cleopatra turned to face him directly. It was as if the sun had fallen out of the sky and landed on him.

Holy tits, Batman.

Trent choked. The tiny scrap of a dress clung to the two biggest, perkiest breasts he'd ever seen defying gravity *sans* bra. The distinct shape of nipples dead in the center of each globe strongly suggested he bend down and suck them until they pulled into hard, tight buds.

The rest of the woman read his mind, and was less than enthusiastic about the direction of his thoughts. Her raccoon-rimmed eyes flared wide with outrage.

He jerked his attention away. It'd been years since he'd been near a woman, and he wasn't about to break his celibate streak with this one. If she was a woman and not a confused teenager. She looked very young.

"Here." He held out the suit jacket he was carrying over his shoulder. "I overheard the security guys saying they'd bring your things out if you stick around."

She sniffed and reached for the jacket. Then, she turned away to push her arms into the sleeves so he couldn't get a second look at her.

Trent turned away, too, trying to erase the image of Cleopatra's rack from his memory.

"Thank you."

He spoke over his shoulder, not trusting himself to keep his eyes where they belonged. "You're welcome. I'm staying at the hotel across the street. When you get things sorted out here, you can leave it at the front desk."

"What's your name? So I know what to tell the clerk."

Right, she didn't care to know the name of the guy who'd shown a little kindness. He didn't want to know hers, either. Trent knew she'd caught him checking her out, but he hadn't been a complete asshole about it, and she probably got that reaction all the time. Understandable if she wasn't in the mood for a pickup line, but he hadn't offered one.

"Mason."

"First or last?"

"Both." The less Cleopatra knew about him, the better. The less anyone knew about him, the better. "Here's the guards. Good luck with everything."

"You too. Thanks again."

Clearly, she was a nice girl. Well-bred, probably had two married parents and a nice suburban upbringing. Like he'd had once. Before they'd died, and he'd gone off the rails with grief and teenage hormones. He was old enough now to know better than to get dragged into whatever trouble she was in.

Trent was here for business, and it was time he got back to it. He waited at the curb for the traffic to clear. The Las Vegas strip was always busy, but if you caught the lights right you could make it across

Chapter Two

the street without walking to the corner. He'd hit them dead wrong, so he was still standing there, eyeballing cars, when Cleopatra's outraged voice rang out.

"Son of a fucking *bitch*!"

Whew. The girl could cuss. Trent chuckled. It was almost funny to hear the string of foul language come from a cute chick. Maybe she wasn't as young as she looked. Whoever she was, she reminded him of Penny, only with a worse attitude.

"Goddamned bastard *stole* it. Wait. Come back—my wallet's missing. My driver's license, my debit card, my phone. They're all gone. How the hell will I get home? Wait!"

Trent turned to see the guards manhandling her away from the Astoria's front door. One of two refrigerator-box-sized men grabbed her by the collar of his favorite suit jacket and dragged her back to the little pile of items on the sidewalk. He winced and hoped it hadn't torn.

"Stop touching me, you oaf!" Cleopatra fought the good fight, but it was hopelessly one-sided and she was losing.

There was a tearing sound, and then the giant shoved her away. Trent closed the distance in two strides to steady her. Cleopatra gaped up at him with fierce green eyes that stole his breath.

"You won't win," he told her. "Do you want to file a police report about your wallet?"

She pulled away hard, out of his grasp. "No."

"Why not?"

"I can't."

Oh, shit. Now he for sure didn't want to know what she was into. "Is there someone you can call?"

"No. I have to figure this out on my own." Her hands shook as she bent and rummaged through her scant belongings, searching desperately for something that didn't appear to be there.

Pride. Trent recognized it, and pitied her for it. If she was into drugs, or prostitution, or any variation of those problems, he couldn't help her. He couldn't go down that road again.

Cleopatra stuffed a jumble of soft fabric back into the small duffel bag and slung it over her shoulder as she stood up. She heaved a great sigh. It would've done wonderful things to her breasts if they hadn't been obscured by his ruined jacket. It covered more of her body than her dress did.

But he was trying not to think about that.

"You've been very kind, Mason. I hate to ask this. May I borrow your hotel room for a few minutes to clean up and change clothes? I'll get out of your hair right afterward. Promise."

Clean up, as in wash the makeup off her face.

Change clothes, as in get naked before putting on something less slutty. Or not. She could hang out naked and a certain part of his anatomy wouldn't mind a bit.

He'd bet his left testicle Cleo shined up like a new penny.

Bad Penny. Bad memories. A good reminder, though, of why he had to get Cleopatra Trouble Tits out of his life immediately.

"Sure." Well. His dick had won control of his mouth, and his brain was left flashing silent red warning signs.

You'd have wanted someone to be kind to Penny if she was in a bad situation.

Yeah, and she'd have made them regret it.

History might not repeat itself, but as the saying went, it often rhymed.

How the ever-loving hell had she gotten herself into this mess?

Janelle hunched her shoulders down inside the too-large suit jacket. It smelled of Mason, which was strangely comforting given she'd met him barely ten minutes ago. The warm, faintly spicy scent and the breadth of the jacket's shoulders were the ghost hug she desperately needed to get through this humiliating shit show.

Unlike Crystal, she hadn't gotten a Barry for a sugar daddy.

On the last night she'd had her own internet access in her own apartment, Janelle had submitted a brief and thoroughly halfhearted application to the website Crystal had sent. The application fee was fifty bucks, but it was refunded if they didn't accept you. There was no risk, and she was desperate enough to try it.

Chapter Two

Janelle's money had bounced back to her bank account a few days later.

Rejected.

We look for sugar babies of your age who are either enrolled in graduate school or pursuing non-remunerative employment (i.e., internship). Your credit report is an additional source of concern. Babies with poor credit have been known to attempt blackmail or other illegal extortion of their Daddies.

Of course. Her entire life could be reduced to a three-digit summary: not trustworthy.

But…her age? She'd just turned twenty-five, and she was *too old*?

Rage of a kind she'd never experienced had blinded her for the last few hours of unpacking at her parents' house. It wasn't that she wanted to screw some guy having a midlife crisis for money; it was the principle.

This should've been the nail in the coffin of her sugar baby experience, but pride had intervened. She was not too old, and she was going to prove it. In a fit of fury, she'd gone online and filled out applications at two other, less reputable-looking websites. One rejected her.

The other called a week later.

"I see you have some boundaries. No married men," the woman on the phone noted. "No bondage, no threesomes, no more than two encounters a month, no anal sex, no rough play, no…is there anything you *are* willing to do?"

"Oral sex," she offered begrudgingly. "If I have to."

Janelle liked giving head, but the concept of doing it for a stranger was too weird to be more than abstraction.

"Role play?" the agent countered.

"I cannot imagine adults getting off by playing dress up. No."

"You're limiting your prospects," the woman replied crankily.

Yeah, well, Janelle was used to not having a lot of options.

"Is there anything else you're willing to do?"

"Travel," Janelle said immediately. "But the, uh, daddy has to pay for all expenses."

Thus, she'd been matched with exactly one prospect. She'd spoken with Kyle, aka Rich Jerk (aka her new sugar daddy) on the phone twice, and bought a plane ticket to Las Vegas at his request. He'd

Chapter Two

promised to pay her back when they met. Janelle had scheduled a Friday and a Monday off from work and flown into McCarran International Thursday evening, ahead of Rich Jerk's arrival. Since then, not one thing had gone according to plan.

Now she was trotting after a tall, broad-shouldered, extremely good-looking man with only one name, while looking like she'd fallen off the back of a paddy wagon full of hookers.

"Mace," a male voice rang out. Her protector turned. Janelle kept walking as though she didn't know him, eyes glued to the hideous hotel carpet. She turned the corner and waited out of sight.

A minute later, "Mace" Mason appeared. She inhaled and finally took a good look at the man who'd gone above and beyond to help her. He had to top six feet, and Janelle was certain his muscles had muscles. Thick biceps stretched the fabric of his dress shirt. "Please don't tell me my rescuer's nicknamed for pepper spray."

Her reluctant protector's mouth quirked up at the corners. She'd made him laugh, or at least, almost smile. This was the first good look she'd gotten at his eyes since he'd whipped his sunglasses off on entering the building. They were dead sexy, deep blue and fringed with lashes that would've made any girl abandon mascara for life if she'd been lucky enough to own them.

"No, for a blunt weapon from the Middle Ages," he shot back.

"Too bad it's not the spice." Janelle inhaled, and all it did was send a hit of pheromones straight to her brain. He stared at her a long moment. Yeah, dumb comment. Her mind was busy plotting how to get her wallet and phone back so she could get on the first plane back to Florida. It had nothing to do with the weird drugged sensation that came with being near Mysterious Mace Mason, hottie and, apparently, decent human being.

The world could use a few more of those.

She'd have to meet him looking like this, too. It was too much to ask fate to show any hint of mercy.

Janelle followed him into the smallest hotel room she'd ever seen. Instead of the usual double queen beds, there was only one. Shoved against the far wall was a two-seater couch, next to a chair and a table that could be used as a desk. Facing the bed, there was a clunky

Chapter Two

dresser topped with a large television. In other words, it was a normal hotel room except for the size.

Small hotel room. Muscular, attractive man. What could go wrong?

"I'll just be a minute." She pushed the bathroom door open, hung Mason's jacket on the back of the door, and upended her sloppily packed bag. Then she ripped off the skimpy dress she'd packed to make an impression, never once imagining it would be seen outside the confines of a hotel room, and stuffed it down to the very bottom of the bag. The gold heels almost chipped the tile wall, she kicked them off so hard.

Janelle cringed at the sight that greeted her in the harsh light over the mirror. The toiletries by the sink were still wrapped. Janelle tore the paper off a small bar of soap and rubbed her hands in the water, then scrubbed her face until it was clean of makeup. Afterwards, she tugged on a bra, t-shirt and leggings and finally stuffed everything back into her bag and squared her shoulders.

The least she could do was try to mend Mason's torn jacket.

"Feel better?" he asked as she emerged.

Janelle nodded, hardly able to look at him. "I think I can fix this."

Mason plucked the fine wool from her hands. "Right now, you have bigger problems. I'm going out for a sandwich. Want one?"

"I don't have any money. It was in my wallet." She was always broke, but she'd never been penniless until now.

"It's a sandwich. Don't worry about it." He'd rolled up his sleeves so his sinewy forearms showed. His hair was short on the sides, a little longer on the top, like someone in the military who'd recently been discharged and hadn't quite adapted to civilian life yet.

"Why are you being nice to me?" Janelle pulled at the hem of her shirt. It was a V-neck and clingy, not her usual style, but all the clothes she'd brought were revealing. By her standards, anyway.

"Good question. Maybe I should throw you out of here, like those bouncers did."

Mason took one step closer, and for a second she thought he'd do it. Her heart flapped like a pigeon desperate to take flight, but all he did was reach for her shoulder bag and drop it onto the couch.

"I'm leaving my phone here, unlocked. If there's anyone you can

Chapter Two

call for help, do it while I'm not here to listen. I'm here for a conference, and I can't babysit you."

"I'm self-sufficient."

Mason raised an eyebrow. Janelle ducked her head. His skepticism was warranted.

"Go to your conference, I'll figure something out. Promise. I'm not a mooch." The instant Mace departed, Janelle reached for the phone. She sucked in a hard breath and dialed her own mobile phone number.

A familiar male voice answered. "Janelle?"

She shivered as the air conditioning chilled the sudden sweat that broke out over her neck. "Kyle."

"If you want your wallet and phone back, get back here and get naked. Now."

"I'm not doing that."

A beat of silence. "I'll ruin you."

Janelle's teeth caught her lower lip. The words were punch in the gut. "I'll report you."

He laughed. "For what? Rape? Assault? You consented. In writing."

"For being an asshole," she seethed, knowing full well she'd have a hard time convincing anyone she'd resisted, and he'd insisted, even after she'd emphatically told him no.

Kyle laughed, that rat bastard. "There's no statute against hurting your feelings. But prostitution is definitely illegal. So is breach of contract. I can sue you."

"I didn't—"

"Oh yes you did. If you want to go crawling back to your pathetic life in Florida without anyone knowing what you've done, you'll come back to this hotel room and get on all fours. Naked. You'll pretend to enjoy everything I do to you or everyone in your contacts is going to get a copy of the little video I made this morning. Check your email."

Call terminated. Janelle's mouth hung open, a tangle of retorts about revenge porn being illegal dying unspoken. Even if it was, he could say she'd consented and what then? She set the phone down carefully. Her stomach heaved as a fine cold sweat covered her forehead. She'd never wanted a stiff drink so badly in her life.

Chapter Two

The door clicked open. "I hope ham and cheese is okay. You're not vegetarian or anything...Did something happen?"

Janelle felt her head move as though she were a puppet dancing on a string. "No. I called my phone. It's fine. I'll get it back."

Eventually. Right before she was arrested for Kyle's murder, just long enough to make her one phone call to a lawyer. Crystal was in law school, maybe she'd handle it pro bono. Janelle figured Crys owed her a favor for her role in this debacle.

Janelle unwrapped the sandwich on the table and stared at it until Mason's voice called her back to the present.

"You have parents who can help?"

"And tell them how I ended up here? No way." She picked up the sandwich and took a bite without tasting it.

Mason's appetite was in fine form. He tucked into his sandwich and licked a bit of dressing off his thumb. "How bad is it?"

"The mess I'm in? Pretty bad."

"Drugs?"

Did she look that strung out? "No!"

Drugs were one problem she didn't have. Though she'd sure looked like a potential addict in the excuse for a dress with makeup running down her face. Janelle shifted uncomfortably and examined her sandwich.

Mason, on the other hand, perked up considerably. "Sex?"

"How'd you guess?" The return of her habitual sarcasm was unbelievably welcome. She bit into the sandwich. "Was it the outfit?"

Mason's mouth ticked up at the corners. "Money?"

"The root of all evil." Janelle rubbed her forehead. Now that her anger had leached out, fear, failure, and loneliness had stolen her appetite.

"What's your name?"

"Jan-" *Hey, wait a minute.* "Janie."

He crumpled the paper of his sandwich and waited a beat. "No last name?"

"You gave me one name, I'll give you one name. If you want to know more, spill."

Mason stood up and tossed the ball of sandwich paper into the

Chapter Two

trash can by the desk. "You're cheeky for someone in a fix."

"You like it, though." *Whoa.* Where had that come from? This was no time to get flirty.

He chuckled but admitted nothing. Instead, he stood up and pulled out a wooden door on the dresser. Inside was a dorm-sized refrigerator. Mason removed two airplane bottles of gin and a pint-sized bottle of tonic.

"No limes. You want a gin and tonic anyway?"

Mysterious Mace Mason was her guardian angel. She must've done something right in her life if he was offering her the drink she needed. "Yes, please."

"Are you twenty-one?" he asked skeptically.

Oh, for fuck's sake. She was too decrepit to sleep with a dirty old man but appeared too young to drink? "I'm twenty-five."

"You look younger." He cracked open the bottles and mixed the contents into matching hotel glasses. "A lot younger."

"Especially without makeup." She took the glass and downed half of it in a single gulp.

"You looked like a baby raccoon with all that shit on your face. I thought you were sixteen."

"Nope. Completely of age. Next milestone is running for President, and then AARP discounts here I come."

The sound of Mace Mason's startled laughter was a balm to her pride. The gin and tonic was the perfect temporary antidote to threatening Rich Jerks and hot, untouchable guardian angels. The booze went straight to her head and took every pleasure synapse of her brain hostage.

She had a problem to solve. Except that instead of thinking through how to get her wallet and phone back from Rich Jerk, all she could think about was Mace Mason's broad shoulders and narrow waist. "How old are you, Mace?"

"Thirty."

"Cheers." Janelle held up her glass. He tapped hers, looking straight into her eyes as he did. Everything inside her went hot and soft. But attraction wasn't going to get her a pass.

"What happened this morning, Janie?"

CHAPTER THREE

Janie's expression turned as sour as a lemon. "Why should I tell you?"

Exasperating woman. For a minute there, she'd gone relaxed and flirty. Now she'd flipped like a switch back to wary and defensive.

At least it wasn't drugs. Sex, well, he could be broad-minded about whatever she was into. He had exactly zero moral standing to judge anyone on that point. Money, though, the jury was still out.

Trent glanced at his watch. "I'm leaving in fifteen minutes for the afternoon half of my conference. If you want to stay here and figure out how to straighten things out, I need to know that it's not going to boomerang back on me. What kind of trouble are you in?"

"Big trouble," she said softly through pink lips.

"How big?" Trent wished they were talking about sex. This conversation could play out so many dirty ways. His rational brain was holding the door against lusty ideas like a doomed character about to get eaten in a zombie flick.

Without makeup, Janie's fine bone structure was clearly visible. Large green eyes rimmed by dark lashes, a manicured sweep of dark eyebrow, the straight slope of her nose above the perfect philtrum that led to plump, pink lips. Below, a stubbornly pointed chin that spoke volumes about her frankly shitty attitude.

Chapter Three

In addition to that face, Janie was blessed with a long, elegant neck, and he'd not forgotten the one instinctive glimpse he'd stolen of her incredible breasts. He was only male, after all.

And it had been a long time.

Janie, if that was her real name, licked her lips and dropped her gaze to the floor. "I came here to meet a man. For sex."

"Turning tricks?"

"No!" Her eyes searched his, pleading and outraged. "He was supposed to be my…my arrangement."

"An arranged encounter," he repeated, half understanding and half perplexed. His cock was certainly enjoying the diversion of talking about sex with an actual woman after a years-long, self-imposed drought. Her t-shirt dipped at the center, showing a couple inches of bra-trapped cleavage. Trent didn't look lower than her neck, unless you counted a furtive check of her legs. Encased in thin cotton, they were toned and slender. She was slim everywhere, except for the chest.

"I was supposed to be his sugar baby," she blurted, high cheekbones flushed red.

Oh. That's what the kids were calling it these days. "He was older, I take it?"

"Much. And he's an asshole. I arrived last night, but I was out when he checked into the hotel this morning. He left a note to wear the sexiest thing I'd brought and be ready around noon. You saw how I was dressed. I tried, but I couldn't go through with it. He threw me out of the room."

"That's it?" Mason sat back on the bed. "You almost screwed some old guy for money but didn't?"

"I couldn't!" she almost screamed, tears welling in those green depths.

"Why not?"

"Because…" She downed the rest of her gin and tonic. "Because I've only been with one person before."

One partner at the age of twenty-five. By his low standards she was practically a virgin. "I assume that was true going into the situation?"

Janie hung her head. "Yes."

"What changed?"

Chapter Three

She shrugged. "Up to that point, it hadn't felt...real. He told me to do a strip tease and tried to stick his dick in my mouth, and I told him I couldn't do it. I wanted to go home. He tried to pin me to the bed, but I fought him off. He called security, which I guess is where you pick up the story."

Janie raked her hand through her dark hair. It was a soft, rich cloud glinting with reddish highlights. Probably dyed.

"Now he has my cell phone and wallet, and he's threatening to send some video to everyone on my contact list." The words came out in a whispered confessional rush. "He says he emailed it to me."

Internet security. Sex tapes. Those were things he could help her with. As long as she wasn't into drugs, he could help her without dredging up memories that could send him spiraling downward in this most dangerous of all cities. "Was he paying you?"

If Janie blushed any harder she'd turn into a tomato. "Not directly. He'd offered a stipend. A thousand dollars a month for two weekend encounters."

Trent sighed. This girl was a babe in the woods if she thought it was a fair deal. She was stacked, attractive and clearly educated. "You'd have gotten more working at a crappy escort service."

"Plus travel expenses," she replied indignantly.

As if that made any difference. Trent downed his drink and set the glass on the table. Between a beautiful woman crashing his hotel room and him standing in the hot sun for a sandwich, his shirt was sweat-damp and wrinkled. He'd have to change unless he wanted to chase off any prospective business contacts with BO. Pushing off the bed, he went to the closet and slid the door open.

"You can stay here for a few hours. Make some calls. Get your ID replaced. Call your parents to get money for your own room. I'll be back around five." He unbuttoned his shirt, aware of her watching him.

Cute little Janie who'd only slept with one person. Person, not man. Maybe she was a lesbian?

Judging from the way her eyes were riveted on the mirror before him, not a chance.

The placket opened gradually. Her eyes widened. How long had it

Chapter Three

been since any woman had watched wide-eyed as he undressed? He'd lost count. Trent knew he should stop now, before innocent little Janie's eyeballs popped out and stood on stalks. Instead, he unbuckled his trousers to pull out the hem of his shirt.

Janie's mouth went slack. She swallowed, and he bit back a smile. Totally innocent. How the hell had a chick like her gotten mixed up in quasi-prostitution?

The world could be an incredibly shitty place. Trent tossed the shirt onto the floor of the closet with the small pile of dirty laundry growing there. Then, he pulled up the undershirt he wore and chucked that too. He balled it in his hands and looked over his shoulder.

"Enjoying the show?"

Janelle coughed and grabbed her drink. "Sorry."

Trent tossed the wadded undershirt onto the heap and went to the bathroom. He couldn't exactly tug one off with her out there listening, but he wanted to.

"Your tattoo's interesting." Janie declared the instant he came out of the bathroom. "I apologize for staring."

She sounded properly contrite, which was disappointing. Trent supposed nice girls from the suburbs didn't see a lot of half-naked ex-Army guys with giant tattoos spread across their backs. He'd enjoyed her momentary interest for what it was—momentary—and didn't want her feeling bad about checking him out. After all, he'd done the same to her, and he didn't feel remotely bad about it.

"It's the story of Icarus, isn't it?" The ice cubes clinked against the glass as she took a long, fortifying sip.

Yeah, she was educated.

"No. It's my story." He pulled a fresh undershirt over his head and a new shirt out of the closet before conceding, "There's a few similarities."

"For a minute there, I thought you had actual wings."

Like he was some sort of angel. Which given where he'd found her, maybe he was. Her crappy luck if she believed for one minute he was any kind of savior. Dressed, Trent ventured over to the table she sat behind and picked up the hotel stationery and pen. "Here's the guest password to use my computer."

Chapter Three

She accepted it with small, lovely hands. Trent took Janie by her stubborn chin and tilted her face up. "I am an expert in cyber security. If you attempt to do anything other than check your email, I'll know. I will nail you to the fucking wall if you attempt to hack into any other system. Understand?"

Wide-eyed, she nodded. He let go, but the sensation of her soft skin under his fingertips stayed with him.

The video was bad. She'd been out of the room when he'd arrived, and Kyle had clearly planted a camera in her absence. That required a coldness of calculation that implied he'd done this kind of thing before.

Everything she'd done up to the point he'd dropped his pants and tried to shove his semi-hard dick in her mouth was caught on tape. It was grainy, but there was sound and there was no point pretending it wasn't her, there willingly at least up to that point.

Mason seemed like a nice enough guy, provided she didn't attempt to hack into his computer—which she wouldn't know how to do even if she wanted to—so she helped herself to another drink from the mini bar. Vodka cranberry this time since the gin was gone. He'd understand. Janelle jotted an IOU on the hotel-branded notepad.

Then she used the hotel phone to call the agency hotline. She wasn't going to let Kyle get away with this. If he was doing it to her, he'd probably done it to someone else, and he'd probably to it again. *Solidarity, ladies.*

"Your contract doesn't specify no filming, and oral sex was something you agreed to perform," the woman on the other end replied unhelpfully.

"I didn't sign any image rights release forms. I read the paperwork before signing it," Janelle seethed. She was fucking literate, after all. *That is beside the point. The point is that Kyle stole your personal property and is threatening you. Focus.*

It wasn't easy after she'd consumed the gin and tonic and half of the vodka cranberry, but she voiced her complaint anyway. "Revenge porn is illegal."

Chapter Three

She wished she'd been quick enough to point that out she she'd been on the phone with Kyle. Stupid.

"We don't get involved in personal disputes," the woman on the other end of the line replied. "I recommend you call the police."

So much for female solidarity. "He is threatening to send an illegally obtained video to my friends and family to force me to have sex with him."

"You *agreed* to have sex with him."

"Well, that was before I met him, and now I want my goddamn wallet back so I can get home!"

"I am not a law enforcement agent. I have no authority to assist you. I can call him, that's it."

"You could throw him out of the program. I doubt this is the first time Kyle's done something like this."

Click. Janelle gave the phone a dirty look. *She* was dirty. She was such a pathetic failure; she couldn't even succeed at screwing an old guy for cash. She sucked at being good. She sucked at being bad. She was a waste of a human being. *Ugh.*

Janelle needed to wash the thoughts away as badly as she needed to rinse off the lingering creepiness of Kyle's hands on her body. A faint bruise marked her left wrist. Another bloomed over each bicep, though they were probably from the guards. She took a quick shower, since Mace was out of the picture for a bit, and she didn't want to impose later. Then, she put her clothes back on and braided her hair while considering her next move.

A next move that definitely shouldn't involve sleeping in his bed, but it did. The sheets smelled of bleach, clean but impersonal. She rolled out of bed, plucked Trent's undershirt from the pile, and sniffed it.

It was, hands down, the weirdest impulse she'd ever given in to. Nevertheless, she rolled it into a ball and hugged the wad of cotton like a teddy bear while she rested, unable to fall asleep for fear Mason would return and find her cuddling his dirty laundry. The spicy, deodorant-scented bundle made her feel safe, and a little bit stronger. Janelle needed the comfort, and she wasn't going to overthink it.

After a while she got up, returned the shirt to the pile, and made

Chapter Three

the bed. She turned on the TV and pulled out her toiletries. While the TV ran in the background, she removed the chipped nail polish from her toes and fingers. Then she applied a new coat of pale pink instead of dark red. One day she'd be able to afford salon mani-pedis.

Along with a new car.

Fake it 'till you make it.

She was never going to make it. She was going to die here of boredom in this weirdly small hotel room, and all alone. Janelle shoved her misery away and booted up the computer to research her options.

CHAPTER FOUR

Midway through the afternoon in a fascinating but highly technical panel discussion of two-factor security weaknesses, Trent realized he'd been sitting there for forty-five minutes without absorbing a thing. He hadn't paid two grand for the privilege of sitting in a stale conference room in the middle of the desert for four days to rescue green-eyed sirens with other resources to fall back on, like caring parents.

Business contacts were the only reason he was here.

A sharp elbow in the ribs brought his attention back to the present.

"Captain," he replied, sitting up straight and nodding.

The dark-skinned woman to his left smiled slyly. "Daydreaming, Sergeant?"

"No ma'am."

Old habits died hard. He'd served for three years in Afghanistan under Captain Olivia Davidson, the last two working cyber communications for military intelligence's field operations. Now they were both on the outside and partners...of a sort. She'd been out for eighteen months now, and she'd built up her own company by going after government contracts with a ruthless strategy honed on the battlefield.

Trent had declined to re-enlist. He'd thought he was ready to get back to normal life, by which he meant an approximation of Olivia's

Chapter Four

life before it had cracked against the rocky shoals of divorce. Married. Children. But once he'd severed from the military and gone on reserve duty, he'd drifted for a few weeks before deciding to follow Olivia's path.

Within a few weeks, Trent knew he didn't have the same talent for managing people and growing a business. She'd helped him win a few government contracts and generally get off the ground. She'd been the one to recommend this conference as a potential source of contacts.

He'd followed her like a duckling waddling after its mother. Olivia was not his mother, but she was his mentor. The very last thing he should be doing was mooning over the dark-haired nymph hiding in his hotel room when he ought to be making the most of this opportunity. Yet his body kept flushing with heat at the memory of Janie watching him undress.

"May I confide, Captain?" he asked.

"Let's get a coffee. This speaker's been droning on so long I can't even remember his point." She stood up and made her way past a full row of scowling men who didn't like being interrupted by a woman, especially a black one. Olivia never let that shit get to her, though.

Outwardly.

They found a pair of comfortably overstuffed chairs in the lounge area and availed themselves of free, terrible coffee. Considering the deprivation they'd endured on the base, neither complained.

"What's on your mind, soldier?"

Trent gave her the thumbnail sketch of his predicament. He imagined most people would've laughed at his problem—most men didn't think a pretty girl taking refuge in your room would qualify—but Olivia was a mom through and through. If there was one person in the world who knew him, it was Captain Davidson. She understood why this was a serious challenge for him.

"Well. You can't turn her out into the street," she finally said.

There went that plan. "Can I hand her off to you?"

"No you cannot, soldier. I'm already sharing a room to keep expenses down, and there's no space for a third. Why don't you give her the other bed for a night?"

Because there is no other bed. Though the names and décor of hotels

Chapter Four

changed, Trent knew most of the Las Vegas venues from his days as a professional poker player. He'd thought he was being smart by choosing the awkward line of smaller rooms to save a few bucks and, more importantly, give him some breathing room between long days of socializing. He hadn't counted on Janie.

"Who are you rooming with?" he asked, sidestepping Olivia's question.

"My twin," Olivia deadpanned. It was an inside joke. People frequently mistook her for her roommate, another black woman, though they looked nothing alike.

Trent winced. "You still get that shit?"

Olivia snorted. "You might be the only white guy here who can tell us apart. So, what are you going to do about the gate crasher?"

"I have no idea. She has no money. I can't keep feeding her all weekend."

Olivia grinned widely, her teeth a little gapped in the front. "Lucky for you, I'm not attending tonight's dinner. I have other plans."

"Oh yeah?"

"Gotta get back on the dating train sometime. I'll drop by your room with my dinner ticket later."

"Thanks."

That took care tonight. Maybe Janie would be gone when he got back. Trent ignored a little stab of disappointment at the thought.

If she explained the situation rationally instead of retreating into sarcasm, Mason would let her stay. Probably.

Maybe.

She hoped.

The door opened softly and her pulse leapt. "You're still here. I was hoping you wouldn't be."

Janelle swallowed. "Me, too. As I have yet to invent teleportation, I'm still stranded. I'd have left a thank-you note, though. So long, thanks for the sandwich, have a nice life. And for the drink. And for the second one I made after you left. There's an IOU on the table."

Chapter Four

Mason sat on the edge of the bed, since she was curled up on the small couch. Loveseat. She could hardly even think the word. His knees splayed open and he leaned back on one hand. Her attraction had sharped to a knife's edge. She cleared her throat and continued.

"I called the agency. They talked to the sugar daddy. He says he doesn't have my wallet, and the agency told me there was nothing they could do for me. Without ID, I can't check into a hotel room even if my parents agreed to rent one for me."

"Your parents wouldn't help you?"

"They would if I told them about this situation, but frankly, I'm too embarrassed to do that if there's any other way to fix this mess. My plane ticket isn't until Monday. I can probably talk my way past security at the airport, but I'd rather not have to."

Mace rubbed his forehead. "How did a girl like you get into this mess?"

"A girl like me?" What the hell did he mean?

"Pretty. Smart. Capable."

Right now, Janelle felt like none of those things. "Student loans. I missed a few payments early on and my credit's trashed and my debt load's high."

"How about getting a job?" Mace demanded.

"I have two, thanks for asking." Ah, sarcasm was not her friend here.

Mason made a face. "Sorry. If you're employed, why are you so broke?"

"My loans take up a huge chunk of my monthly income. It makes managing the loans damn near impossible. I've paid a lot of it down since I graduated, but my credit's still in the gutter. I've had job offers rescinded because of it. My boyfriend moved to Texas and broke up with me shortly after. Now he's getting married to someone else." Janelle gritted her teeth hard enough to almost crack her molars just to keep her chin from wobbling.

"He was the one partner I take it?"

"How'd you guess?" Janelle watched Mason slowly collapse backward on the bed and for one embarrassed moment she wondered what he'd say if she told him she was ready for partner number two. He lay

Chapter Four

back with such controlled motion that even if she hadn't already checked him out with all the subtlety of a bride picking out housewares for her wedding registry, she'd have known his abdomen was solid muscle.

Mason clapped both large hands over his eyes and rubbed them. "What is it you need?"

Not sitting here ogling a guy who wasn't her type at all. She liked nice men. Not too big, not too tall, a little earnest, kind and funny. Guys who'd remember your birthday, your mom's birthday, and your anniversary without fail. Like Ben, her ex.

Mason was none of those things, except kind. Though her presence was wearing on him, and his patience seemed ready to snap. "I need a place to stay for a night or two until I figure out how to get my wallet back from the Rich Jerk."

Mason made a crack between his fingers and peered out. "Rich Jerk?"

"That's what I call him."

"There's a simpler term. They're called johns."

If he'd smacked her across the face it would've hurt less. "You know what? I think I'll take my chances with the police. There's probably a women's shelter I can check into somewhere around here." Janelle snatched up her bag from the floor beside her and headed for the door.

Only to nearly ram into his chest as Mason rose and blocked her path. Janelle stumbled back two steps and peered up at him.

"What does the Rich Jerk want?" he demanded in a low growl.

"What do you think he wants? A belated Christmas card?" *Mayday, mayday. Do not burn this bridge. It's the only one you have.*

Mason watched her. "What's your full name, Janie?"

"If I tell you, will you let me stay?"

He sighed. She had the feeling that he'd been doing that a lot since meeting her this morning.

"I promise I'll sleep on the couch," she offered, cajoling.

"No one can sleep on that couch. It's tiny. We'll figure something out. But first you have to tell me your full name."

"Do I get to know yours?"

Chapter Four

"Janie," he growled. Irrationally, it made her smile.

"Janelle Carlisle from Verona Harbor, Florida." She stuck out her hand. "And you are?"

"Trent Mason."

"Pleased to meet you, Trent." His hand engulfed hers and pumped it once. When he let go, a tingly aftershock made its way up her arm and reverberated throughout her body. Trent wasn't her type. But she wasn't blind, either. He was all kinds of gorgeous.

Just not her kind.

Really.

Even if he was, the chance that he was single was nonexistent. She'd already checked for a wedding band. Nothing. That didn't mean he didn't have a girlfriend, though. A girlfriend who wouldn't take too kindly to a strange woman crashing in his hotel room, no matter what the circumstances. "Are you seeing anyone?"

He jerked around, blue eyes startled. "What?"

Ask without sounding like you're trying to get in his pants. "I don't want to get you in trouble with a girlfriend, if you have one. I'll understand if I can't stay."

Trent Mason shook his head. "No girlfriend. I got out of the Army about eight months ago. Listen. Before you decide you want to crash here, take a few minutes on the computer and do a background check."

He reached over to the computer and raised the lid. "Go on. I'll wait."

By the time Janelle recovered from her total shock that some lucky girl hadn't snapped him up, Trent had returned to lounging against the headboard. Earlier, she'd noticed a dog-eared copy of *The Iliad* on the nightstand. He picked it up and thumbed to the center.

She dropped her bag and sat in the chair, fingers perched over the keyboard. Typed his name into the search bar. It popped up instantly.

"You have a Wikipedia entry?" she asked, bewildered.

Trent nodded once, without looking up.

Janelle clicked the link. The entry included a picture that looked an awful lot like a younger version of the man on the bed. "It says Trent Mason was the youngest top-ranked poker player eight years ago."

Another silent nod.

Chapter Four

"Left the game circuit after losing…" *Jesus.* "After losing millions of dollars in a high-stakes game of top-tier poker champions. World Series of Poker?"

Nod.

Her money problems seemed puny in comparison. Janelle kept reading. "Dated adult film star Penelope Roberts, who performed under the name Bad Penny."

Terse acknowledgment from the vicinity of the headboard.

"After an arrest for drug possession, spent time at the Glen Harbor Rehabilitation facility in Colorado for a rumored cocaine addiction."

Holy shit. Her guardian angel was a drug addict and gambler into dating porn actresses. How could this get any worse?

"Mason appeared in a sex tape with Ms. Roberts…" Oh. *That* was how it got worse. Her fingers were as sturdy as Jell-O, hardly capable of scrolling down the page. "After a year of legal disputes, the film was formally released and distributed. Mason subsequently joined the Army and served in Afghanistan."

"Two tours," Trent added without glancing up from his book.

"And now you're here for a cybersecurity conference?"

"I'd rather you didn't update the entry with that information. There's a reason I only use my last name. The point of this exercise is that if you want to click your heels and go home, Dorothy, your best bet is calling your parents and telling them everything. It won't help your case if they find out you're shacking up with Trent Mason."

Janelle couldn't look at him, that six feet of sexy brawn sprawled out over the bed she'd napped in a couple of hours ago. Desperate for anything that would make this better, she clicked on the next link.

The video began playing immediately. *Maybe it wouldn't be so bad…*

Her eyes widened. Her cheeks flamed. Her entire body throbbed as though she'd swallowed a bucket of jalapeños. Raw.

Trent Mason was *hung.*

Also, she'd never realized a woman's body could bend like that.

The video went on and on and on, the sounds of two people going at it like a pair of enthusiastic, horny rhinos echoing in the small room. He hadn't had the tattoo across his back then, although there was one on his hip right below one well-defined oblique. Young Mason's body

Chapter Four

wasn't as bulky, though he'd been built even then. The Army must've chiseled away any remaining fat.

When Janelle looked up, Mason's expression was contorted with emotion. Pain. Pleasure. Sadness. It struck her that he might not feel as casual about the video as he let on.

She fumbled with the keyboard until the video stopped. "I don't know why anyone would be into that…that dirty stuff. I don't understand the appeal."

When Janelle looked up again, his eyes were locked on her. Hot emotion seethed in those dark depths, but his voice was even and cool when he spoke.

"Heard Penny say a lot of things, not one of them a complaint."

Fair enough. Janelle swallowed and clicked the window closed. The blonde woman had been pretty into everything he'd been doing to her. Then again, she was a porn actress. They had different standards, or something. Bad Penny done a fair number of pulse-revving porny things to Mason, too.

"You actually enjoyed doing it?" She was trying to play it cool, but she had no idea what the social protocol was here. Everything she said came out as an insult, when she was equal parts mortified and dying of curiosity.

"Didn't hear me complaining either, did you?"

His phone beeped, and he rolled over on the bed as he gave her a very good look at his taut behind. Along with an excuse not to respond.

"Nice little girl from the 'burbs, educated, good family. I bet missionary sex once a week was all there was to it." He shot the words over his shoulder, casually insulting.

The barb hit home. "Some of us are happy to be with the person we care about and don't need to go looking for distractions. I like it sweet and gentle. Besides, at least I didn't wind up in a porn video on the internet."

You may well end up in a porn video on the internet.

"It's a sex tape. There's a difference. It's meant for personal enjoyment, not public consumption," Trent shot back lazily.

"Either way. It's sick." She picked up her bag. She'd made a

Chapter Four

mistake, but he'd done the same thing and more, on purpose. If he was going to be a dick, he didn't get the benefit of the doubt. Teasing her about her sex life was just mean. No, she'd never had anything like what he'd done in that video, and it made Janelle uncomfortable. How many bad decisions did she have to make before she learned her lesson? Mason wasn't the nice guy he'd seemed.

"Where are you going?" Mason demanded. Trent. A name like a curse, hard in the mouth, easy to spit when angry, like she was now. Trent.

"I'll take my chances with the cops," she declared, desperate to get away from her second hotel room catastrophe of the day. This time, he didn't try to stop her.

Instead, he went to the computer and opened the window she'd used to view her own unwitting sex tape. He hit play.

Janelle got the message loud and clear. *Don't you dare look down on me.* "Turn it off."

The sound stopped immediately.

"I know exactly how badly a leaked sex tape can screw up your life, Janie. Going to the cops won't protect you, and it'll invite all kinds of questions about how he came into possession of it. I don't think you want their noses up in your business. With a little time, I can help you neutralize the threat. Everything goes back to the way it was before. You can go back to wherever you're from—"

"Florida."

"Right. You go back to Florida, get on your feet, keep digging out of your student loan debt, and move on with your life. Put this whole thing behind you."

He closed the computer. A knock at the door startled Janelle so badly that her shoulder bag slid down her arm and snagged on her elbow.

"Your choice." Then he moved to answer it.

CPSIA information can be obtained
at www.ICGtesting.com
Printed in the USA
FFOW02n1028250518
46858725-49083FF